MAUREEN DUFFY

was born in Worthing, Sussex, in 1933. Educated at the Trowbridge High School for Girls, Wiltshire, and the Sarah Bonnell High School for Girls, she took her degree in English at King's College, London, in 1956. She was a school teacher for five years, and in 1962 she published her first novel, *That's How It Was*, winning immediate acclaim. Since then she has published ten novels: *The Single Eye* (1964), *The Microcosm* (1966), *The Paradox Players* (1967), *Wounds* (1969), *Love Child* (1971), *I Want to Go to Moscow* (1973), *Capital* (1975), *Housespy* (1978), *Gor Saga* (1981), and *Londoners* (1984). She has had six plays performed and has published five volumes of verse, including her *Collected Poems* (1985). She has also written a critical study of the supernatural in folklore and literature, *The Erotic World of Faery* (1972), a biography of Aphra Behn, *The Passionate Shepherdess* (1977), a social history, *Inherit the Earth* (1980), and *Men and Beasts: An Animal Rights Handbook* (1984).

With Brigid Brophy she made and exhibited 3-D Constructions, Prop Art, in 1969. Maureen Duffy received the City of London Festival Playwright's Prize in 1962; she was co-founder of the Writers' Action Group, and Joint Chairman of the Writers' Guild of Great Britain 1977-78. She is Vice-President of Beauty Without Cruelty, Vice-Chairman of the British Copyright Council and Chairman of the Authors' Lending and Copyright Society. In 1984 she became a fellow of the Royal Society of Literature. She lives in London and is currently working on another novel.

VIRAGO
MODERN
CLASSIC

NUMBER
99

That's How it Was

Maureen Duffy

With a New Preface
by the Author

Virago

For G.R.W.
because I said I would

Published by VIRAGO PRESS Limited 1983
41 William IV Street, London WC2N 4DB

First published in Great Britain by New Authors Limited,
Hutchinson 1962

Virago edition offset from first British edition

British Library Cataloguing in Publication Data
Duffy, Maureen
That's how it was.—(Virago modern classics)
I. Title
823'.914[F]   PR6054.U4

ISBN 0-86068-291-9

Printed and bound in Great Britain
at Anchor Brendon Ltd, Tiptree, Essex

PREFACE

In 1961 I had been finished with university for five years. During that time, and while teaching in a series of schools in South London, I had written three full-length stage plays and joined, in so far as there was a semi-official membership, the Royal Court writers' group which included at that time John Arden, Edward Bond, Ann Jellicoe and Arnold Wesker. The year before I had been commissioned to write a television play and with the £450 fee I had bought a houseboat to live in cheaply and retired from fulltime teaching determined to take the make or break chance and try to live as a professional writer.

A group of people, several of them working at Hutchinson's publishing house in various departments, used to gather in the Albany pub on Monday evenings on the corner of Great Portland Street. They included among the writers J.G. Farrell and Heathcote Williams and among the publishers Graham Nicol, editor of Hutchinson's New Authors series. It was he who first suggested one Monday night that I should give up the writing of plays that no one could be persuaded to produce and write a novel.

At first I said no. I didn't like novels much and I thought of myself as poet and playwright. But the seed had been dropped and there is nothing like being wanted. Almost in spite of myself I began to think in terms of writing a novel. The next time I saw him Nicol repeated the suggestion with the bait attached that New Authors would certainly publish it.

This was the purest con trick since neither he nor I had the least idea whether I could produce anything publishable, especially after years of wrestling with the problems of playwriting. The trick, however, began to work. A writer needs a public. Shaw had done the switch from novels to plays. Should I try the reverse?

Nicol's prompting coincided with one of those watersheds in my emotional life when, as those who are drowning physically are said to experience, the whole of life passes under review. Many novelists start with an autobiographical novel and circumstances conspired to pitch me into this common entry. I was trying to make psychological sense of myself and to do this I was rerunning those events and emotions that had formed me. Consequently when the editor next asked me what I was doing about his suggestion I said that although I didn't want to write a novel, didn't much like novels, if I did write one it would be about this girl who . . .

'You write it,' he said, 'and we'll publish it.' I did and so did they.

The germ of my first novel, and indeed the title, *That's How It Was* already existed as a short story I had published in *Lucifer,* the magazine of King's College, London, while still a student there. That short story with some embellishment became chapter five. I had tried in my plays to deal with working-class life in language as concrete and evocative as I could write it, to create a kind of neo-Jacobethan that was based on precise observation and this was the style I carried over into the novel.

The roots of any work of art are deep and knotted. I wanted to celebrate my mother but I also wanted to show how a personality and a relationship that in the world's eyes were brave and fine could produce a psychological result which, also in the world's eyes at the very beginning of that socio-sexual revolution that has come to be known derisively as the Swinging Sixties, could be labelled sick or perverted and thought of as at best a great handicap.

The book is a novel rather than an autobiography because of its structuring towards this end, with the consequent selection among characters and events, and the heightened language used to evoke them. If I couldn't invent facts, which I couldn't because I wanted to tell a particular truth, the art must be in the style, in a language that was colloquial, with I hoped the energy of the demotic, and charged with imagery.

Among the human characters of the book there is one not human who was nevertheless as real to me and my childhood as any of the more conventionally flesh and blood beings. She had flesh and blood but it was others' not hers. I called her in my mind *la belle dame sans merci.* She was Tuberculosis, always referred to in my family as

TB, the earlier Consumption that had consumed the young lives of John Keats and Aubrey Beardsley.

In the year that my mother died, 1948, she was one among nearly 23,000 recorded deaths from TB of the respiratory system. Another 27,000 died from bronchitis, 20,000 from pneumonia and 7,000 from other respiratory infections. The pneumonia and bronchitis figures often conceal deaths actually the result of TB but immediately attributable to a secondary disease of the lungs. The post strepto-mycin figure for 1979 for deaths from TB of the respiratory system was 552.

In 1948, as now, cancer and heart disease were still the greatest killers but TB although not statistically the most important had a significance, almost you might say a culture, all its own. Hardly any family was untouched by it and in some, like the Keats' family and my own, it raged. When my mother died she was the fifth of the sisters to have had or die from TB. (One was accidentally killed by a bomb on ticket-of-leave from the sanatorium.) It seemed to attack particularly those in their teens and early twenties. Many died within a year or so of 'galloping consumption'; some like my mother, D.H. Lawrence, Mansfield, Weber and Orwell lived with it for years in a state of siege.

Known then as 'the white man's scourge' it seemed to cut down malevolently those with their lives just opening out. There was something peculiarly offensive to people in seeing what should be the bloom of youth eaten away by wasting sickness. Country people had long thought of it as a form of bewitchment. My mother lived with this phantom for nearly thirty years, beating it off by a continual act of will until she haemorrhaged and died in the street at the age of forty-two.

The world of *That's How It Was* as well as being pre-National Health was also pre-free state secondary education. It was a world too, documented by Tony Harrison in his sonnet sequence *The School of Eloquence,* where the grammar school was the key to escape from poverty that at the same time brought with it alienation from the escapee's working-class background if not from the family roots themselves.

Education in my mother's words was 'the one thing they can't take away from you'. It usually meant, for the first generation to have more than the old elementary schooling, an elevation to the teaching class. Of my peer group of parallel cousins four became teachers as the first step up or out. No member of our family in the over four hundred years I have traced us back had ever gone to college before or indeed stayed on beyond the statutory leaving age. Some had even taken the examination that allowed you to leave early. Literacy itself among us was only sixty years old.

To 'pass the scholarship' as it was described was, after my mother's health, the most important concern of my childhood. I can't remember at precisely what age it became so but it probably dated from about six when I learnt that my eldest cousin had won a place at West Ham High School For Girls. Certainly I locate my concentration on my own educational progress first at that age. From then until I reached my goal and sat down in Form Three of the grammar school at ten years and ten months, I existed in a state of alternate anxiety and confidence. On good days I knew I was near to top of the class of sixty at Newtown Junior School and would pass; on bad no rational argument could overcome the terrors of possible failure. Until the very last minute and the opening of the fatal letter that contained the news, I swung to and fro on this hook, for I had to win not just a place but a free place since the Education Act abolishing fees didn't come into force until the following year, and it had to be a place at our own town grammar so that there would be no fares to be paid.

Entering Trowbridge High School For Girls I was absorbed into a different world every morning. The to and fro on the hook was continued by the conflict between these worlds which was only partly resolved when I went to university, and in some ways never will be. It is perhaps one of the crucial tensions out of which artists of my generation and background make their art.

The education we were given was in the most enlightened liberal humanist tradition which exactly suited my needs and temperament. I took to it as if my family had been enjoying it for generations, so much so that it increasingly set me apart from my step family, home and even my mother who had been the main instrument in winning this new life for me.

Although I steadfastly refused to tailor my accent, my vocabulary and frames of reference, my intellectual, aesthetic and emotional orientation were all changed. Life at home was nasty, brutish and might be short; it was no wonder that the pleasures of learning, of music and the visual arts took me over.

Above all of course there was literature in Latin, French and English. We were encouraged to write poetry, short stories and essays, some of which found their way into that first publication outlet for so many writers, the school magazine. Poetry in particular was a source of the intensest pleasure. A great deal of my time was lived in a dream of verse writing, reading and learning. Much of it was spent in impersonating John Keats and imitating his odes.

My family alleged, and with reason, that I hardly lived in the 'real' world at all. They thought that my absorption was a desire to show off, to be different just for the sake of it. For them the siren's song that I had heard was an unintelligible, boring jangle and we grew progressively further apart.

The great enemy to advancement for working-class girls was to become pregnant. This was the terror that kept so many chaste, not moral qualms or a lack of adolescent lust. Pregnancy was the great trap and once in there was no way out except by abortion. It's important to remember how this problem obsessed women in the pre-contraception era. For that for them was effectively what it was. Men might buy 'something' if they could overcome their embarrassment, carelessness or distaste. They might or more likely might not be persuaded to use it. Most women knew nothing about female contraception beyond a few old wives' remedies.

When the worst happened all the traditional methods of gin, scalding baths, jumping off the table and assorted noxious medicines would be tried. The really determined and hardy would take themselves to an abortionist but my deeply respectable mother knew of none such. To be 'caught', as one of the euphemisms for being pregnant put it, was to be ruined not in reputation although that went with it but in life and job prospects. There was nothing beyond but marriage and the home or no marriage and the factory. It was certainly the end of books and a distant prospect of college.

My desperate striving for an education and another way of life made me for a time a kind of emotional fascist in self defence. I couldn't allow myself to show tolerance of or to understand my step family, whose needs and aspirations were so different, because theirs were a constant threat to mine. The pressure to conform, to leave school and go into the mill or factory, to get a chap was unremitting except when I was at school or alone with my mother. I believe that part of her intention in sending me away just before she died was to secure that education she had fought for. Alone in the house, with her influence and strength removed, I might have been forced to give in.

As I had gone along with the educational process my goal had receded towards the glorious heights of ambition: to go to university and to be a writer. This last I hadn't really confessed to anyone. I disguised it under the professed intention of becoming a teacher. It was asking a lot to be the first of the family to go to university. Then to propose to throw away everything that had been struggled for in the vain hope of being that most despised thing, a poet, was unmentionable. Yet this was what I was secretly proposing to do. I had determined by the age of fourteen, which is when effectively the book ends, that I wouldn't marry or have children but would follow in the penprints of my hero Keats.

To write was for me to be a poet and it was with great reluctance that I turned to prose to tell the story of the making of a poet. Such an undertaking is no doubt a manifestation of hubris and I have been appropriately punished for it. To be told that your first book is your best is galling and depressing for a writer, and when readers praise *That's How It Was* at the expense of my other books I feel like a parent defensive of less bright and beautiful children.

Those who ask for a sequel have, I believe, failed to grasp its purpose and structure. They believe too that its vividness and intensity were a welling up from memory rather than the deliberate exercise of style. In truth I couldn't repeat the book in a form that they would recognise without writing a pastiche.

Yet because the roots of fiction are deep in childhood there are many ways in which I have repeatedly returned to the matter of my first book. I have for example written again and again out of my long love affair with London which is one of the main themes of *That's How It Was*. My last novel, *Gor Saga,* has as its hero a person of two worlds, animal and human, which translates into speciesism that class and cultural division I have always lived with, and when I wanted to create a future world of mass unemployment in an era of high technology it was back to that earlier experience that I turned in the belief that although human structures may seem changed out of recognition humaness remains the same at the heart of them.

The core of my first book, the relationship to the mother which John Fowles has singled out as the basis of all fiction, I have mined repeatedly in later work. *Love Child* can be read as a myth which is the *déclassé* mirror image of that earlier theme; mother and child effectively open and close *Capital;* they are recurrent figures in *Wounds* and *I Want To Go To Moscow* where Scully's mother is the presiding goddess as is Mrs Bardfield in *Gor Saga*. All nativities are the Nativity.

My first book is also about truth and fiction, history and the selectiveness of memory. It is a political book in the sense that national and international politics govern the physical conditions of Paddy and her mother's life, and in this sense politics have remained a major element in all my later writing. Those conditions aren't just a piquant background to a moving image of mother and child. They are a documentary about man-made poverty and they are in the book to be remembered in the spirit in which the Great War, the Last War as we called it, was to be remembered as the war to end wars in *All Quiet On The Western Front*.

The writing of *That's How It Was* was a deliberate exercise in craftsmanship, a flexing of professional muscles. As with many of my books it was constructed towards its very last line, the question: 'And what the hell do I do now?' It is Paddy's question, not mine for when I wrote it I had already decided on my own answer. It is a form of ending to which I have often returned in the book's successors. It can be called merely a fashionable device of openendedness but I suggest that such a label misses the point. I believe it is the contemporary equivalent of the Shakespearean endstop of order restored. As his was appropriate for his age with its particular philosophical and political cast so the ending which leaves the reader to answer is appropriate for our times of rapid change and the need for constant existential decision. The philosophical progenitors of *That's How It Was* were Sartre and Kierkegaard.

A book is written not in a vacuum but at a precise historical moment which will affect not only the stylistic dress in which it is clothed but its moral and political underpinnings. I hope that twenty years on my first novel can still say something about that moment as well as about the abidingness of its central theme.

Maureen Duffy, London 1982

PART ONE

Child out of the womb torn I saw,
Out of the curled darkness,
Bathed in the love and pain of my birthday,
The blind awakening to my years,
The world turn in your hand . . .

I

LUCKY for me I was born at all really, I mean she could have decided not to bother. Like she told me, she was tempted, head in the gas oven, in front of a bus, oh a thousand ways. But there I was, or nearly. She'd done the washing in the afternoon. 'You shouldn't be doing that, my dear, not in your state,' the landlady said.

'I'll be alright,' and she reached up to the line, stretching her guts on every peg. About two o'clock she woke and the bed was brimming with blood.

'Paddy, Paddy!' Quiet in the dark, shadows of stark furniture rampant in the room, he didn't stir. Not at first anyway. 'Paddy, Paddy!' Insistent now, he must hear.

'Unh!' Sleepily.

'It's coming, I think it's coming.'

'Jesus save us!' He swung his legs over the side of the bed. 'You hang on, just hang on. I'll be back soon as I can with a doctor. If I have to drag him out of bed.'

He woke the landlady, who came running to exclaim, 'I told you so! Never should have washed and so close to your time. Hang on, dear, the doctor'll soon be here.'

And she must have twisted and writhed there in the drab, furnished room. I don't know, of course. It was all my fault after all and she could only tell me after. Hell, I must have guessed how it could be, I was most unwilling to come.

Paddy persuaded the first doctor he found out of his warm bed with a shower of gravel at the window.

'You silly young fool. You could have broken the glass!'

'And I will yet, if you're not down here quicker than thought itself.' The head was withdrawn suddenly and presently he appeared at the door.

'Why do women always choose the middle of the night? Is the midwife there?'

'There's no midwife.'

'And who's going to help me then, boiling the water and cleaning up after?'

'The landlady'll help.'

'More trouble than she's worth, I expect.' And so he grumbled his way through the dark October streets and up the creaking stairs.

'You stay outside. You're no use in here. Say your prayers or something.' And he did.

'Holy Mary, Mother of God, pray for us sinners now and at the hour of our death. Amen.'

'She'd do a lot better with a pulley,' said the landlady.

'For heaven's sake give her a pulley and stop nagging me.' So the landlady tied a sheet to the bed-head and put the end in her thin brown hands.

'You hang on to that, my dear.'

It was six o'clock when I finally made it, the late autumn night growing grey and haggard overhead.

'I said she'd do better with a pulley.' She took me over to the fire and began to wash me.

'Are her feet alright?' my mother asked. They thought she'd gone light in the head.

'Beautiful little feet, my dear.'

'Let me see.' I was held up for inspection in the hissing gas light, bald as a coot and red as sealing wax. 'Thank God for that!' She leaned back against the pillow. The doctor and the landlady swapped knowing looks.

'You rest now, you'll feel better when you've had a sleep.' And she was too tired to tell them how brother Dick, and old Uncle Walter, and long passed-away Daisy had been born with their feet turned backwards, like the ghosts of poor Indian women died in childbirth, always trying to escape their own failures.

'What is it?' Paddy asked when they let him in.

'A girl, a lovely little girl.'

14

'Ah well, you can't order these things I suppose. A boy would have been fine. Michael we'd have called him.'

'It'll have to be registered,' the doctor said. 'I suppose you're the father,' with a shrewd look.

'Of course I'm the father. Who else would be? I'll be along first thing in the morning.'

'No need, I'll look in later. A very narrow pelvis—you're lucky she's alive.' He left them to think it over.

The certificate was a small pink one, with some strange business about being still-born or live. It took me a long time to sort that one out.

A fortnight later, she wanted to get up. 'Other girls get up after a fortnight. Why can't I?'

'Alright,' the doctor resigned himself, 'sit up and try.'

She put back the crumpled clothes and dangled her legs over the side. The room swung sickeningly, the rag rug flung its tatters in her face. Gently he lifted the thin legs, like brown sticks, the ankles permanently swollen from a childhood of chilblains, and laid them back in the bed, pulled down the pink nightdress—she would never go naked to bed and Paddy could never see why.

'Oh go on, sure there's no harm in it.'

'It's not right somehow.'

The doctor straightened the bedclothes. 'Now do you believe me?'

The easy tears of great weakness ran down her face.

'You've been very ill, you must understand. You're not like the other girls; you're lucky to be here at all.' In a month she was right as rain again.

They called me Patricia Mary, but fell out over the christening. My mother stood out like a little bantam, the brown eyes big as gob-stoppers darkened with determination. 'She's not being let in now for something she can't understand or say yes or no to. She wouldn't thank us for tying her up like that when she wakes up one day and finds what we've saddled her with. She shall choose for herself when she's old enough to know what it's all about.' Paddy swore and slammed the drawer shut. She was unimpressed. She knew she'd won.

'He never raised his hand to me,' she told me later, 'he knew he'd better not.' But then, no one ever did. She stood there, thin as brown paper, her bird's bones and lean flesh held together by a steel-wire will. It would have been like trying to fight a small fierce flame. Instinctively you knew you could only either smother it, put it out forever with a clumsy fist or acknowledge the supremacy of an elemental spirit. Either way you couldn't win. So at seven weeks I was started on the never-ending search for self-knowledge before my little cross-eyes could focus and while my lolling head was just a signal-box for the reflexes of hunger, nappy rash, wind and longing for the warm, moist-dark comfort of the recent womb.

Maybe if Paddy had had his way over the matter of my christening things would have been different. My Aunt Lyddy says it would have been different if I'd been a boy. She's the only one now who'd know, but memory is a funny old thing, with one deaf ear that doesn't catch half the questions you ask and has put the answers in a safe place and now can't find it, just like my gran used to. By the time truth's been strained through someone else it's not the same colour anyway, that's why I'm putting all this down now. It's like trying to catch a flea on a sheet. You pin it down under your forefinger and just as you shift ever such a bit, it's away and the chase is on again. When you finally catch it and crack it between your thumbnails, there's a little pop and a nasty mess and that's that. So I feel that even if I do manage to pin down my side of the truth it'll probably be dead as a doornail, or hop away if I shift ever such a little. Sometimes I just can't tell any more what happened to me, and what I was told by my mother or someone else, or what I just would have liked to have happened. If there's a race memory there's certainly a family memory, a rubbish-tip of anecdotes, jokes, tinsel phrases, tarnished photographs, out-at-elbow arguments, obscure chronologies—'If you're twenty-seven now, my mother died just before you were born and Dodge was twenty-six when she died. That means she'd be fifty-three this summer.' Only she never lived beyond twenty-seven.

'It's no good, dear, I get things so confused,' Aunt Lyddy says, and I'm left once again with family memory, that rag-bag, to sort through, and my own twisted skeins and rags of remembrance. And in this strange trade of rag-picking a kind of idealization takes place because naturally it's the brightly coloured scraps of near poetry, the gay threads of laughter, that catch the eye, not the dull browns and dun duckerty everyday, and I remember that the night before he left they had pink shrimps for tea and he sat there stripping off their armour-plating, one of the few things he had the patience for.

'Who'll peel your shrimps for you, Alanah, when I am gone?'

She wasn't the woman to make a scene. He explained that the other woman needed him more. 'You can look after yourself, she can't.'

'If I'd been the clinging type I might have kept him, or if I'd bothered to pretend, but it's no good, I'm just not like that,' she told me. The next day, he left. I was two months old and they had lived together for nearly two years. She sat by the table, one hand nervously smoothing the side of her face from temple to chin, and thought. She looked at the oven and considered. Then she looked at me in the cot. The meter showed just under fifty and there were no shillings in her purse. Suddenly the whole idea seemed ridiculous. She wrapped me in a shawl, put on her hat and coat, laid me in the pram and walked out into a roaring December day, wild with water and wind, and fought her way against all nature crying despair, along the sea-front. At Splash Point the waves threatened to fling us both into the sea but she battled on for two miles before she would turn back. Coming home, the wind bowled us along merrily like bits of torn newspaper along the gutter. She let herself into the musty, old-maid-smelling passage, already gloomy with the midwinter dusk, and took me upstairs. I howled desperately with hunger and cold. Soaked to the skin, her hair hanging in rats' tails around her small face, she took off her coat and began to unhook her blouse.

'Louey, Louey!'

'Yes, Miss Seary?'

'When you're dried off a bit there's a cup of tea and a nice bit of fire down here.'

Soon she sat by the blaze, me asleep, replete, in her arms.

'So he's left you?'

She nodded in reply.

17

'Let him go. You don't need him. Men, they're more trouble than they're worth, I learnt that long ago. You make him pay though—there's no reason why you should be left holding the baby, though she is a dear little mite, and good as gold.' I must have looked it at that moment. She laughed, delighted with her own joke.

'Don't you worry about rent, my dear, til you're on your feet again. You stay as long as you like. I like the company and who could I let the rooms to this time of the year? 'Course, I guessed you weren't married when you first came, four months ago. Men.' She prodded the fire into vicious flame. She had long ago decided that there was only one sex worth bothering about. I think even I would have gone out into the cold, cold snow if I'd turned out to be a boy. The one exception was her old tomcat, Billy. He was an old rogue with frayed ears who sprayed the passage regularly every evening before going out on his nocturnals. She would stand at the front door—the back already open—and exclaim, 'Billy want to go out the fronty or the backy?' A howling draught clawed through the house while Billy cocked his leg over my pram, parked in the passage, and deliberated. I suppose he was wondering which of his girl friends to go yowling after that night. Billy accounted for half the old-maid smell in the house, the other part came from the moth-balls in which Miss Seary kept her strange array of dresses, passed down without modification from her mother, and a prized fur collar complete with fox mask and brush. The dead eyes gleamed malevolently from her breast when she went out shopping. 'Very fashionable at that time,' my mother said.

'He's left me some money. He says he'll pay a pound a week towards the baby's keep.'

The landlady sniffed. 'That won't last long, you'll see. Promises like pie-crust, they're all the same.'

But she was wrong. He kept it up for a year before he disappeared for good. Or was it for good? My mother thought she saw him once, years later, in a workmen's café sitting with a mob of Irish labourers from a nearby building site. 'I looked at him and he looked at me and I went all weak inside.' She never got over him and she never blamed him.

'What was he like, Mum?' I'd ask.

'A dapper little man, I suppose you'd call him, slim but tough, with fair hair and blue eyes like yours. Always very clean and well dressed and sang in that light tenor street-boy's voice, like John McCormack. But, oh, he was the loveliest dancer and the most terrible liar I ever met.' And that was all I could find out. Because of his love of a tall tale you could never credit a word he said.

She met him at a dance-hall, so what else could you expect? you might say. She was a lovely dancer too. I only once saw her dance, when I was about ten, and the styles were all different anyway. It was a fox-trot, the real test of a dancer. Her little feet in their size-three high heels pivotted, trotted like circus ponies' hooves kicking up magic sawdust, stardust. Her partner, a young all-American G.I., who'd done it for a laugh, suddenly grew serious, concentrated, disciplined his gangling legs to pilot her through the wash of dancers. When it was finished, he brought her back to me and she sank down on the hard chair provided by the village hall, puffing and coughing.

'I shouldn't have done it.' The pale touch of rouge glowed against her sallow skin. 'But it was lovely. Oh, I could dance once.'

In her dancing days it was the Big Apple and the Black Bottom, strange exotic names, and the Tango, the most exotic of them all. 'They only want to do it so they can bend you backwards and rub their legs against yours.'

She demonstrated at dance-halls in the intervals and the management provided her a partner, their most skilful regular as a rule. This evening, the manager introduced them.

'Miss Miller, Mr. Mahoney.'

He took her in his arms and they moved off in perfect rhythm. There was never any question of turning back. As Aunt Lyddy says, 'If a woman really loves a man, he only has to crook his little finger and she'll come running right or wrong.'

He came, he said, from the barren tip of Ireland where there was only potatoes, mist and rocks. His sisters were praying in every corner of the world—having decided husbands were hard to get they'd married God. He'd been taught by Benedictines to read and write and make plaster mouldings. Once he took her to a hotel and showed her angels' heads and leaves in relief round the walls, that he'd done, but he was such a liar. He couldn't marry her yet because he was in the army.

'The army?'

'The army of Ireland. The I.R.A. I've sworn not to marry for five years.'

One night, when he was asleep, she brushed against his coat hanging limply from the brass bed-knob. There was a smothered thud. Hardly thinking, she put her hand in the pocket, whatever it was would spoil the shape and he was very particular with his clothes, and drew out a gun. She looked at it incredulously for a moment then put it back and climbed into bed beside him. He murmured in his sleep and reached out for her. She lay awake for a long time. That night she felt my first faint kick.

She never knew where he went when he left her, often for days at a time. Once, picking her way through the streets to the churchyard, where she ate her lunch sitting on a warm tombstone in the sun—'They don't mind, I'm sure, I know I shouldn't mind, and it's quiet in there. You can get the fresh air'—she was stopped by a crowd in the streets.

'What is it?'

'The hunger-marchers.'

She stretched her five feet to their fullest extent and craned her neck. They were going past now, lines of grey shuffling men putting one foot before the other with the abstracted concentration of inanition. Suddenly, she saw him, shabbily dressed as the rest, not his usual smart self at all, trudging along, hands hanging loose. She turned away quickly, hoping he hadn't seen her and lost herself in the crowd.

I would try to get her to blame him, but it was no use.

'He wasn't a bad man,' she said, 'only a little weak.'

'I'll never forgive him,' I said, 'never, and if he turns up one fine day, I'll say, "We don't need you, we're alright." I'll never forgive him.'

'You mustn't say that, he's your father.'

'I don't care,' I thought. 'I hate him. He left you in the lurch. One day I'll make him pay. I'll never forgive him.'

My mother shook her head. 'Perhaps he's dead—though it's hard to believe.'

'He's not dead. Somewhere he's walking about still.'

Maybe he still is.

2

SHE was born number nine of a batch of ten, alternately boy, girl, with eighteen months between—Grandfather had a good head for figures—in the warren of railway cottages run up at the end of the nineteenth century and sometimes seeming nothing more than extensions of the running sheds themselves, with only the wall of the works between, that mark the last surge of the East End proper. Beyond, to the east, are the cheap thirties suburbs, to the west the Jewish tailors, kosher cooking smells, rabbis with long curls, every nation under the sun, with a babel of tongues and only the length of their noses in common. But the borough belongs to the English. They clustered round the railway in search of work, drawn in from labourers' cottages and agricultural poverty in Essex villages to workmen's dwellings and industrial misery in the city. They exchanged rat-infested thatched roofs for slate, and that was about all the difference there was. They kept to their large families, their odd dialect phrases and themselves to themselves. They were smart and undersized, stuck to their principles and their mates, hard-working and drinking. Their children's children are teachers and nurses and television playwrights.

She was number nine and she should have been a boy. Grandfather tried again, another girl, decided he was losing his touch and gave it up as a bad job.

'There'll be no more,' he said, and settled his feet back in the grate. He always kept them warming on the hob, they were cold as stone since his last stroke. He didn't go to work any more, of course, the eldest children provided most of what money there was and the rest of the family was on the dole, a seven-pound loaf and a jug of soup a week. The soup went down the drain when the chickens wouldn't eat it.

'What isn't good enough for them isn't good enough for us,' said Granny. Breakfast for the children before school was a sop, bread mashed in the dregs of Mother's tea with a few grains of sugar. The milk bill was a farthing a day—enough for Mother's cuppa—fetched in the jug. Bread and marge and jam was the staple food but there was always a hot meal a day, usually stew simmered in the black iron pot with plenty of pearl barley and dumplings and a flour pudding boiled in a cloth with a dob of jam or treacle or sprinkling of sugar. Once a week the lucky one whose turn it was would be given the top of Father's egg or the tail of his bloater. Jam was an important feature of most meals, at a halfpenny a basin.

Granny was out at six every morning to scrub out offices, whatever the weather. In the winter of the silver thaw she pulled stockings over her boots and ventured out just the same. She slipped and cut her head open on the tram-lines, had it stitched at the hospital and carried on to work. She couldn't afford to feel the pain. With such an early start to the day she was always home to tan Dodge's backside when she came home from school escorted by Louey and her sister a step above, Ada, known as Dinge because of her continual whine.

'Why didn't you ask teacher if you could go?' Gran would say as she heated the water and stood the galvanized bath on the table.

'Every day it's clean britches for you. I blame you,' she swung round on Dinge. 'You're the eldest, can't you see she goes at the proper time? Too busy with your nose in a book, I suppose.' Dodge was lifted bodily into the bath, the red finger-marks burning on her child's thin backside, knock-kneed with embarrassment.

When it came to washing-up time Dinge would be missing again, this time shut in the lavatory with her foot against the door and a book in her lap.

'It's not fair,' my mother would wail, 'she always gets away with it, just because she's older.'

There were benefits of being the eldest too. When Lyddy's

young man came courting at the weekend he would distribute tuppence between the three youngest girls, a penny to Dinge and a halfpenny each to the others.

'Is that all you ever had?' I would ask.

'It was a lot in those days.'

I had sixpence a week and thought myself hard done by.

'Tell us some more.'

'What about?'

'Oh, when you were little, what you used to do.'

'I've told you ever so many times.'

'Never mind. Tell us about when Dodge put her bum through the window.'

And the stories would run on through the thick grey winter evening, a fire-light legend of people whose lives were so much more vivid, who did more exciting things, who were more daring and clever than I could be.

'And so I went to the door, and it was getting dusk and slightly foggy, just like it is tonight, and I opened the door and there was this terrible old man in a long overcoat down to his ankles and an old green hat pulled down over his face and a moth-eaten scarf wound round his neck. And he thrust his face into mine and said, "Is your father in?"'

I would shout.

'And I flew up the passage and said to Granny, "Mum, there's a funny old man asking for Father." And when she went to the door——'

'It was Aunt Lyddy dressed up in Grandfather's clothes and she got a clout for frightening you.'

Louey was scared of the chickens too and Dick, her youngest brother, would chase her round the garden with a terrified clucking hen held under one arm while she screamed and cried for Gran. When she was eight, a thunderbolt fell on the school during a storm. The children were shepherded into the hall and marched to safety in the playground. When the register was called Louey was missing. Teachers dashed into the building, calling and searching. The desperate headmaster called at the house in Ghant Square to break the news to Granny, but he found Louey was already there, cowering in the cupboard under the stairs. She had scaled a five-foot wall, crossed several gardens at record speed and run on home. She never recovered from her fear of storms.

I had a clear picture of the girls' bedroom in my mind as a child; I still have. There was a big brass-railed bed that the three girls slept in; they lashed their pillows to the foot-rail and played camels, riding so hard that one Saturday morning Dodge slipped her foot in the stirrup and dented the window, a favourite tale, and the morning queue waiting patiently for its quota of marge—this was during the last war, World War I, but always the last we hoped—was treated to a view of that little bare bottom, so often tanned by Granny.

'But didn't she cut herself?'

'Not that I remember.'

Then the bed would become a tent, the girls' garters warping the sheet to the bed-knobs, the curtain-rail holding up the middle. Dick would creep in from his room next door and practise his 'darneys' on the top of the furniture, a complicated balancing act which once landed him in his new sailor suit in the sea at Brighton when he tried a weed-slippery breakwater instead of the mantelpiece. They would giggle and fight until Granny's feet were heard purposefully slow on the stairs and her long cane rapped on the wall.

'Dick, are you in bed?'

'Yes, Mum,' he would answer. Dinge would haul on the sheet, the pole collapsed in the middle of the bed, the garters flew to the four corners of the room and Dick crouched among the girls' feet.

'Ada, are you asleep?' No answer, while the girls held their breath and tried not to giggle. Then Granny's feet and stick would retreat down the stairs and Dick creep back to his own room. It was a ritual that all understood. But in the morning at school-time there was a sudden wail of despair.

'Where's my garter? You've got it!'

'No, that's mine.'

'It isn't, it's mine. I'll tell Mum.'

'Go on, tell-tale tit, tongue's gonna split. It's mine.'

'Mum, I can't find my garter.'

'Don't ask me,' Granny would say. 'You had it last night. What did you do with it?' And there was no answer to that one.

'I can't go to school without me garter.'

'Well you should look after it then.'

All day one dismal stocking would concertina down the leg to be inched and wriggled surreptitiously up the thin shanks.

'Ada Miller, don't fidget.' That evening there would be a frantic search until it was found, dusty in the farthest corner behind the chest of drawers.

Why were they so important to me, those stories my mother told? True, she was a good tale-teller.

'Oh, Mum, is it true?'—the agonized question.

'Of course it's true; it was me.'

And she never forgot any detail or varied the magical sequence, no matter how often she repeated them. They were my mythology, and all the people in them lived with daring and laughter and died tragically. These, long-buried for the most part or grown a middle-aged spread, aunts and uncles had a Peter Pan youth. They were forever there under the gas light of Ghant Square, plotting who should knock on old Mingy Minters, the chemist's, door.

The things she did I played in my turn—rat-tat ginger, two door-knockers tied together and a piece of black cotton leading round the corner so I could knock on two doors at once, my heart thudding, my breath harsh and cold in my throat, tasting of ashes and coal gas from the November fog. I tried religiously to relive her childhood but I was alone, no brothers and sisters to laugh with and dare each other on. Not that I cared. It was a kind of rite I was performing, an attempt even then to perpetuate times past which always seem gayer than the present through someone's rose-coloured spectacles of remembrance.

Such tales she told me that she peopled my past with heroes and made a mythology for me out of stories of dead children and fairy tales she read me, sitting by the fire or lying easy and warm in bed, and these are the real past.

She grew up then in this legendary era and I could add end on end, like a game of dominoes, one thing leading to another, the things she told me. Maybe it was an attempt to compensate for my own companionless childhood where everything seemed so commonplace, though perhaps dignified by time now, like old buildings with moss and ivy grown on them, it may have the same charm hers had for me.

She went to the school just round the corner where they all went and she passed through all the different grades. When she reached Miss Nightingale's class the war was on and the children ran out into the streets to watch a Zeppelin sink blazing through the sky.

'I could see their faces, real Germans,' she told me, 'at the end of our road.'

'Now, children,' Miss Nightingale said from the piano stool, 'Number 7 in your song-books.' They turned the pages and she struck up a fine rousing march. Quickly Louey scanned the words and the whispering began.

'It says Fatherland, pass it on.'

'Now,' said Miss Nightingale, 'I'll play the tune through the first time and then the second time we'll all sing together.' As she played, another murmur flickered from lip to lip.

'Fatherland means Germany, sing Motherland.'

Miss Nightingale pounded out the preliminary chords and the class came in with strength.

> 'Glory and love to the men of old,
> Ready to fight and ready to die
> For the Mo—otherland.'

Miss Nightingale paused in mid-cadenza. 'Now, children, try again.' This time, as she drummed out the opening phrases, the word went round again.

> 'Ready to fight and ready to die
> For the——'

Complete silence. She'd seen, of course, the eddies of rebellion rippling out from Louey.

'Louisa Miller, come out.' Obediently she pushed her way past the thin knees in their cotton skirts and bony stockinged shins.

'Now, what's all this?'

'Well, "fatherland" means Germany, and we're fighting the

Germans and my brothers are in the army,' she said, with a child's twisted logic.

'You must come to the mistress,' Miss Nightingale sighed. This was insubordination and something must be done.

Presented with the problem, the mistress wisely gave in. 'I think, Miss Nightingale, in the circumstances, for the duration of the war the words could be modified so that they sing "motherland". One can't expect children to understand that art is international.' Like everyone else, she probably thought the modification would only be necessary for six months.

It was everyone's war for perhaps the first and last time. In a wave of enthusiasm, Louey's two eldest brothers had joined up and been shipped to India. They came back six years later, little, brown, shrivelled old men intent on getting on now they knew there were whole nations lower on the social ladder than themselves and with strange new words in their mouths. One made it, and became a little round polished filbert of an uncle for me, the other was less successful and wrinkled like a walnut.

The third brother was only seventeen; a fine tall boy, the recruiting sergeant summed him up.

'Run round the block, laddy, and come back a year older. Then maybe we can fit you in.'

He died eighteen months later in France of pneumonia. Granny travelled abroad for the only time in her life to watch him die.

'We're very sorry, Mrs. Miller. It seems his heart didn't develop after the age of twelve,' the officer told her. It was all so unreal that she should be in France anyway. God knows how they found the money, though three of the girls were at work by then. Lyddy's young man was out there too, somewhere in the front line, so maybe she didn't feel quite so alone. The war dragged on with no more major tragedies for the family, food was scarcer, Granny, widowed now and working harder than ever, added interminable queues for the very barest essentials, bread, potatoes, marge, to her day already stretched thin to breaking point.

But Louey would soon be leaving school and adding to the family resources. She could write a good hand, modified cursive script they were all taught, Aunt Lyddy still has hers unspoiled; she could add and subtract, divide and multiply both with figures and money, rods, poles or perches, tons, gills, centimetres, yards, feet and inches, furlongs and chains. She knew all her tables up to fourteen times, the Kings and Queens of England, the stories of the Maid of Norway, the princes in the Tower, how King Charles hid in the oak tree and all about the Great Fire and the famous battles of the last century; the Factory Acts somehow got left out. She could sew and knit beautifully, she read ravenously in compensation and knew *The Legend of Bregenz* and *Barbara Frietchie* by heart. She was going to be a tailoress. Then suddenly the war was over.

3

IT DIDN'T make much difference, not at first, any more than it did the second time. I remember walking down the hill over the railway bridge thinking, 'The war's over. I ought to be glad but it doesn't seem to mean much. It means nobody will be killed any more and rationing will end,' and all the time I was trying hard not to tread on the black lines between the paving-stones in case I married a black man. It was a blazing day and I was going swimming. I hugged my costume and towel under my arm in a neat swiss roll, jam and cream, and tried hard to concentrate on the fulfilment of the one thing I'd wished for with every stir of the pudding and every first taster of the year since it began.

'I wish, I wish for the war to be over.'

But it was still meaningless. I was twelve.

My mother was fourteen and out to her first job. It lasted exactly a fortnight. Each night she came home and cried with the misery and fatigue. It was a sweet factory where the air was a blizzard of flying starch and the youngest girls carried hot iron trays of sweets from one floor to another so that they could be decorated and wrapped by the expert older women. She might have gone on there, after all you have to get used to a job, to put up with it whatever it is, coughing a little in the dusty atmosphere and panting up the twisting iron stairs, her thin arms strained as if the sinews would fray and tear, but there was a sudden panic. The eldest sister, now wife and mother, felt strangely languid, coughed a little softly, turned over and died; the second, in her early twenties, became ill in her turn. The whole family was carted off to the doctor, where they stood thin and brown and large-eyed in a row. They were all pronounced 'weak-chested' and Louey was freed from the sweet factory for-ever. Only Aunt Lyddy with her mess of fair hair and pink skin was branded fit. She was her father's girl.

'But I thought I had it, my dear. When Ada and Dodger both sickened and Maisie was dead and Minnie dying and your mother always such a poor little, thin thing, can you blame me? I could feel it clutching me by the throat and I'd come running downstairs to Granny and cry, " I've got it, I've got it!" And your uncle, only we weren't married then, would comfort me. He was very good, not like the others.'

I knew what she meant. In spite of their sickness they were all happy, bright girls, full of devilment, and there were plenty of boys who found them attractive. But understandably, the boys' mothers weren't so keen and the romance usually with-ered as soon his mum found out. There was Lennie, who came courting Ada. He played the violin and was an ardent Socialist. They argued endlessly, for she was secretary to one of the directors of a food-processing firm which had been under-standing and helpful throughout her long illness, so she was inclined to be pale blue at that time. In the course of one such argument Lennie swung his feet carelessly under the bed. There was a resonant chime. With great presence of mind, 'Tea-time, I think,' said Ada, but it was all spoilt by my mother and Dodger, who were in the room too to see fair play, and collapsed in giggles, before they bunked out of the room and downstairs. Poor Lennie, his mother's influence was stronger than his principles and he stopped coming with a dismal attempt at an apology.

'Poor Dinge,' my mother said, 'she was so upset. I think she was really fond of him, but he hadn't the guts of a louse. She was worth two of him any day.'

'And what about Green Trilby?' I asked.

'Oh, he was just as bad. His mother wouldn't let him have me, though I met him once when you were about three and the old woman was dead, and he asked me to marry him then. But he didn't want you, another man's child, so that was that. Anyway, think of being Mrs. Perkins, and married to that silly green hat.'

All the girls were ordered fresh air and food, of course, as soon as they became ill. Granny did her best. Better food was beyond her, there was no money, or to send them to the bracing sea-air which might have helped, but the shed in the garden was turned into a summer-house where they took up residence one after the other, so that they could get more of the smoky city air, heavy with clinker from the big engines that stood cooling and puffing in the nearby yards, before cleaning and repair work could be done on them.

And so when it puts its white, dead hand on her in turn, my mother knew what to expect. She was the last to get it and in a sense it braced her up and brought out all the cocky, fighting-bantam spirit in her. After the sweet factory, she had gone to do what she always wanted—dressmaking, or rather tailoring ladies' costumes, coats and skirts, piece-work, two-and-nine-pence for every one they made, two shillings for the coat, nine-pence for the skirt.

'And the buttons had to be sewn on properly, none of this hot needle and burnt thread that you get nowadays.' The first advertisement that she answered was for machinists experienced with electric machines. She'd used Granny's old treadle Singer at home, so of course she tried for the job. She got through the interview alright but on the first day the machine ran away with her and pinned her finger neatly on the needle. She fainted before they could get it out, but they let her keep the job. She was happy there, it was what she'd always wanted to do, and she worked hard even though, as she said, sometimes when you were catching up on back work in a slack period, and you turned a sleeve inside out, there was a nest of small furless mice inside.

At night she would rush through her tea and go upstairs to the bedroom without even taking her hat off and sit on the bed with bright bits of a new dance dress or blouse all round her, the needle running cleanly through the cloth in a plumb straight line with no hesitation. I've seen her do it so often; her hands smoothing the stuff, almost loving it, and the tiny, tinny click of the needle against the thimble, and as she sat there, picking out the pins as she went along and sticking them in the bed in a prickly hedge all round her, the evening would deepen into the gold city haze, sunset red and blurred behind the crazy skyline of chimney-pots, swinging cowls and dolls-house silhouettes, until she couldn't see even white tacking cotton any more, and she fell asleep still with her hat on.

'I wonder you don't do yourself an injury,' Granny said in the morning when the hat couldn't be found and she had scratched her leg on a stray pin in the night. However it paid dividends. When the manager, Ben Rose, set up his own firm she went with him as overlooker and he would have taken her back any time, though she walked out on him when I became too obvious.

They were the gay twenties alright. The girls would buy a few yards of stuff at two-and-eleven, three, a yard, and run up something new and fashionable, to wear the same evening with a quick press before they went out. In the drawer is a mound of photographs from this time. They took their holidays by kind permission of Ada's boss, she had made herself indispensable and ran the sports and drama clubs, at Gorleston. There they all are, sitting in front of a beach-tent, Ada, Louey and Dodger, unmistakable sisters, my mother always the little one who somehow got into the picture at the last minute, the boss and his wife, and Granny as well, smiling all over her country pippin face, two cheeks like a little bottom and the turned-up nose she passed on to all the girls and me, too, in my turn. Then there are snaps of all the girls taken in turn with Gran, in front of a seascape, and a couple of mad period pieces showing a row of boys, their backs bent double, their arms round the waist of the lad in front, and the girls, roaring with laughter, jockeying along over their backs, yards of silk stocking, pointed one-strap shoes, tunic dresses and cloche hats.

And this'll show you another side of her, too. They'd gone to the pictures, she and her girl friend Lillie, a timid thing with doughy face and flaccid skin who followed Louey's lead in everything. They'd settled themselves in, with a bag of grapes to pick at and rustle, when a large man in a big black trilby with a turned-up brim plonked himself down in front of them, wheezed, shuffled and prepared to enjoy the film without taking his hat off—it was winter and maybe he was bald and afraid of draughts. As I've said before, she was short but she had a long, supple neck which she craned from side to side in an effort to see round. It was no good. He effectively blocked the whole screen and since there was no sound, as yet, to go by it meant the extinction of the whole film, action, captions and all.

She leaned forward and tapped his shoulder. 'Would you mind removing your hat please? I can't see.'

'Yes, I would,' he replied calmly, and turned back to the film. Infuriated and frustrated, she tried to think of some brilliant way to get her own back.

'Let's move,' whispered Lillie.

'Why should we, we've paid just the same as he has.' Then she thought of the grapes. Methodically she began to pluck them from their branchy stems, dry and thin as birds' claws, break the sweet fleshiness of the fruit against the ridged roof of her mouth with her long, thin tongue, spit the pips and skin into the palm of her hand and delicately arrange them around the black trilby brim.

'Oh, Lou, don't!'

'Why not, miserable old beast.'

They never swore in that family, I don't know why. When my mother was hard-pressed, later in life, she would let a chaste 'Sugar!' escape. Really driven, with her mouth full of pins and dealing with an obstreperous bit of cloth which wouldn't take the pattern papers she jigsawed on it, 'Bum!' she would say. I think I heard her say 'Bugger!' three times in my life, but then she had her own brand of verbal wit that could demolish a situation, without lowering herself to effing and blinding.

'Come on, you eat some too,' and poor Lillie was forced, all wobbly like a pale shuddery blancmange, to eat her share. She wouldn't put them round the brim herself—her hand would have shaken too much anyway and upset the lot.

When all the grapes were gone, the stalks went to join the pips and skins, and, satisfied, Lou allowed Lillie to find them new seats. But she kept an eye on her victim and when he got up to go she dragged Lillie out after him.

'But why?'

'I want to see what happens.'

Outside it had begun to snow and as the flakes settled on the

34

remnants of the half-pound of grapes, they formed a Christmas-card forest landscape. The girls followed him for half an hour, giggling delightedly when passers-by turned to stare, nudge and point at the man in the funny hat. Then, avenged, they left him to return home to his wife, the stuttering explosions of fury, and the explanations which could only make the whole thing worse.

She was tough and resilient. She bent this way and that with chance and change. After every crisis she was still there, the bones worn a little more through the skin like boulders eroded out of their bed of soft earth on an exposed hillside, the eyes more prominent and bright, but she was there. With the other girls their decline had always started in their early twenties from a cold, caught in a too-thin dance-frock or a winter nip unprovided for. Louey got her packet through running for a bus. Every morning she stood by the lights and jumped for the platform as it slowed down. This morning she missed her footing and was dragged along the road, hanging on to the hand-rail. She would have let go, but behind her reared the four great horses of a brewer's dray, the leaders reigned up tight, battering the air with their iron-shod hooves that slipped and struck sparks from the cobbles and tram-lines. She could see the brushed fringes of white hair and count the nails in their shoes as big as dustbin lids.

They stopped the bus and dragged her on board. She seemed alright except for a graze or two. She said she was alright and dusted herself down, lamenting a tear in her stocking. The conductor tinged the bell and the journey was resumed. Four days later, she lay in a coma with pneumonia.

'I'd say it's due to shock,' the doctor told Granny, snapping his little bag shut. 'Has she had any bad news, or an accident, something that might account for it?'

'Not as I know of.'

Granny had told her again and again not to jump on at the lights but walk the extra hundred yards to the proper stop. As far as I know she never was told what caused it.

When the crisis came, Granny sat through the night holding her hands and talking, pouring the slightest details of family news and legend into ears that seemed to be deaf to anything but the screaming images that swirled inside their own head.

'Dick's found a young lady, we reckon, a girl who plays the piano in the pictures, a big girl and a bit older than him, but plays the piano beautifully and wears a purple cloak. You remember when your brother Harry brought his girl home for the first time and she was such a well-brought-up little thing and you lot piled all the pots from under the beds on the table, with enough empty beer bottles to start a bottling stores. Hold on, dear, hold on to me. I'm here.'

And the thin brown hands in her swollen red fists would writhe and clench as will and flesh struggled together.

'You've pulled her through, Mrs. Miller, I didn't think she'd make it but you've pulled her through,' the doctor said when he found Louey sleeping, quiet but exhausted, the fire sunk to a steady glow, on his regular morning call.

That was how it started, that fantastic running battle she kept up for twenty years. It was an enemy she kept at bay with her only weapon, the will to live. Sometimes she turned and fought doggedly for six months from a sanatorium bed while her brief hospital friendships died around her and the grotesque image darkened the pine woods and clear skies outside the ward windows, but mostly it was a cold war. The evil little pot, smelling deathly of disinfectant, always stood by the bed with the floating cotton-wool blobs of phlegm that turned my stomach. Her own cutlery and crockery lay apart from mine. Occasionally, at moments of long parting, I kissed her forehead while she turned her breathing mouth away. Every year we waited through the early winter for the January visitation of pleurisy that had me boiling the kaolin and spreading it, with a stick from the fire-lighting bundle, on the pink lint, and slapping it, all hot and reeking, on the caging ribs. She was the castle under seige and I was the desperate defender boiling the oil to send the attacker howling back to cover. No human enemy this, but a monstrous hydra, a fantastic beast that glowered and threatened, that took the throat in its choking hands, thrust its hand into the side and tore at the finely woven lung tissue, that could never be finally defeated, only driven back for a time to strike again in a weak moment, that muttered and grumbled in its underground refuge. So it seemed to me, as she softly eased a cough in her throat or fumbled hastily for the little tin that held a thousand tiny black Nippits, like beetles and tasting worse: anything to stop that final racking cough that would tear the frayed lungs—lace curtains, as she called them—to shreds, and let the blood, bright with the precious charge of oxygen, well up and choke her.

'I'd eat shit with sugar on it if it'd do me any good.'

'Oh, Mum! But why didn't you go like the rest?'

'Ada and I were the lucky ones, I suppose. The other three all got the acute sort, ours was chronic. Your poor old Granny had a lot to put up with. Then Dodger was ill and I was in trouble, as they say.'

'I never knew, my dear,' says Aunt Lyddy. 'One day when I went to see Mother I found her crying. "Whatever is it?" I said. "They're only living in rooms and the baby coming," she said. I didn't understand. I was living in two rooms, had been since we married and Gilly was nearly seven then. "They'll be alright. Lots of people have to manage in rooms," I told her, but she wouldn't seem to be comforted. Of course, I saw why later.'

Granny didn't have to worry much longer. She didn't feel well herself. There was a nasty pain in her innards but she hardly had time to see to it. They took her into the local hospital, where you only go to die, legend says, but this was nothing to worry about, the doctor told her family.

She was very restless before the operation, talking feverishly about her little dark daughter.

'She'll be alright,' they reassured her, as I said Dodger was ill at the time, 'she'll soon be better.' But she wasn't comforted. My mother had come up to stay while Gran was in hospital. In the middle of the night she woke suddenly, hearing her mother call her. She sat up in bed.

'Louey, Louey!' The door was open. 'Don't worry, I'm going to be alright now.'

Peacefully, she lay down again. Gran died on the operating table at one o'clock in the morning. Two months later I was born.

37

4

THEY must have been strange years for her, those first years of my life. My first memories aren't much help in piecing a whole together, disconnected images that won't be tied to time or place. We moved from town to town, from one set of rooms to another. That family that had seemed so complete was all scattered. Dodger died soon after I was born, Ada, ill in her turn, went off to the clean air of the Isle of Wight at the firm's expense. It was six years before she came out. Out of the family of ten, six were left and two of them were ill.

They say your character is fixed in the first six months of your life, like young fruit set on the twig, that it all depends on the relationship you have with your mother's breast or something. My mother fed me herself. Later on, I wondered how, she was so thin and flat-chested.

'Nothing but a couple of press-studs,' she would joke.

I know I won first prize in the baby show after they'd entered me as a laugh. I seemed very pale and slight, set beside the fat, bottle-fed offspring of the mothers who looked at mine so pitying, wondering how she'd had the nerve.

'D'you think you'll rear her?' one of them asked.

'Of course I'll rear her.' My mother was indignant.

'Is it a little boy or a little girl, you can't tell when they haven't got no hair.'

'You want to brush it more,' another chimed in.

'There's no sense in brushing a bare scalp,' my mother replied.

The prize, when she carried it off, was a guinea—enough

to buy the canopy for my pram that you can see in so many of the early snaps.

I did everything children do: I fell into a bed of nettles; I pulled a seven-pound pot of mayonnaise down on top of me as soon as I could climb; I crawled into the boot-blacking box under the table when I was left for a minute all togged up in white to go out; I screamed at the elderly and influential lady who leaned over my cot flashing her teeth and glasses; I stripped the new wallpaper cleanly reach-high all round the room because I'd been allowed to help with taking off the old; oh all the things kids do, I did.

We moved all the time—I've got more homes than years to my credit—up and down the south coast, always sea and pebbly beaches. Once she was cook for an asylum where the boys, set to help her as part of their therapy, tore the paper for laying the fire into scraps half an inch square and chopped the wood into matchsticks. Then we lived in one room in a fireman's house. I still remember the excitement when he was called suddenly to a fire, seeing him running down the stairs with his helmet on and his little axe in hand. There was a bungalow we had for a winter, one of a pair, Sunrise and Sunset. We got it for a song, provided she would light the fires and open the windows and cook the meals when the captain and his wife came down for weekends. Once he put his shoes outside the door to be cleaned, but only once.

'I'm no skivvy, you know, to clean your shoes. You may be used to little black boys in India, but I'm not one.'

Then she fell really ill for the first time in my brief life. The enemy advanced on all fronts, she was forced to retreat to a sanatorium for three months. I was three years old and packed off to a home in the country.

It was torture, hourly misery. We slept in a long dormitory and were wakened at twelve o'clock to queue up and take our turns on the china pot in the middle of the room. Thirsty, we drank from the dog's trough and were punished. It was a hot summer, I remember, and we played with rusty tin cans, muddy ditch-water and last year's brown leaves in the scruffy fields, and lined up before the window with wooden spoons to swat our quota of wasps before we sat down to eat. Stung by gnats in the evening lanes, I scratched with my dirty fingernails. Sores appeared instead of bumps, jelly-like blobs followed which were hastily covered by plaster.

My mother came to fetch me at the station. I remember her, plumper, brown-skinned as ever, her dark rough hair waved to her shoulders, an immaculate, tailored costume, the restless brown hands and moist-bright, bulging eyes, tall she seemed to me at that age but really short in comparison with the people around. A black train huffed and puffed behind her as I was led forward. She hardly recognized me. I was pale, unkempt, my hair with the dull matted look of stacks of blighted straw; my face, arms and legs covered with pieces of sticking plaster, concealing the sores beneath. I wasn't sure quite what to do, I felt leprous and disappointed, but quickly she took my hand and led me away.

I learned afterwards that she lodged a complaint, but I only remember sitting on the edge of the scrubbed-wood table in our new rooms in London and crying, while she scrubbed the enormous sores on my legs with sulphur soap and applied biting sulphur ointment. Yet somehow I knew it had to be done. I felt unclean and understood this brutal going-over.

I can't remember the shape of the rooms we had there, or what was in them. I know they were upstairs and there was a towering railway arch nearby. The street is still there. I often pass it in the bus going to see Aunt Lyddy, and there's always the temptation just to go and look, but I know that if I did it would have no meaning any more. I remember two kinds of weather there: bright sunshine and running out into the street to the Wallsie man on his tricycle for three-cornered snow fruits and snow creams, and thick pea-souper, trundling down the main road on winter Friday nights with a bag of brown shrimps in my mother's hand, going to visit Aunt Lyddy, me driving the tram from the platform, ting-ting, watching the river of muddy fog flow past my noisy craft.

It was winter too and early dark when I woke suddenly as children do and found my mother had gone out while I slept on a blanket in front of the fire, that had blazed and flared and now threw dancing goblin shapes on the walls. Terrified, I stumbled to the door, groping down the stairs in palpable, velvet darkness and saw a sliver of light under the door of Mrs. Downstairs. I rushed in, blinking, ready to cry for sympathy. My mother was there of course.

The more I think about that place, in fact, the more I remember, because this was where I first became conscious of myself as distinct from other people, of us as apart from the rest, us and them. The world suddenly took on a pattern, outlines of things were clear and hard. Before, actions had gone on in the blurred and nebulous regions over my head, actions which didn't concern me and hardly affected me. Now I was the hard core of my own world. I knew I was me. I mesmerized myself with my own identity, chanting my name in a hypnotic ritual.

'Paddy, Paddy, Paddy, Paddy, Paddy . . .'

'Why,' I asked, 'why, Mum?'

'Because,' she would answer.

'Oh, Mum!'

On my fourth birthday I was given a blackboard and easel so that when I went to school six months later I could already read and write. My mother was very relieved. She had been offered a job which she took as soon as I could be bundled off to school, the last one she ever had.

Call it pride or independence that sent her out to work again. She couldn't keep it up, of course, but for a short while there were no weekly visits to the relieving office for the couple of pounds that kept us through the week. The notes they gave us were always changed quickly and the coins brought home to be parcelled out in little piles on that same scrubbed kitchen table, each pile covering necessity, giving a feeling of security, rent first of course, insurance, coal, gas meter, the Co-op club for emergencies like shoes, and finally food. I only remember one of the officers who dispensed our weekly supply of life-blood. He was a thick-set man with horn-rimmed glasses and one arm shorter than the other. He wrote the details in his book with a curious circular motion, approaching the letters from the top of the page. There was no hint of charity in his dealings with my mother. They treated each other with great politeness, as if she were drawing the dividend from her handsome annuity. They discussed the weather, books, events in the news, and somehow she had signed in the right place and crude money had changed hands with no resentment on either side.

Once she lost her purse on the way home from the relieving office. I can feel the blind terror of that search still in my stomach like a cold sickness. It had been handed in intact at the baker's. She leant against the counter, pale and shaken, holding the big brown purse, a proper mum's purse, with three compartments held together by a clip and a flap that snapped shut on its popper fastenings, the sound of security.

'You have a little sit down,' said the lady behind the counter, 'gives you a nasty turn it does. Bad as a fall.'

But now for a brief while she was at work and I was at school, the first of my six junior schools. It had a high wall all round the small playground where we did the country dancing, which I hated because of the grimy little boy who was my partner. In the afternoons we were put to sleep in canvas cots with hard pillows. Craftily, while the other dozed, I eased up my pillow and read on, turning each page soundlessly, the latest episode of the adventures of Monty Mouse, my comic hero of the moment.

For the first time I had a feeling of belonging in a place. That I remembered the sea, that my feet were hard as horn with running over pebbly beaches, meant nothing. This was where I belonged, in these dirty streets with the railway close by, the street markets, the lighted shop windows, the pavements that splashed with mud and sodden papers, cartons, tissue paper from the oranges around Christmas-time; that blew like a sandstorm in summer, with grit and dust that stung your eyes, and whirling bus-tickets, sweet papers, litter of all sorts in August. These were her streets where all the legendary family had lived and dared, and I was one of them. I was a Londoner, an East Ender. Deliberately, I wove that conviction into my conscious thought so that it could never leave me. I would always have a place, I would always belong.

And then we moved again. Her last attempt to earn her own living ended in a dangerous exhaustion. The winter fogs choked her, the cold shrivelled her skull until the brain seemed ready to burst out like cotton wool; the March winds howling along city streets like wind tunnels, knocked the breath out of her body and left her gasping. It was back to the coast with its mild, clean air and gentle winter sunshine. For the first time, we were to live in a house which was all ours and even if we let some of it, as my mother said, we should be the ones who could tell people to go. At first anyway, there would be just the two of us.

The house was part of a terrace, with two gardens, back and front. An alsatian called Rex lived next door with his invalid master. There were two rooms and a kitchen downstairs, three rooms and a lavatory upstairs, and the sun always shone in that house. The walls all seemed to be pale yellow. There was a large, bulbous-legged, circular dining-room table of polished mahogany and my mother's machine—one of the constant factors in my life; there was always a machine and pins and stray pullings of cotton; my clothes were all made on it and most of hers too and, from time to time, clothes for other people who actually paid her money. It stood under the window where the light was good. Shopping always meant a visit to the remnant counter where a future dress, blouse or skirt might be hiding under the tossed and fingered pile of folded velvets and satins, shaggy tweeds, store curtain and chair covering.

I was dressed in a white blouse and little grey pleated skirt with navy coat, pair of plimsolls, sixpence in Woolworth's, in a shoebag, to go to my new school. It was a modern building, all windows, with light airy rooms which disappeared way above my head. The headmistress, a tall muscular woman with a brush of short, sandy hair and blue sandals, soared above my mother.

'She has plimsolls for indoor shoes? Good. You can change into those now.'

I bent down, took off my one-strap button shoes with the round toes—I always wanted liquorice patent leather but Mum considered it flash, Cousin Gilly had them though—pulled on the new plimsolls, smelling of buses on a wet day, and fumbled with the strings.

'Can't tie her own laces. She'll soon learn,' the voice sergeant-majored high above me. 'Let's hear you read.' I don't remember what it was I read. 'That'll do. Class 3A. I'll take you along now.' My mother was delighted.

43

In that school I grew up. Miss Wilkinson, energetic and determined, with junior and infants schools under her care, expected intelligence, tidiness and good behaviour. You were in the 'A' stream because you had ability which it was your duty to cultivate to become the responsible citizens of tomorrow. I see her striding the platform at assembly, exhorting us to have a springy step.

'If you want to country dance, you must learn to country walk.' She pranced across the platform like a spirited horse. No one laughed. It was accepted that education was a good thing *per se* and Miss Wilkinson its shining local protagonist.

Then the whole of 3A was sticked. We had been left alone for a staff meeting. The other two third forms, B and C, had become noisy and bored. We had left our places, sat in each other's desks, chattered. The whole class was lined up in the corridor. Miss Wilkinson progressed solemnly down one side smacking the outstretched palms with the flat of a ruler. The smacked hand rejoined the other on the top of the head, until she passed along the left side and it was punished in turn.

'Because you are the A class and should have set a good example.'

I never told my mother. I knew I should get no sympathy there. I was no longer a baby; I was six.

That year I was Robin Hood. I had a green tunic with brown lacing up the front, sent me by Cousin Gilly, it had got too tight and short for her, a bow and arrows cut from a bush and strung with a precious piece of string, and a green-and-red scooter Aunt Lyddy had given me for Christmas. I roved through the quiet little seaside town, where retired ladies and gentlemen had come to dine with dignity and comfort and as slowly as possible, captured castles, fought bitter hand-to-hand conflicts at every street corner, fled the sheriff through the forest avenues of plane trees, clattered over the railway bridge, my horse hooves ringing bright and clear in the frosty air.

One dim evening, I was riding home, a bundle of faggots for the camp-fire across my saddle-bow, when I was set on by robbers, thrown from my steed, trampled in the dust, my carefully gathered bundle scattered in the path. Bruised and bleeding, I stumbled to the door.

'Whatever have you been up to?' my mother demanded, shock making her angry. 'Just look at you. You're not going out on that scooter again. I told you to be in by six and it's half past and nearly dark.'

Fortunately for Robin, it was not considered sissy to show emotion in those days. My chin wobbled, I screwed up my face and began to wail on a rising note. By this time the gravel embedded in my minced knees was stinging worse than wasps; I was hungry and tired.

'I was bringing you home some wood for the fire. You said yesterday when we saw all those branches blown down in Selby Road what a lot it'd save if we could carry them home. Well, I got a lot of them and I had them across the handlebars and I was hurrying not to be late and they caught in the lamppost and I fell off and I've lost 'em all!' I howled like a beaten dog that doesn't know what it's done wrong, because I was misjudged and there was no justice in the world and I'd lost the sticks and was a failure. I'd tried to do something to help her and it'd all gone wrong and now instead of praise there was blame.

My mother put down the book she had been reading, and walked to the front door.

'Let's have a look.'

'That's where I came off.' The scooter was lying in the gutter, dead branches were scattered forlornly over the road.

'You've bent the handlebars a bit, but we can straighten them out,' she said, and she picked up the scooter and leant it against the spiteful lamp-post. 'Now let's pick up the wood.' Patiently and calmly she began to gather the sticks together. Soon I joined her and the bundle grew again.

'My goodness, what a lot you got. I don't know how you managed to bring them all the way from Selby Road. You carry them in and I'll wheel the scooter. They'll be a big help.'

I grew six inches under the light touch of her hand on my head.

5

Mr. MUNNINGS, who worked in the garage opposite
our front-room window—there were thousands of
snap-dragons that hot, dry summer in the garden
under the window, I pulled them off their plump green calyxes
—grew like weeds they did my mother said so it was alright—
and pushed my fingers down their gaping throats—Mr. Munnings had hanged himself. It was something to do with some
money he'd looked after too well for someone. Breakfast-time
there was a small, still crowd of neighbours outside the green
garage doors. The police arrived in a black clean-shiny car and
went inside.

'Come away from the window,' said my mother.

'Oh, Mum!' Would they bring out the body?

'You heard.'

Reluctantly, I left the window. It's a hard world when you're
six, everything nice is wrong.

'Can I go out to play?'

'When you've wiped up.'

That morning, I bounced a cup. I felt my mother's wedding
ring, loose on her thin fingers, nick a tiny piece of skin from the
tip of my ear as she clouted me.

'Give me the cloth. You're like a cow with a musket. Pick
up the bits and get off out of it. If you want something done
properly, do it yourself.'

My ear was still bleeding a little as I let myself out, but I was
free till dinner-time. The crowd was all gone.

Jessie Munnings was my friend, not my best one but we were
in the same class together, only I'd joined the public library

46

and was reading Thornton Wilder, about Little Jerry Muskrat, Peter Cottontail and Granny and Reddy Fox, and she was only on number five Beacon Reader, you know, with the stories about the gingerbread man and little half-chick who was going to the Dovre Fell to tell the king the sky was falling. I found Jess playing hopscotch with her mouth open in concentration. What should I say?

'Play fivestones, Jess?'

'Our dad hung hisself,' she answered. I waited while she hopped to the double-end square and turned. 'I'm not going to school Wednesday, it's the funeral. Our mum says I got to have a black band on my sleeve and go too.'

She flipped a stone along the pavement and began again, hopping and landing slap on her sandals with her feet apart.

'You coming to school Monday?' I asked.

'Maybe, it depends how I feel. My mum says it hasn't really hit me yet. She says I mayn't feel like school by the time Monday comes.'

I considered this carefully. Jessie was all of a sudden someone of stature, a tragic figure with deep feelings that might well up violently and swamp her whole being so that she couldn't come to school on Monday. Soppy little Jessie Munnings; 'Your nose is running,' the other kids shouted after her and, as so often, it was cruel but true. Jessie's mum didn't believe in tampering with nature, so she breathed adenoidally through her open mouth and in the winter had two shiny candles on her upper lip.

'Jessie Munnings, blow your nose,' our teacher would say.

'Please, miss, I haven't got no handkerchief.'

'You mean you have got one?'

'No, miss.'

'Come out and get a piece of paper and go out to the lavatory and blow it. And do try to remember "two negatives make an affirmative, two no's make a yes," ' to Jessie's uncomprehending eyes. Then, sickened by the child's face, 'Oh, get along, child.'

'Yes, miss.'

She was a podgy child, with straight brown hair cut in a fringe. She never smiled, not because she was thinking profoundly but because she hadn't the wit. Her solemn expression

47

hid an abyss. She hadn't even the sense to be afraid. Not like my real friend, Beryl, who was quick, brown and timid like a mouse.

'I don't know what you see in her,' my mother said, 'you always pick such funny people for friends.'

Beryl and me went everywhere together. She was my faithful henchman when I baited old mother Parsons, banging her gate as we passed, because she was a witch. But not on Good Friday.

'Why not today?' asked Beryl.

'Because Jesus is dead and so she can put a spell on us.'

That afternoon we crept past under the screen of her ragged privet hedge.

'Come and get oranges,' said Jess, pocketing her flat stone.

On Saturday morning the men who delivered the weekend's supply of fruit to Mills the greengrocer, stood on the tailboard of their lorry tossing spare apples and oranges to the band of waiting kids. Usually it was a yelling, shoving mob, with whoever had the longest arm and the swiftest eye getting a coveted fruit, but this morning was different. There was a sudden silence among the children when we appeared round the corner. Then a rustle sighed through the group, which parted like the Red Sea for Moses. Unconcerned, taking this tribute as though she were used to it, Jessie marched straight through the middle, took an orange and an apple from the lorryman, turned and walked away.

All weekend, Mr. Munnings swung in my head, turning slowly on his rope, with an upturned chair beneath his feet. His head was jerked to one side like Mr. Punch, his tongue stuck out and his eyes bulged.

On Sunday afternoon, I decided to go fishing. I wouldn't wait for Beryl to come and call, I'd go by myself. She wasn't any good for fishing anyway. She liked playing hospitals and schools best, silly girls' games.

'Can I have some bread and paste, Mum?'

'What for?'

'Going fishing.'

'Alright. Mind how you cut the bread. If you cut your fingers off by mistake you won't be able to hold the rod.'

I collected my equipment, piece of bread and paste, for bait, if I didn't eat it first; jam-jar with string handle; a couple of bent pins for hooks; bamboo rod which was really an old curtain-rod, and a twist of black cotton round a piece of paper.

'Don't come home with your boots full of water and your socks all wet. And be in for bed by six,' my mother said. 'Aren't you going to wait for Beryl?'

'She's no good at fishing.' I swung on the door-handle.

'I see, who is it this time? Off with the old, on with the new, that's you. Poor little Beryl.'

'I'm going by myself.'

'And what am I supposed to say if she comes round for you?'

'Say I'll see her Monday.'

'I'm glad I'm not one of your friends.'

Miserable but defiant I took my gear over the railway bridge, through the fields, hot and sweet-smelling of grasses with a tang of sorrel, down to the sombre green coolness of the river bank, overhung with stunted willows, I could climb and make my castle. I set up my rod, ate some of the bait and wandered out from under the trees into the full sun of the meadows, and threw myself down on the grass. I peered into the dry stalks. A leaf-hopper clung to a stem in front of me, undisturbed by the earthquake I must have caused by my sudden entry into his world. Perhaps he thought he was disguised by his flat, green wing-cases. Cautiously, he twitched a leg. An ant hurried towards me looking for some grotesque burden to take upon himself. I felt like Gulliver.

Dazed with the beating sun and fixed staring into the microscopic, insect world, I staggered to my feet. The meadow swung round, the day darkened, then, as I shook my head, grew bright again. I went back to the river, picked up my rod and began to trail the bread and paste through the water. I cast out farther and let it sink slowly through the opaque water until it rested on the soft, oozy bed.

'Why should I bring Beryl?' I thought. I wanted to be alone, to let thoughts glide smooth as the lazy slack-bodied river, mind become as dark and soft as the muddy bottom where strange delicate weeds could grow and send their boneless limbs up through the pale brown water, shifting and swaying with every eddy.

Suddenly, the line grew taut and darted away. I had a fish. Must be a big one too, about three inches long judging by the power of its pull and the silver gleam of the upturned belly. I played it carefully as a trout or salmon, brought it gradually in to the bank until it was trapped in the puddle made by the heavy hoof of a drinking cow. Gently I tilted the rod high, higher, until the fish hung gasping above its little pool. I steadied the rod until the silver body hung still and limp, then it began to jerk, twisting from side to side, embedding my mother's bent pin deeper in its throat. Back and forth it leapt, swinging wildly. Then, just as suddenly, it stopped. Once more it hung limp, only this time it was dead weight and it began to twist gently on the thread, turning, turning. I watched until it hung still again; there was no breeze.

Disgusted, I tore it off the hook, its throat ripped open, and threw it out into the middle of the stream where it sank rapidly. When the evening came down with cool shadows and a light breeze, it would drift slowly to the surface, eyeballs thick as the beaten white of an egg, and gently the little fish would nibble the flesh from the hair-thin bones, with the little mouths that broke against my flesh when I sat for a long time with my feet in the water, the toes white and distorted like dead flesh; and the air-light skeleton, like the bones of leaves, would sink back again to the welcoming slime of the dark river bed.

Water had seeped into my shoes, a dark stain was slowly eating up my white ankle-socks.

'Don't come home with your boots full of water and your socks all wet.'

I retreated to the bank, I had wandered into the shallows, and stripped off socks and shoes. The shoes I emptied out, scraped off the thick sole of mud with a stick, and put them to dry. With the socks, I waded out into mid-stream and tried to wash them. Mud squeezed up between my toes and the water clouded in swirls, like tea when the milk goes in last. Then I ran up and down in the hot grass, whirling them round my head like a lariat until they were dry enough to put on. My shoes I blackened with juice from dock leaves. They looked rather dull but the dust would cover that as I walked home.

The sun was nearly down. Soon the dead fish would ride through the muddy stream with its white staring eyes like beads. I picked up my tackle and turned home, the wild rye sticking its sharp arrow heads in my still-damp socks as I dragged my feet through the grass.

On Monday morning, Jess had a piece of black ribbon tacked round the left sleeve of her faded blue coat—'cat's tooth stitches' my mother would have called them. Obviously whatever it was still hadn't hit her. When she got two out of ten for mental, it didn't seem to matter. I got five, somehow I couldn't concentrate on bottles and corks at a shilling and a halfpenny and three dozen buttons at tuppence three farthings a dozen, and only just escaped having to stay in at play-time.

Let out at a quarter to eleven, we roared into the playground, boys and girls immediately segregated to their different paddocks. In the girls' playground the warfare was more subtle, instead of a blow the fear of ridicule, the harsh sting of laughter. Several of the big girls linked arms in a chain that swung and wheeled about the tarmac square, closing in on a trembling victim.

'What's your favourite colour; what's your lucky number; what's your favourite boy's name?'

And whatever you answered they would seize on it, couple it with a surname and scream and point with wild, painful laughter. Only no one picked on Jess.

At the top end, a long rope was being tossed over and over with a smack in the dust. I watched the long-legged girls run in, skip twice, and then out. If they hesitated and the rope slapped their ankles they took the end while the other girl joined the long queue waiting for their turn. Jess was at the head of the queue, she ran in, bounced ready to skip, the rope smacked her on the shins.

'Your ender,' called one of the girls, running forward and then, remembering, she stopped.

'Don't matter, you can have another go,' and Jess ambled back to the end of the line. The whistle blew, we lined up,

Jessie was talking to the girl behind her but Miss Parsons didn't say anything.

At dinner-time, I pushed my food around my plate, cold meat, pickles and boiled potatoes. A disconsolate smell of washing hung about the place, the pegged-out clothes were heavy and languid, sagging in the airless garden. I watched my mother cautiously across the table.

'Mum, Jessie Munnings' got a black ribbon round her arm.'

'Oh yes,' my mother was unimpressed, 'I must say it seems unnecessary to trick the child out like that. I suppose they'll take her to the funeral, too.'

'It's on Wednesday.'

'So I heard. Oh well, some people have funny ways of carrying on, I must say. Eat up, you've hardly touched your dinner.'

'Don't want it.'

'There's a bone in the larder, but you must finish up those potatoes first.'

'Don't want it.'

'What's the matter with you then, sickening for something? I've never known you refuse a bone before.'

'Don't feel like it. Can I get down, please?'

'Better take a mac with you this afternoon, looks like rain.'

'I'll be alright.'

My mother watched me out of the door, her hand on her hip.

'Hurry up, Dreamer, you'll get there for Christmas,' she called.

Supposing, just supposing.

Shadows drifted across the sun all afternoon. We shifted on our sticky seats and left sweaty thumb-prints on our reading books. By going-home time the sky was ready to crack. We dawdled along, shouting abuse at each other.

'Owen Jelly got no belly!'

'Sticks and stones may break my bones
But names will never hurt me.'

Only nobody shouted at Jess.

Supposing, just supposing. And then I'd be all alone in the world, like in the stories.

'Tell us a story, Mum.'

'What one d'you want?'

'The Little Match Girl.'

'But you've heard that hundreds of times.'

'Oh, go on!'

'Once upon a time there was a little match girl, who was all alone in the world . . .'

Then they'd put me in a home for good, and everyone'd feel sorry for me, but I wouldn't stay. I'd run away and live wild in the woods on nuts and honey, or keep a goat on the bare back of the downs. I'd drink the milk and make cheese. Could you make butter out of goat's milk? And when there was a kid I'd kill it and roast it and make clothes out of its skin. I'd be tall and strong and run a mile without getting out of breath and I'd know everything about everything and no one would have to teach me. I watched myself, lonely and magnificent, striding down the years. Then the sky warped suddenly and the lightning ripped it open.

Rain began to fall in big spattering drops leaving dark stains as large as pennies on the grey pavement. She hated storms, she was terrified of lightning and the cracking thunder. I pulled my coat up over my head and ran.

The muscles in thigh and calf seemed as if they would burst, a sharp pain stabbed my chest, my throat was dry and sore by the time I dashed up the alley and in at the back door. I pulled my coat from my head and breathed heavily through my nose to stop the pain of cold, quick air in my chest. Then I listened. There was only the sound of my own breath and drumming blood.

'Mum?'

The sky answered with a whip of lightning that lashed the smarting earth. I only counted three before the thunder spat and snarled over the house-top. Now, in the pause that followed, I could hear the rain flooding the guttering and pouring down the side of the house.

'You've done it.'

The room was very dark.

'You've done it.'

'No, please, I didn't mean it. Please, God, no, please!'

'She's gone, she's lying out there after the lightning. Out there with the rain falling on her.'

'I didn't mean it, you know I didn't really mean it. Mum, please! Please, please, if she isn't dead, let me die instead.'

'You did it. You did it.'

A fist of storm shook the house, the lightning threw up the familiar furniture in grotesque, menacing relief. My shaking hands gripped the edge of the table, slid down the bulbous leg and dropped me, sobbing, on the floor.

'Whatever is the matter?' my mother said when she found me.

'I couldn't find you. I didn't know where you were.'

'But you've never been afraid of storms before. I'm the one who's afraid, not you.'

'I know. I know you are. I wasn't afraid. I ran all the way home 'cos I knew you'd be frightened. Where've you been?'

'I went upstairs to put a pail under that bit in the ceiling where the loose slate is. Then the storm got worse so I drew the curtains and sat in the dark. Come on now, it's all over. There's that bone in the larder still. D'you want it now?'

I nodded. In a dark corner of my mind something hung, turning slowly, but I shut the door on it.

She came back with the knuckle joint of yesterday's roast lamb on a plate. As I sank my teeth into the half-raw meat and sucked out the marrow, a few last tears trickled down my face and salted the flesh. Outside, the storm was nearly over.

6

MAYBE you're wondering how we suddenly had the affluence of a whole house, considering we could hardly afford rooms before, well all this time my mother's elder sister, Ada, the only one still alive apart from Aunt Lyddy, had been in and out of hospital, after Gran died and I was born, and she was dying of it. Dingy alright she was now, her quick brain, brightest of the family, sharpened nearly to the point of madness by years of bedpans, sputum tests, trivial hospital gossip of tantrums, changes in treatment, criticism of sister, all to ignore the continual undertone of death and the slow decay of constant inactivity.

'I shall die if I have to stay here any longer,' she said when Louey visited her. My mother knew what she meant. She'd seen it so often she knew—like the prince in the story who turned his face to the wall. Sometimes they get so much better they're even ready to go home and then the night before they leave they suddenly grow pale, the temperature shoots up, the pulse races wildly, they cough and spit for the first time in weeks—not excitement, but fear. Fear of the outside world and all its demands and responsibilities, homes, families—they who haven't even been responsible for their own bowels for perhaps as much as a year—burns up the last drop of courage. There's no physical reason; the doctors shake their heads and the screens are wheeled round. Oh, Mum knew alright.

But what could she do? Then Ada found the answer herself. In the next bed was a lady who owned two houses in the town where I was born, one by the sea, one on the healthy, high downs. The one by the sea was out for a peppercorn rent if my mother would take poor Dingy out of the sanatorium and nurse her. Ill herself at the time, she couldn't refuse.

Childlike, of course, I didn't realize my aunt was responsible for our sudden rise in fortune—the house was ours, Mum's and mine, and she was just coming to stay for a while.

'Why's all the post always for her?' I demanded, when there was yet another pound box of chocolates from her ex-boss, or a seven-pound tin of fancy biscuits such as I'd never seen before: creams and shiny chocolate coatings, lemon fluffs, puffy marshmallows dusted with flour, brittle ginger snaps and coconut crunches.

'They'll make her cough like Billy-O,' said my mother, 'some people have no idea.'

'I hate her, nothing ever comes for us any more. I wish she weren't coming.' It was like the fanfare before a princess, a showering cornucopia of fudge and toffees and almond whorls in gleaming tin-foil wrappers, festive as flung confetti.

My complaints soon died away when she arrived to share them out among us. Her bed was downstairs, in the front room with the sun-washed walls, so that she could look out of the window and see the usually trivial comings and goings of our side street, and the light was good enough to read by for hours on end, as she turned the pages of a large book propped on a stand across her knees so she wouldn't tire herself holding it. Wet afternoons we sat with the great tray laid flat on her bed doing incredibly complicated circular jig-saws with thousands of pieces, usually half a dozen historical scenes unfolding like a pageant.

'I've done a bit, I've done a bit!'

Sometimes I took a piece and hid it, so that I was the one to have the victory of finishing and she would accuse me sharply, calling my mother to arbitrate between us, like a child my own age. Occasionally, to keep the peace, my mother joined in the game but she was never as passionately involved as my aunt and I, and she often took the chance when we were busy to slip out shopping. When she came back, my aunt would pounce on her with tales of my cheating.

'Can't I leave you two alone five minutes?'

'Where've you been? Who did you see? What did they say?'

Ada would demand in inquisition. The real world of decision and action had receded so far from her in those sanatorium years, once she was even in the care of nuns vowed to exasperating and eternal silence, that in compensation and to give her quick mind something to work on, she had developed a strange faculty for vicarious living. She sucked every savour of interest from my mother's tiny doings and left them like gristle, a tasteless, indigestible mess to be spat out quietly in private. But while my mother shrank and withered under the strain, Ada grew fatter and stronger. One day she announced that she was getting up for the first time in six years. Gradually, she became well enough to take a bus to the sea-front and sit on the stony beach in a deck-chair, with her sun-shade and the crossword puzzle which she did every day, bar Sundays, for nearly twenty years, and once won a fountain pen and a postal order that bought my teddy bear six months before I was born. In our back yard she planted a handkerchief lawn to sit on when next summer came. Its black soil was stuck through with hundreds of frail green pins, when war was declared.

If anyone stops me in the street and sticks a microphone under my nose and says, 'What do you remember about the beginning of World War II?' I shall have to say, honestly, nothing. Just suddenly I was in the middle of it and there were different things to do, an unreality about doing ordinary things and nothing more. I remember my mother being very indignant about people who had the money and stocked their larders with tinned foods of every kind in case of rationing. Exhausted with months of caring for all three of us, by the constant friction between me and my aunt:

'But, Mum, she's a grown-up, she shouldn't be like that.'

'You must realize she's not well. Hasn't been well for years.' My mother fell ill again herself. While she gathered her fragmented will for another assault on living, Aunt Lyddy came down to look after us. At once she organized us for war. The cupboard under the stairs was scrubbed and whitewashed for a shelter, the great round mahogany table became an Anderson, the double bed where my mother and I slept was moved downstairs to the back room.

Now the raids really began. Every night the siren warned

us that the bombers were roaring over our heads towards London. As soon as they had passed, the All-Clear signalled our relief until the early hours of the morning when they would be on their way back. Aunt Lyddy began to worry about her family left behind. Cousin Gilly came down to stay, and together we crouched under the table shield when the siren went.

Only Ada really enjoyed it. She was living at last. With her over-developed capacity for sucking every last drop of significance from what she read or heard, she suffered and gloried in the war. She had a vast map of the world pinned on the wall and daily she charted 'that madman Hitler's enormities'. She rushed from her room in the morning as soon as the paper plopped through the letter-box, and consumed every news item with a wolfish hunger for the details of our every early defeat.

One day she came to the foot of the stairs, crying and calling.

'I thought she'd been taken ill, my dear, I really did, but it was only that we'd shot down a hundred and eighty-five German planes in a night.' The war was hotting up. My mother discharged herself from hospital and came back to look after us; Aunt Lyddy returned to London and her family.

At school we were issued with gas masks in biscuit-coloured cardboard boxes that bumped round our necks on bits of string. I pretended a headache and didn't want to go to school when the day came to try them on, but my mother found out in time and marched me firmly to my fate. In the end I was filled with pride because my head was too big for the usual babies' mickey-mouse mask and I had to have a real grown-up one.

Like my aunt, Miss Wilkinson was in her element. She joined the Civil Defence, learned to fire an ack-ack gun and trundled it round the streets at night. She appeared in her armband and tin hat on the platform at assembly.

'Now, children, we can't all be soldiers and fight for our country but we can all help the war effort in our own little ways. You can help by being economical. You see my blue sandals. I've had them for eight years and they've still got years of wear in them, because I clean them every day. Now that's one way you can all do your bit, by cleaning your shoes every day.

The country can't afford to waste new shoes on lazy boys and girls, when she has to find boots for her soldiers.'

Dog-fights, all-night raids, fire drill had all become part of our everyday existence. The sky above our houses roared and smoked with fighters that twisted and gyred in a crazy dance of death; mad, winged insects set to music by Walt Disney. Occasionally we saw one spiral smoking down, to be swallowed by the heaving sea. One Sunday dinner was cooked and eaten in sorties from the shelter cupboard during lulls in the fighting.

'I think I can just get the peas on,' and almost before the gas was alight, the hiccupping drone of their engines was heard again. Another night, the gasometer was riddled by hit-and-run machine-gun fire. Fortunately, it was empty, but they were getting close. Miss Rouse, a schoolteacher who rented our top back room at this time (there was a succession of strange ladies in and out of our back room, including once a Miss Pound and her sister on a drawn-out holiday from the asylum, who eked out our small living) and was a member·of one of the more obscure sects that flourish in tin chapels in seaside towns, thumped her ancient upright piano with even deeper conviction on Sunday afternoons, when she treated us to a recital of the gloomier hymns.

'If only she'd change her tune,' Aunt Ada wailed, 'can't you ask her for something just a bit livelier, Louey?' But my mother knew where her extra money to tide us all over came from, and Miss Rouse continued to make a glad sound to the Lord.

It was half past five in the morning when my mother woke. Overhead an engine coughed and moaned.

'Don't like the sound of that,' she thought. 'Think I'll get up and make a cup of tea.'

They say you don't hear the scream of a falling bomb when it's coming straight for you. I did. I swear I did; that and the shatter of every window in the house as the card walls crumpled around us—then silence. Heavy iron weights seemed to be lying across my body. I couldn't move even a finger, my mouth was an ashy grate choked with sulphurous cinders and dust. I don't know if I lost consciousness at all. My mother, hit on the head by falling masonry, lay stunned and silent in the dark beside me. Gradually the waves of shock subsided, but when she managed to speak to me it was only in the faintest of whispers. Her voice had gone.

Somewhere, far away in the house, we began to hear sounds, voices, heavy feet, rescue.

'Help!' I shouted. 'We've been bombed. Get us out of here!'

'Sh!' said my mother. 'Listen.' The voices were clearer now, through some trick of acoustics we could hear them although they couldn't hear us.

'Is there anyone else in there?' a low, masculine voice asked.

'Yes, there's a lady and her little girl down there somewhere,' Miss Rouse's high voice cracked with fear.

'We took a woman out of the front room but we can't find no one else.'

'They must be there somewhere.'

'Now you must shout as loud as you can because they won't hear me,' my mother whispered, her words rustling like drops of rain in the booming silence that still roared with the memory of the explosion. And so I shouted; I yelled and hollered the same stupid words again and again.

'We've been bombed. Get us out of here.' We were alive. We had survived; they must find us. Then suddenly they were there.

'You're standing on my leg,' I shouted, as if it mattered.

Carefully they began to remove the joists and masonry pegging us down.

'Don't worry, we'll soon have you out. Good job you've got fair hair, girlie. Saw a little tiny bit sticking up in the dark. Then we heard you shouting.'

The dust and tumbled debris had choked the words in my throat. My mother lay on the outside and they worked towards her.

'Don't bother about me, I'm alright. Take my little girl out first.'

'Alright, lady, we'll have you both out. Don't worry.' But they did as she said.

I was lifted from the rubble and carried out by a fireman. I remember his blue serge jacket. His mother lived at the end of the road and he took me straight there, up the steps, through to the kitchen. The old lady washed me and tried to comb the filthy mat of hair that stood up all over my head. Then she gave me a hard-boiled egg and bread and butter for breakfast. They clung to the inside of my mouth. I couldn't seem to swallow. My nostrils burned and my stomach retched with the stink of explosives. I fell asleep jerkily, in the armchair, and she carried me upstairs.

When they dug my mother out in her turn, they set her on her feet.

'Can you walk?' the A.R.P. man asked.

'Of course,' she answered and began to pick her way carefully over the floor, needled with splinters of wood and glass.

'But you've got no shoes on!' he exclaimed, as her bare feet winced.

'D'you think I go to bed with my boots on?' she said scornfully.

'Come on,' laughed the man, 'put this round your shoulders and I'll carry you. Why, there's nothing of you at all.' He lifted her and strode through the shattered house, his big boots crushing the broken glass like ice cubes.

Outside the morning was pale grey and a dismal draught leaked through the broken street. Ada lay on the pavement, a blanket thrown over the splintered stumps of her legs. Someone had given her a cloth with which she tried to wipe away the blood that trickled down her forehead from the raw wounds in her head.

'I want to go with them. I must go with them,' she moaned repeatedly.

'Put me down,' my mother said. Barefoot on the cold paving stones, she stepped forward.

'Ada, Ada, it's me, Louey.'

'Lou! You won't let them take me away again. I must come with you.'

'It's alright. I won't let them take you away. You're coming with us always.' Two hours later she died on the pavement. It hadn't seemed worthwhile to move her. Wearily, my mother got up. Someone had found her an old pair of shoes.

'You come in here, my dear. Bring her in here,' called old Mrs. Caplin from three doors along, and drew her gently into the musty house.

'It shouldn't have happened,' my mother said bitterly. 'She was doing so well. She was getting better. Better than she'd been for years and all wasted.'

'Drink a drop of tea and then up to bed.'

'But there's so much to do. The funeral. I must send telegrams to Skippy and Lyddy and Dick,' but she was already sagging in the chair.

'Off to bed now, off to bed.'

They told me she was dead. They meant well, of course. They knew the dark lady in the house had died and so they told me.

'My mother's not dead. I won't believe, I won't.' All day I sat in the front-room window, peering up the road. Two days passed, three days, then, in the afternoon of the fourth day, I saw her—a tiny figure far off but I knew it. Every scrap of clothing we possessed had been destroyed and they had clothed her out of the Red Cross store, but she was so small that nothing fitted. It was drizzling. She wore a long mackintosh that flapped and clung around her ankles, Chaplinesque wellington boots, so many sizes too large they seemed to have a life of their own, and a squashed brown halo hat. Her face was yellow and her eyes bolted out of the sockets with tiredness, her hair was strangely, suddenly streaked with grey, but she came on doggedly towards me, as I gazed out of that front-room window, down the road, in those daft boots, and she was alive.

7

THEY told us afterwards that it was a very small bomb. Big enough, we reckoned. It totally demolished two houses and killed two old ladies further down the street by shaking down their ceiling and smothering them in their sleep. The bomb fell obliquely between the two houses, landing at the foot of our stairs outside Ada's door. The stairs vanished completely—Miss Rouse had to be rescued by the firemen from her back window, in full elopement style. She was in the lavatory, being an early riser, when it fell. The door was blown off its hinges in her bedroom, across the room and out the window, leaving her neatly laid breakfast table untouched. The A.R.P. men carried it down just as it was, crockery correctly placed on the white cloth and stood it in the street, knife and spoon forlornly just so. We never saw her again.

Blast plays strange tricks, like a spiteful child. My mother's machine vanished as surely as Miss Rouse, the solid, mahogany shield of the table splintered like ply-board; the old-fashioned marble-topped gas stove was sliced clean through, like a hot knife through butter; the cupboard shelter, so carefully prepared by Aunt Lyddy, looked as if a cleansing wind had swept through, leaving it empty as a sun-dried crab shell above the tide line; the gas meter hung by a thread. Heavy boots had trampled over my aunt's lawn.

The next day, the looters moved in. My mother was too ill to get up.

'Tell me where everything is and I'll see to it,' said old Mrs. Caplin. My mother whispered her instructions and the old lady went into action.

'Young man, young man, there are two pairs of sheets in that drawer. Don't tell me you can only find one. I know there are two.' She directed from the bottom of the ladder.

Mr. Knight, who lived next door, was an invalid. When they found him they had to carry him out, a big man, heavy with years of inactivity. They sat him down in a chair in the street.

'Are you alright, Granpa?'

He mumbled and shook his head.

'What's the matter then, old chap?' The fireman bent his head close to the old man's loose, trembling mouth.

'Me teef, me teef. I can't talk wivout me teef,' he spluttered. They found them where he had left them, in a glass of water by the bed. Then he explained his real concern. Rex, his massive alsatian, my bucking bronco in cowboy days, was missing.

'Run away, most like.'

'Not my Rex, no. He wouldn't run away. He's in there somewhere.' For three days the old man fretted and then finally to convince him they carried his chair into the shell. He called and whistled.

'Give it up, Dad,' urged his son, who'd come up for the occasion. At the foot of the stairs was a great heap of rubble. The old man called again. Something stirred in the heap and whimpered faintly.

'That's him, that's my boy.' Rex was unharmed but starving when they dug him out. It was the early days of the bombing, and we hadn't grown used to the miracle finds that were an everyday occurrence in London.

Like all of us who'd been buried, Rex suffered from cramp and muscular aches for days after his release. I had moved in to Mrs. Caplin's with my mother and every night before bed we had a stinking session of rubbing each other with embrocation, and even now if I catch a whiff of that stinging smell I'm back in the dark little room with the big brass bed.

My mother's eldest brother came down for the funeral.

'What will you do now?' he asked, his polished coconut head shining on his little fat cheeks—'like a little bum,' my mother said—puffed out with the importance of the moment.

'I haven't thought. There's been so much to do.'

I went back to school as soon as I had been fitted out with

enough clothes. We were the first civilian victims in the town and a fund was set up to help us. Miss Wilkinson took me out to morning coffee on Saturday morning to give my mother a chance to get on with things.

I had never been out to morning coffee before—that splendid middle-class institution that was such a symbol in my life—I don't think I'd ever been in a restaurant before. I stared around.

'What would you like?' Miss Wilkinson asked. I read the word HORLICKS on the wall, but perhaps that wasn't the right thing to ask for. I was terrified of showing my lack of knowledge, of appearing badly brought up. Suddenly it came to me.

'Milk with a dash, please.' Miss Wilkinson looked at me oddly.

'You're sure you wouldn't like orange squash or a milk-shake?' she asked.

'No, thank you. I'd like milk with a dash, please.' Miss Wilkinson roared with laughter and then sobered down to make the order.

'Tell me all about it,' my mother said when I got home. I told her.

'It was alright, wasn't it?' I begged.

'What made you ask for that?'

'I don't know. Something you said once. It was alright, wasn't it?'

'Oh yes. That was fine. Did you like it?'

'Yes, yes. I liked it. But I didn't let you down, did I?'

'No, of course not. I like it myself. It was the right thing to do. What did Miss Wilkinson say?'

'She laughed.'

'I see. I expect she was a little surprised that you should ask for anything so grown-up.'

At school it was my turn to play hero. All sorts of strange things were brought that we couldn't possibly need and one day I was given a seven-pound jar of home-made strawberry jam to take home. It was wrapped in old clothes to cushion it and put in a carrier bag.

'Now mind you don't drop it,' I was told.

'Hold it up in your arms in case the string breaks.'

So I staggered off with this thing clutched to me. We had hardly got out of the school doors and were streaming up the drive, out into the wide avenue that led into the main part of the town, bordered with trees and grass and small shrubs, when a plane appeared at the end of the road, very low, coming down the road as if trying to land. We gazed at it for a moment, then there was a metallic, staccato clatter and little puffs of dust zipped up from the roadway. Children scattered in all directions as they realized what was happening. I hugged my monster jam-jar even tighter and dived for the nearest bush. Other children were falling down flat in the gutter too, as they'd been told or read, or saw in a film. As the plane came in for a second time and passed low over my head, I looked up and saw the pilot looking down, peering through his goggles, anonymous in his leather flying helmet, and remembered what my mother had said about the Zeppelins.

'And there they were; Germans, real Germans, at the end of our street.'

The plane zoomed away and the danger passed. We picked ourselves up and started for home as fast as we could, me still clutching the pot of jam. I hadn't got much further when the siren went. I jogged steadily on as its stomach-turning wail died miserably away. As I turned a corner, a couple of streets from home—home was Mrs. Caplin's now—a shrieking wind lifted the hair on my head as something passed over and once again I threw myself down on top of the precious jam. There was a tremendous 'whump' quite close by and a lady ran out of the nearest house, calling out to me, 'You'd better come in here, my dear, til it's all over.'

Strangely, that seemed to be the only one. A little later the All-Clear went and I said goodbye and hurried home. Mrs. Caplin met me at the door, her white hair blown about her face, like old man's beard on an autumn hedge, her face ash-grey. She had been at the front door looking anxiously out for me when a great hand of blast had taken her up and thrown her down the passage to the foot of the stairs.

'Where's Mum?' I wanted to know.

'Out shopping somewhere in the town.'

She'd gone to buy shoes. They were the one thing that no

one could supply, shoes small enough to fit her, and she'd gone out just to get them.

She was on her way home in the bus when the siren went, the new shoes in a box neatly tied up with string and brown paper. She was the only one on board when the bus drew up; they always stopped during the raids. The driver joined his mate in the bus. They must have heard the same almighty 'whump'.

'Don't worry, lady,' said the conductor as she jumped in her seat. 'Nowhere near us, over in the east side of town.'

'That's where I live. My little girl's over there. I must get home. If you won't drive me, I'll get out and walk.'

They looked at each other, and then at her.

'Alright, missus, we'll take you home,' said the driver. 'You can only die once. Come on, Charlie.' And he ambled back to his cab.

They dropped her five minutes' walk from our road and she scurried off clutching the shoes.

'She'll be alright. Don't worry,' the driver shouted after her.

As she turned the corner, an ambulance tore past, bell clanging. People were hurrying down the road. At the end of our street a neighbour ran out into the garden.

'They nearly got you again, Mrs. Mahoney.' My mother leaned against the gatepost, her face staining yellow with fear.

'Here, come in and sit down a minute.'

'No, I'll be alright. I must get home,' but for the moment she couldn't make her legs work. The woman disappeared inside and came rushing back with a little glass of pale, cold tea.

'Drink this. It'll do you good.'

My mother choked down the brandy and handed back the glass.

'You sure you won't come in for a bit?'

She shook her head. 'No thanks, I must get home. Thanks for the drink,' and she was already scurrying away.

At the door she fumbled desperately in her bag for the key, then beat frantically with the knocker.

'That'll be her now,' said Mrs. Caplin. She made her way slowly up the passage, her legs still crumbly with shock, and opened the door.

'Where is she, is she alright?' My mother pushed past the old lady into the passage.

'She's alright. Nothing wrong with her. We've been worried about you.' But my mother didn't hear her. She reached the living-room.

'You're alright, you're alright. I've been so worried.' She threw her shoes on to the table, slumped into a chair, put her face on her arms and cried, great dry sobs that shook me through.

'I'm alright,' I said. 'Look, I'm alright,' stroking her wiry hair that would never be its dark, dark brown again, but always after threaded with grey, as I remember it best.

'Shoes on the table, new shoes on the table. That's un-lucky,' scolded Mrs. Caplin. 'I never did. What we all need is a cup of tea.'

'I don't care. You're alright.' But she took them off all the same.

That decided us. We'd had enough. After all, you can't be lucky all the time. That land mine had fallen in the street back-ing on to ours, demolishing a whole block, killing and injuring twenty people. Anyway, what was there to stay for now? We couldn't live with Mrs. Caplin indefinitely. She and her husband were over seventy and the patter of tiny feet on the lino or the thump as I jumped from slip-mat to slip-mat in the carefully polished passage soon got on their nerves.

Used to the discipline of an earlier generation, they thought my mother was too lenient with me.

'You can't hit me, you're not my mother,' I said one night when the old lady raised her hand to me because I wouldn't go to bed. 'You're a silly old woman.'

Mum was called at once and my rudeness repeated.

'She's quite right,' said my mother. 'No one punishes her but me. On the other hand, I won't have you being rude. Come here.' I knew what was coming and began to cry as I walked towards her. She pulled down my pyjama trousers and tanned my bottom hard.

'Now upstairs to bed,' she said, pulling them up again and tying the cord. Up in the bedroom she sat on the edge of the bed and held me close.

'Don't cry. It's all over,' but she was crying too now. 'I know you're naughty sometimes but you're all I've got. I won't have other people punish you. They don't understand. Don't worry, we're going away. We'll be by ourselves again. It'll be alright.'

'Where are we going?'

'We're going to Wortbridge to stay with Brother Rob. We'll be alright. Only you must try and help me and not get on Mrs. Caplin's nerves. They're old. They don't remember what it was like to be young.'

'When are we going?'

'Next week. As soon as we're packed. You'll have to help me pack.'

'I will. What's it like?'

'I don't know, I've never been there before. It's country. You'll like that.'

'It'll be my birthday in a fortnight, I'll have my birthday in Wortbridge. I'll go to a new school. I'll be seven.'

8

WHEN the famous poet was appointed vicar of Wortbridge in the eighteenth century, he wrote:
  'And so I have come to this thriving industrial
town.'

By the time we first saw it, nearly two centuries later on a
misty October afternoon, the industrial tide had receded far
out, leaving it like the stranded towns of the south coast, with
a smack of the sea and strange flotsam and jetsam from an
earlier prosperity. I think of other towns left high and dry by
change—the dozing village in the Essex summer heat with only
the huge church, too big for the shrunken congregation, and
sagging timbered guildhall left to prove it was once the centre
of the cutlery industry before Sheffield was thought of; the
houses of wool merchant princes in Suffolk, memorials of
comfort and prosperity, vanished four hundred years.

Wortbridge still had three mills, boasting finest West of
England cloth. As we turned up towards his house, my wrinkled
walnut uncle carrying the case, my mother and I stared in
horror at the tumbled buildings, old cottages overgrown with
weeds, littered waste ground fenced with rusty broken wire,
where a tribe of scruffy children shouted and clambered.

'Have you had bombs here, then?' she asked, thinking we
had come all this way to get away from them, just for nothing.
My uncle laughed.

'No fear!'

'But all those houses?'

'They just fell down.'

His own house was in a new estate of semi-detached, stone-dashed villas on the edge of town. It seemed very posh to me. But we didn't stay long. It was too small for two families and my mother liked her independence. She soon found us a couple of rooms in Clarence Street, the one with the broken-down cottages, of course, and we moved in.

I think I hated Wortbridge from the beginning. I was different from these people. I knew it and they knew it. Later on, rationalizing, I said the place had all the worst characteristics of town and country. The people seemed to me slow and thick, in speech and in the head. My accent marked me out at once as a vaccy. I gloried in it. I cherished and cosseted my cockney ways. I wouldn't become a moonraker, a swede. Once they refused to serve my mother in the fish-and-chip shop because she was a 'bloody Londoner'.

'And who's winning the war for you?' my mother replied. 'The bloody Londoners. You don't know there's a war on down here,' and she marched out, all five feet one and a half inches rigid with fury. That's how our private war was declared.

In their turn, of course, the Wortbridgers distrusted the vaccies with their quick ways and sharp, pinched faces. They said they were all dirty, all had fleas, were sewn into their clothes for the winter, that they were light-fingered and only out for what they could get out of you. Oh, an endless list of complaints. I reckon they'd've been nicer to the enemy, certainly there would have been more in common between the average young German soldiers and these solid Saxons.

As it happened, we didn't stay for long that first time. It seemed no sooner we were moved in to a couple of rooms in Clarence Street than my mother was ill again and whisked off to hospital in another part of the country. I was billeted out.

I often think that most of the people who took in evacuees did it in a thwarted missionary spirit. If their lives had been ordered otherwise they would have gone off to convert the heathen to cleanliness and godliness, in that order. We were a heaven-sent chance to use up all those latent talents. I know how the natives in a newly discovered tribe feel now, with their own traditions of combing and dressing their hair and oiling their skins, suddenly told to give it all up in favour of soap and water. All at once they are made to feel unclean, social out-casts, savages in spite of their most complex and subtle codes governing individual and communal behaviour. Mrs. Avery was convinced from the beginning that I was a thief and a liar, and it was her duty to reform me.

'Tell the truth and shame the devil,' she shouted at me, thrusting her face into mine, when I'd dropped a bottle of milk I was bringing home from the dairy.

'A boy jumped out on me from behind a hedge and made me drop it,' I lied, face like a beetroot. What would she do to me?

'You're a wicked little girl and you'll go to hell.' But if I'd said I'd dropped it, which was true, she wouldn't have believed that, either. She probably thought I'd sold it or drunk it all myself.

Ron Avery, her son, was seventeen and a credit to her. He worked in a garage and spent most of his time at the pictures or cycling round the town whistling after the girls.

I'd made a friend in Clarence Street, before we left, Lucretia Smith. Cretia was a Londoner like me. One late November evening, we were playing hide-and-seek in the street, all the gang of us. Terry Dicks was on 'it' and the rest of us started up the street to hide while he leaned up against the lamp-post, hiding his eyes and counting—'Twenty-two, twenty-three, twenty-four . . .'

I dashed off at once, with the rest of the kids fanning out on all sides, and was halfway up the street when I looked back. Everyone else had disappeared. It was getting really dark now, the air smelling rotten with damp and the only light the yellow gas lamp. Terry Dicks was still counting, 'Sixty-six, sixty-seven, sixty-eight . . .' and rocking up the road, going all out, came Cretia, stiff-legged, her big feet flapping in all directions.

'Come on,' I shouted.

'Give us your arm.' And together we bowled up the road til we found a doorway to hide in.

'You're a Londoner, aren't you?'

'Yeah. So are you, ent you?'

'Yeah.'

We stayed in our doorway til the long melancholy call, 'All in, all in,' rolled sadly down the street like the thin November mist and then we made for home, the lamp-post. We were both caught of course, but it didn't matter—I had a mate.

No one ever used the word 'cripple' on Cretia. She had a double dislocated hip and that was all. It was no different from having brown hair. Sometimes the other kids got a bit cross when she was slow, but no one ever laughed or called her names. Mr. Smith had kept a toy shop in London, which had been bombed, and the stock that was left had been passed on to Cretia. Most of all I envied her her army of lead soldiers. I spent all my pocket money, threepence a week, two weeks to a soldier, but I could never catch up. Her prize piece was Kingy, who was bigger than the rest, made of some kind of plastic wood, and led the army on his charger. He could even come off and sit on a throne. Day after day, we sat in the shed at the back of Mrs. Avery's and waged miniature war, not on each other but on an invisible enemy, the Spokespees. We deployed our forces, set up camps, laid ambushes, sent messengers and spies into enemy territory and Kingy received their reports and issued orders. Only Ron Avery had a bigger army than Cretia, not that he played with them much now, but there was a machine-gunner who came away from his gun, almost like Kingy.

We were playing in the shed one Saturday afternoon, Mrs. Avery was out shopping, when Ron tapped on his bedroom window and beckoned me to come up. When I reached his bedroom and went inside, he said, 'Shut the door.'

I pushed it to behind me and looked at him. He was lying on his back on his bed with something big sticking out of his trousers, wrapped in a handkerchief, with his hand round it. I was worried. I didn't know quite what to do.

'Come over yer and do something for I,' he said.

'No.'

'I'll give 'ee the machine-gunner.'

'No.'

'Alright then, watch.'

He moved his hand quickly up and down. I was amazed. He folded the ends of his handkerchief over it, squeezed it clean and put it back inside his trousers. Then he got off the bed, went to the drawer and got out the machine-gunner.

'Here y'are. Don't tell our mum, then, will 'ee?'

'No.'

'Go on, you do take it. I'm giving it to 'ee.'

I took the lead soldier, warm with his hand, and backed away.

'You do come up next week and I'll give 'ee the gun to go with 'un.' I hurried downstairs and back to Cretia.

'What did he want?'

'He gave me this.' I showed her the gunner.

'What for?'

'Nothing, just gave it to me.'

'Now you've got a King, too.'

'I don't want it. I'll swap it for Kingy.'

'Oh no, it's not worth Kingy.'

'I'll swap it for one of your stretcher bearers.'

'Alright then.' She handed me a blue walking soldier with tin hat and gas mask.

'Touch leather, no backs for ever,' I said quickly, glad to have got rid of the thing that seemed somehow contaminated.

'Let's play draughts; I'm sick of old soldiers.' But I was worried. What could I do?

During the week he managed to whisper, 'Don't 'ee forget, Saturday, when Mum's gone out.'

'I'm not coming.'

'Thee do want the gun, don't 'ee?'

'No. I don't want it.'

'To go with the soldier?'

'I've swapped it.'

On Wednesday, my aunt took me over to see my mother in hospital, for the first time. I was nervous and miserable.

'There's a cheerful face to come and see me. What's the matter with you?'

'I don't like staying at Mrs. Avery's.'

'It's only a little while. I'll soon be home again.' I hung my head and scuffed my feet on the wooden floorboards of the hut she lived in, in the hospital grounds.

'What don't you like about it?'

'Ron wants me to do nasty things.'

'What sort of nasty things?'

74

I didn't look up. I knew I couldn't tell her. I should be soiled, nasty in her eyes if I did. Still less could I tell her what had already happened. She didn't press me any further.

'I don't promise, but I'll see what I can do.'

She was omnipotent. Within a week it was all arranged from the hospital.

'You'm going to be with your mother,' Mrs. Avery informed me. 'Maybe she's got some control over 'ee. It seems a good, Christian household ain't enough for 'ee. I dunno what lie you bin telling.'

My things were packed up and I was fetched in an ambulance.

'Kiss I goodbye,' said Mrs. Avery, but I turned my face away. 'You'm an ungrateful little thing.' There was no sign of Ron.

I sat up front with the driver and his mate. The back was full of my things, which meant everything we had except a few bits of furniture in store, and an ever-increasing tribe of miserable, howling children we picked up at the different villages, all spotty and sore with scabies.

That night I slept in the scabies ward with the new arrivals, sobbing and sniffling all around me in the eerie blue light. They had been scrubbed ruthlessly in hot medicinal baths when they arrived, smeared with fiery ointment and bandaged to stop them scratching.

'Why wasn't 'ee bathed?' they demanded.

'Oh, I'm not ill.'

' 'Tain't fair. Now you'm getting up and us have got to stop in bed.'

When I left, three days later, for my new billet in the town, they howled again.

'And now she'm going home. 'Tain't fair.'

9

THAT Christmas it snowed. I'd prayed for snow like all kids do, and there it was when I woke, that opaque brilliance in the little sloping-ceilinged attic room at the top of the tall, thin house in the High Street, as if I was the core of an ice crystal. The small window was half drifted-up with snow and my breath had frosted delicate crochet work on the inside of the glass, like the intricate doyleys my mother's flicking fingers wove. I froze the point of my thin, pointed, family tongue—Dinge could touch the tip of her nose with hers—tracing the fronds of the hoary ferns, watching them dissolve under its warm touch. My breath steamed in the chill air. I hopped back into bed, feet aching with cold and pulled my pyjama legs down over them; it wasn't time to get up yet.

Soon, gaunt Mrs. Mortimer would be up to wake me with her morning greeting:

'Good morning, miss,
  Your hair's atwist,
  And your petticoat
  Shows your garters, miss.'

She had a store of little rhymes for every occasion and two splendid long narrative poems she had learned in her youth. They fascinated me and I'd beg her again and again to repeat them. Neither were very edifying stories for a child; one was about a certain farmer's daughter pouring some old cherry brandy out of the window where the geese drank it and fell down stone drunk; thinking they were all dead, the farmer

76

had them plucked. No sooner were they goose flesh all over than they got to their feet and waddled naked away. Immediately, the farmer's wife and daughter set to work to make them little jackets to wear until their feathers grew again.

The other tale was about drunkenness too, strange because Mrs. Mortimer never touched even a medicinal teaspoonful of brandy. This time it was John Dodd, tippling in the Rose and Crown, who got into trouble, being picked up by a phantom coach on his way home and found in the morning fifteen miles away. This one was my favourite.

They were an odd, old-fashioned couple, the Mortimers. In their late sixties, they seemed very old to me. He was short and tubby with a drooping, sandy moustache and bright, kind eyes. I loved to watch him at work in his cobbler's shop up a narrow alley on the upper side of the High Street. She was tall and thin, like the house, with big bones, knobbly elbows, and great red knuckles from constant washing in the scullery down the yard, with its perishing stone-flagged floor. She wore long thick skirts, lisle stockings, brown slippers with ear flaps and stud eyes, and a cotton blouse pinned with a scotch pebble on her scrubbing-board of a chest. I can't remember the colour of her hair; I see her always in the mob-cap she wore all day about the house.

My present from the Mortimers was a pair of white bed socks she had knitted and a shining shilling. From the sentimental old lady who kept the glove shop next door I had a book about Mickey Mouse, printed in red and black, and a new-laid egg. I ate the egg for breakfast and read the book in twenty minutes.

The Mortimers began buttoning themselves into great coats and winding long woolly scarves around their necks, in preparation for church. The roast pork was already spitting and hissing in the oven. I was spending the day with my mother in the hospital.

'Take this to your mother and give her the season's greetings,' Mrs. Mortimer said, giving me a pot of marrow jam. And then I was out of the house and on my way.

The hospital was quite a walk, up the hill, past the little church school that I attended now, and over the common. It was the common I longed for, the common I had wanted the snow for. There I should be alone, no one to see me, and first. I walked deliberately, not hurrying.

Then I stood still on the edge and held my breath. It was a white waste, where only birds and small animals had set their prints. Cromwell's Knoll, a circle of oaks, black bare now, stood up on their mound, scratching the grey, snow-filled sky with twiggy fingers. There was no wind, no sound but my own breathing. I advanced a few yards, feeling myself warm and fleshy in this cold kingdom, like cattle snorting hot, moist breath and stamping in a freezing, midnight stable.

Supposing I lost my way? No, I could steer by Cromwell's Knoll, keeping it well to the right. I clumped along the path, turning again and again to look back and see my own footprints hurrying after me. Now I was in the heart of the frozen world. I stood still and looked about. It stretched away from me on every side as far as I could see. I was quite alone.

I scooped up a handful of snow and tasted it. Explorers without water and Esquimaux eat it instead of drinking water. Then I dug my hands, wet and stinging, into my coat pockets and trudged on. Here there was more wind. I bent my head against it and it nipped my ears spitefully. Base camp was a full day's march ahead. Soon the long arctic night would close in around me. My food was all gone. My companions were dead. I mustn't fall asleep in the snow. I must keep going at all cost.

A little path branched off to the left, too small for human feet. I bent down. Narrow tracks, three thin toes and a following spur arrowed towards a clump of dry grass stalks, doubled back and were joined by others. Here the tracks became confused, the ground trampled by many feet. I leaned on my rifle and considered. In the dead of winter, starving wolves would come bounding over the plain and even attack a man. Not a tree for miles. Had I enough ammunition? My shots might bring help. More likely have the Sioux down on me. Better get along. The sky was darkening. With luck I might make the post before nightfall. Just one more look at those tracks.

Birds' feet, rabbit prints, etchings of the wind on the surface of the snow; grasses bent with the crystal weight of ice drops that chimed faintly like sheep bells, or the walls of the Emperor's palace, minute trees, their branches bowed under the weight of an inch of snow: now I wandered tall in an elfin land.

I stood up and dwindled at once to a little black figure on a dazzling snow plain, with the grey bending arch of sky overhead. A few flakes began to fall. The spell was fading. I was cold, my shoes soaked, my nose dropping off with frostbite. I squinted down it. It was bright red. The flakes fell faster, hardly drifting in the still air. Suddenly I threw myself on the ground and rolled over and over, crushing the tiny trees and the bird tracks, making a broad road of packed snow with the weight of my body. Then I leapt up and began to run, faster and faster, catching up great fistfuls of snow, jamming them tight and hurling them into the distance; scuffing and slurring, leaving black, giant spoor in the untrodden snow.

At the edge of the common, I stood still and looked back. Already the falling snow was covering my tracks but I signed my name with my toe in a corner of the huge white canvas and ran on down the lane, my blakeys ringing on the hard road, sharp and clear after the carpeted common.

At the hospital gates I slowed up, brushed off my coating of snow and ran on through the grounds. I pushed open the door of my mother's hut.

'Hush,' she said. She was sitting up in bed, in a pale blue bedjacket. The window was wide open and a big black starling, iridescent as an oily puddle, was standing on the white bedspread, pecking crumbs from her outstretched hand. Startled, he flapped his wings and blundered out of the window.

'Now you've startled him and it's taken days to get him this close. Still, he'll be back when he's hungry.'

'Mrs. Mortimer sent you this.' I pulled the jar of marrow jam out of my coat.

'Look at you. You're soaked. Take that coat off, and those shoes.'

It was bitterly cold in the hut. Two coloured streamers were stretched diagonally across overhead and cards decorated the locker top.

'Can I come in with you?'

'If you like.'

I undid the bottom of the bed and crept in between the

blankets beside her, until I could feel the warmth of her thin legs.

'It's time they changed the hot-water bottles but the nurses don't like coming across in this weather. I don't blame them. Still, it must be very healthy. I don't reckon even a germ could stay alive very long out in this. There's a parcel for us from Aunt Lyddy.'

'Can I have it? Let me open it.'

Impatiently I cut the string. There was a letter and a postal order for my mother and presents for me, the *Chatterbox Annual* and a magic painting book, that only needed a brush and water to bring out the colours hidden in the paper, and you couldn't go over the edge.

Her own present to me she had got one of the nurses to buy in the town, since she was still confined to bed all day. In a month or two she would be allowed up for a little and then later to catch the bus into town.

'What've I got? Tell us. Go on.'

'What did you want?'

'Oh, a book, a book!'

'But you've got lots of books,' she teased. 'And now another one from Aunt Lyddy. Surely you don't want any more. What about a doll?'

'You know I don't like dolls.'

'Open it up then,' and she pushed a flat parcel towards me. I knew at once it was alright, by the shape. *The Golden Adventure Book* it said and the cover showed three bandits sitting on top of a mountain in South America.

'And here's something extra. One of the nurses gave me this for you. It used to be hers when she was young.'

It was a huge book, *The Big Christmas Wonder Book*, with small print, big pages and thin paper. It was illustrated with line drawings based on Arthur Rackham, so that the trees are all spiky and have faces in the trunks and all the young men have plumed hats and pointed faces and shoes, and the girls have flowing hair and garments like water. It was stuffed with stories, extracts from novels and dozens of poems. The cover was rather faded and battered and it would take me weeks to read all through just once.

'I've got three new books.' I made a pile of them to prove it.

'And what did you get me?' I took a little box out of my coat pocket and a crumpled envelope. She opened the envelope first. It was a card I had made at school with a Christmas tree cut out in coloured sticky paper, stuck on the front of a piece of white paper folded in half. Inside was printed, rather messily, St. John's didn't do real writing yet,

'Best Wishes for Christmas
and
The New Year
To Mum with love
from
Paddy'

'That's very nicely written,' my mother knew what was expected of her. 'Now I wonder what's in here.'

By this time I was frantic with excitement.

'Open it!'

She unwrapped the little box, tuppence in Woolworth's, and took off the lid. Inside, bedded down in cotton wool, was a little blue plastic unicorn that had cost me a whole sixpence. Gently she picked it out and stood it on the locker. It toppled over at once.

'He's like me, a bit wobbly on his pins.' Patiently, she stood him up again. This time he stayed.

'There!'

I sighed with relief. 'Do you like it? Is it alright?'

'It's fine. I shall be able to look at him and think of you. I think I'll lean him against the clock-face—he seems a bit tired.'

'But he does stand up, doesn't he?'

'Oh yes. He stands very well.'

That little unicorn toppled from every available flat surface for years, until he finally broke his leg. It was mended with sticky paper and after that he stood up steady as a rock.

The door blew suddenly open, the wind was rising outside, and a young nurse staggered in with a tray, heavy with plates and hot-water bottles, her blue cloak blown out like great wings behind her.

'Here's your dinner now and don't blame me if it's all cold and the bottles too, coming all across here. I wonder you're not all blown away or die of exposure.' And she was gone. I pictured the hut blowing away through the sky like an aerial Noah's Ark, and us in it. She was right about the dinner. I ate mine but my mother tipped most of hers out of the window.

'There's a party in the children's ward this afternoon. They've invited you.'

'I'd rather stay here with you and read.'

'You can't refuse if you're invited. You'll like it once you're there.' And so I did, of course.

When I'd had my present from Father Christmas, a nurse tapped me on the shoulder.

'Your mother says it's time you were off.' I left the brightly lit ward with its blazing tree and paper chains and made my way across the darkening yard. My mother had been asleep but now she was propped up in bed reading. Her face seemed all hollows in the poor light.

'Did you have a nice time? You'll have to hurry home now, it's getting dark quickly.'

'I wish I didn't have to go. I wish I could stay with you.'

'Never mind. It won't be long now and then I'll be home. Run along now. I want you to get across the common before it gets dark.' I knew it was no use complaining.

I saw her wave to me through the glass as I ran off into the falling dusk, my books hugged to me. The blue unicorn was propped against an empty mug, watching.

10

IT WAS late afternoon when we finally knocked on the door of the house where we had lived before my mother was taken to hospital. She had written a couple of weeks back to ask if our old room was available, saying there was no need to answer unless it wasn't. She knew Vi Jenkins wasn't good at letters. The woman who opened the door was a stranger.

'Mrs. Jenkins moved out six months ago. No, I don't know where she's gone.' She watched us curiously.

Mum picked up the case and took my hand.

'Never mind,' she said briskly. 'We'll just have to find some-where else.'

At the gate she paused. The sun was going down. It was getting chilly and the case was heavy. Across the way a neighbour leaned on her gate, a big fat woman in her early thirties. My mother knew her slightly as a friend of Vi Jenkins. Her husband was Welsh too, away in the army at the moment. From time to time he came home on leave, bounced her in the big double bed and then rejoined his unit, leaving her to cope with the latest addition to the Rees family; there were four now.

'Still, I enjoy it just as much as he does and I can't stop in the middle to bother with one of them things. So I reckon I'll just have to go on falling for one every year.'

Now she called across, 'Looking for Vi?' My mother opened the gate and crossed the unmade lane. 'She'm gone back to Cardiff, six months ago.'

'So they said. I wrote a couple of weeks ago asking for my

old room back, but there was no answer. I can see why now, of course.'

'You got nowhere to go then?'

'Not at the moment. We'll find somewhere. I'll pop down to the Greyhound, see if they can put us up for the night. Then I'll have a look round tomorrow.'

'Why not stop the night with us? There's the front room. Joanie can sleep with me tonight.'

'I don't want to put you out.'

'No trouble. Come on in then.'

And so we moved in with the Reeses. I don't know how it was all arranged but there we were. We had the front room to ourselves, Mum's machine was moved in and the familiar clack of the treadle and chatter of the foot soon made it home. I went back to the old school, where Cretia was now in the top class, one above me, and taking the scholarship.

'But it's no good, even if I pass they won't let me go to the High School. Mum says I can only go in London and Dad says I'm not going up there while the raids are on. So that's that.' She sat on a chunk of tumbled masonry on the piece of waste ground at the back of the house and jiggled her foot up and down, one leg over the other.

I said nothing. The whole subject was a quagmire with only a few safe tussocks of grass here and there that would take the heavy weight of question and answer. At school I was way behind my class except in reading. I'd changed school so many times, switched my writing from print to script to cursive, back to print, then to cursive to suit the demands of different teachers that now it looked as if a drunken fly had fallen in the ink-pot and dragged its erratic feet over the page, plopping great blodges off its wings. I had worked and reworked the same arithmetical ground til there was no idea of logical development. Figures were mad things that could be added and subtracted, thrown about in wild confusion, converted into pounds and ounces, shillings or square feet without rhyme or reason. The only thing that made sense was what I read, or better, learned by heart. That I knew. It was fixed and sure.

And next year it would be my turn for the scholarship. In the meantime we moved again. This time, though, only to the other end of town. Dilys Rees's mother-in-law kept a pub. Being wartime, she was short-staffed. She needed help in the bar and she loved her grandchildren with a possessive smother-love that expressed itself in quarters of sweets and money for the pictures. She was quite sure that Dilys didn't look after them properly.

In some ways this was true. She let them run wild but they seemed healthy enough on it. Before we came to live there they never sat down to a meal. My mother soon stopped all that, running around with a 'piece' in their hands.

'Gi's a piece, our mam,' and they would run off with a door-step of bread and jam. But that all had to change. The table was laid, newspaper for a cloth, a knife, fork and spoon were put for everyone, salt, pepper and sauce in the middle of the table, the food was dished up in the kitchen and we each brought our own plate in and set to work.

I was a faddy child, picking at a small plate, refusing to eat fat or margarine on my bread, turning up my nose at marrow, swede, and turnip, but the little Reeses polished their plates after every meal.

It was decided that when Dilys Rees took the children to live with Nanny Rees in the Lion, we should go too, at least for a time. Dilys would take a job, my mother would help with the children and sometimes in the bar.

For the first time I shared a room with someone other than my mother, and fine old times we all had when we were supposed to be in bed asleep. The two eldest Rees children, Ivor and Joanie, and I were at the curious, sniggering stage. We danced around half-naked, feeling very wicked and eyeing each other's bodies curiously. Meanwhile my mother was down below in the bar, walloping up the pints, doling out the under-the-counter whiskies and rationing the fags.

Dilys had a friend who came often to the house. He was a Londoner, a widower, working on the aerodromes, filling in the holes in the runways, a short, dark man with a big nose and small eyes, thinning at the temples and on top. He was always well dressed and clean, with his hair slicked back with Brylcreem, but his hands were thick and his fingers like little sausages. He cleaned and cut his nails with a penknife and carved great callouses from the palms of his hands, that seemed to grow again overnight, like Prometheus's liver. The little Reeses called him Uncle Ted.

When we first went to the Lion, Ted had rooms there, but he was asked to leave by Nanny Rees. She said she didn't want him hanging round her daughter and he was forbidden to come into the bar. My mother was told not to serve him.

One day a strange rumpus blew up that I didn't understand though I sensed the tension in the air. Nanny Rees was sorting through the communal bag, back from the laundry. Suddenly she held up a big white handkerchief, with a flourish.

'I don't know what to do with this,' she said. Then, turning to my mother, 'Still, I expect you can give it to him, can't you?'

My mother stepped forward and took the handkerchief. 'Yes, when I see him, I'll let him have it.'

'I thought you would.'

Quietly my mother left the room. I followed.

'What did she mean?'

'She's a nasty-minded old woman. I know what she means.'

Soon after this, she told me we were leaving the Lion. We were going to have a whole house to ourselves. Once again we took up our cases, the battered grey wooden one that weighed a ton before you put anything in it, and the two brown cardboard ones, whose locks could never be relied on. I was pleased we were going back to live in the same street as Cretia.

'It'll be very near the High School. You must work hard and get the scholarship. You know you can't go if you don't pass, there's no money to pay for you. I'd like you to go to college. It's the one thing they can't take away from you, education. You're not going to be pushed about as I've been.'

We toiled up the hill and over the railway bridge—all my life I seem to have lived on the railway bank.

'Here it is,' she said, pushing open an iron gate. A path ran along the embankment. There was no sign of a house. She led the way along the path, a train roared past, spitting out steam and gritty smoke, we turned a corner and there was a pair of cottages. Ours was on the left.

There was one room up and one down, with a scullery tacked on. There was no electricity and the water was a shared

86

tap in the middle of the yard. The lavatory was outside of course but that has never seemed a particular disadvantage to me. The floorboards downstairs were rotten through, but as soon as we found a spot was dangerous—you found out by putting your foot through—we put a chair over the hole and tried to avoid the area. There was a larder and a coal hole under the stairs where the black beetles lived. At night the house was theirs. They scuttled about the floor in dozens and didn't even disappear if you came down with a light. At least there were gas lights and a cooker. We paid eight-and-sixpence a week.

My mother soon got the place clean and to rights. Our few sticks of furniture were brought back from store. There was nothing to put on the floor but that made it easier to see the danger spots. The garden was beyond us. It needed deep digging before anything could be done. Next door lived a young widow and her little girl of six. The husband had been killed in the war.

When summer came I took my usual eight weeks' trip to London, to stay with Aunt Lyddy. The raids were still on. In fact, Aunt Lyddy's first house had been demolished while they were in the cellar and they now had another a few streets away. Every night when the siren sounded we trooped down to the shelter in the garden and there we slept or played cards or read, while the bombs dropped around, til the All-Clear sounded at dawn and we trailed back in the first grey light, the new spiders' webs gleaming with dew slung between the hoary leaves of Uncle John's tomato plants and the air fresh and damp.

But I don't remember any more. I swear I don't, maybe because I don't want to, although Aunt Lyddy says there was nothing to remember, that I didn't seem to care anyway, as she says I don't really care about anything. But I don't remember. I can only see them both standing there in Aunt Lyddy's kitchen and then my mother calling me away into the middle room and explaining that she'd done it for me so I could have a chance in life, so I could go to the High School because she was sure I was bright and was going to pass, and she couldn't afford it by herself. She'd married Ted Willerton.

PART TWO

Pale children's faces, whisped with straggling hair,
Vanish down furtive alleys which enchain
Their shadowed childhood in a murmuring fear . . .

II

THE new life began almost at once. Together, the three of us went the long ride on the top of the bus, through the tunnel, to see the rest of the Willerton family. I'd never been in South London before and I was unimpressed. The doors in the street, Willerton Street they called it locally, so many of them lived there, stood permanently open and dirty children ran in and out of each other's homes. Blowzy women with straggling untidy hair and thick arms dropped in on each other for cups of stewed tea or to borrow anything from a cup of sugar to a big black saucepan.

We went to Ted's mother who was looking after his eldest child Gladys, a dark, snub-nosed, big-breasted girl of sixteen. The old lady was thin and sharp with grey hair, and ran the whole clan from her kitchen chair where she sat straight-backed, stabbing her points out with a bony forefinger.

'She don't listen to me, don't take no notice of anything I say. She's out to all hours with all the fellers and Gawd knows what she gets up to. I can't be responsible for her no longer. You must take her yourself. I can't put up with it no more. I'm too old, too old for the young uns' carryings-ons.'

What could my mother do? As his wife it was her duty to take the girl and so it was arranged she would come to live with us.

'Maybe she'll be better when she's with us. You can't expect old people to understand youngsters,' my mother comforted on the way home. There had been two empty seats together when we got on the top of the bus, and a lot of singles. We had to go on top now because Ted wanted to smoke but the thick

91

air made her cough. As usual I went for the double seat, then paused and swung my way forward to an empty single beside a woman with a couple of bulging shopping bags. It wasn't my place any more beside her. I gazed out of the window and wisps of their conversation drifted past me like smoke.

I was glad when they had to go back and I was left to finish my holiday with Aunt Lyddy. We went to the park in the hot afternoons and I went on the swings and the grinning red-and-green dragon that rocked to and fro, while Aunt Lyddy sat chatting and knitting on a seat and the rows of potato plants, where the lawns and flower beds had been, stood up thick and straight under the metallic sky and a pot-bellied silver barrage balloon swung high up, catching the sun like a tethered cloud. Cousin Gilly was playing tennis with her friends from the High School. At four we met her outside the pictures and forgot the war watching Alice Faye's long slim legs high-kicking in the latest musical.

With the beginning of September it was time for me to go home. They both met me at the station. I kissed my mother's soft cheek and then Ted bent down and I had to kiss his rather wet lips. He picked up my case and we walked home together to the cottage. The garden was already looking in better shape, deep dug two spades' depth, and there was a curious trench from the outside kitchen wall to the water tap.

'Ted's putting in a pipe so we can have water inside,' Mum explained. My clothes were laid out, all ready for school next day.

'Remember this is your last year. You must try as hard as you can to get the scholarship. I want to be proud of you.'

Some things we did that year were beyond me, or at least quite meaningless, geometry for instance that we started, and problems about water tanks and trains rushing through stations. Mr. Evans, the master of the top class of sixty, was a little, fierce, dark man with a bristling tooth-brush moustache. He beat the boys unmercifully but never touched the girls. The wickedest boy in the class, Peter Shaw, red-headed, thick-skinned and skulled, once ran the length of the room with old Evans hanging on to his ear. Then he threw the boy across a desk top and caned him til he cried. But he had a voice for poetry.

'Tlot, tlot in the echoing night,
Nearer he came and nearer,
Her face was like a light.'

I can still hear those hoof-beats on the still air as Mr. Evans'
tongue clicked against his palate and see the wild gleam in his
eye as, his voice sunk to a breath, he described the girl's
fingers, wet with sweat or blood. Then crack! We all sat up
rigid with fear when the musket shattered the silence and her
breast.

Within a little while Gladys was packed off by her grand-
mother and came down to us. She got a job in one of the local
mills and soon progressed to a spinner, being city-sharper than
the local girls. Like her father she smoked heavily and the rest
of her spare money was spent on clothes. At sixteen she was a
woman more knowledgeable than my mother. Every night she
was out, often till one in the morning when Ted would call her
in from the gate where she had been clinched with one of the
local lads since eleven o'clock.

Just after I was ten, news came from Wales where the rest
of the Willerton family, three boys all older than me, was
billeted. Somehow Ted had forgotten to mention them in his
whirlwind courtship. Arthur, the middle one, was in trouble,
on probation and unhappy in his foster home. Gladys and I
were deputed to go down to see the boys.

We arrived in Tonypandy when it was growing dusk. From
there we had to take a bus to the tiny unpronounceable village
where the Willerton boys lived. A thin mizzle was falling as we
came out of the station and began to look for the bus.

'Llanfodian. You want the bus to Gilvadd and change
there.'

Gilvadd seemed nothing but a crossroads in the middle of
wild, high country, sooty with coal dust and lowering slag tips.

'Llanfodian, no there's nothing going there til tomorrow
morning.'

We trudged through thickening rain to a group of lights in
the distance. The blue light above the cop-shop door for once
meant safety. Inside was warmth, tea and sliced cake, madeira
like sweet sawdust in the mouth.

'Don't worry, we'll get you there.' The coppers seemed much friendlier, perhaps because we were strangers.

'Who've you come to see?'

Gladys told them.

'Your brothers are they?'

She nodded. 'D'you know them?'

'Yer, Dai, do we know the Willerton boys she wants to know?' They all laughed. The duty sergeant appeared in the doorway.

'Come on now,' he said. 'There's a car outside, take you where you want to go.' He looked Gladys up and down. She looked much older than her years. 'You tell young Fred to behave himself a bit better. Tell him I'm watching him. I got my eye on him.' He led us out to the car and we roared off through the dark, the driver and his mate chatting in their sing-song voices that made me want to fall asleep.

We stayed the night in the local pub. In the morning I looked out on a long grimy street, climbing uphill, with houses that were smudged and stained under a sky that wept soot.

My three step-brothers were all older than me, the youngest, Billy, by eighteen months, Arthur, the middle one, eighteen months up on him and Fred another year and a half step up. They were all dark, like their sister and father. Fred was already out to work, helping the local milkman. He was a fine healthy animal with very dark eyes, polished mahogany skin, like a gipsy boy. Arthur was a sad boy, quiet with a putty-coloured face, short and thick-set. Billy, the youngest, was a little snivelling boy with pinched, ferret features.

It was Arthur we had come to see about. He was miserable with his foster parents who locked him out of the house and starved him. They said he was a liar and a thief. He was on probation for the last, like Fred. They had pulled a job together, taking cigarettes from a café. We walked up the dirty street, the boys slouching along, heads down, hands thrust in pockets, big boots scuffing. Only Billy's were clean. He lived with a religious old lady who took him to Salvation Army meetings, kept him clean and well fed. She wanted to adopt him but he led her a terrible dance, stealing from her purse, playing hookey. He was a sly boy with a mealy mouth, yet she loved him in spite of it.

94

Gladys fished out a packet of fags from her bag and they all lit up. Fred had difficulty with his and swore fervently.

'What's she like?' he asked.

'Alright,' Gladys answered very cautiously.

'Tell our dad I want to come home,' said Arthur.

'Yeah, we're sick of it here. Tell him we want to come home.'

We took Arthur first. His foster parents couldn't get rid of him fast enough, and then of course the other two clamoured to come. So there we were seven of us in the two rooms originally meant for Mum and me. We all slept together in the bedroom, Mum and Ted in one double bed at the top of the stairs, Fred on a camp bed under the window, Gladys in another by the banisters, and Billy, Arthur and me in another double against the only wall left.

Gladys was nearest the stairs because, as I've said, she was last in every night. She took no notice of her father or of Mum when she tried to make a stand.

'I know what you get up to,' she said. 'I'm not daft so don't think it. I do the washing, don't forget. I see your knickers before they go in the bag even though you try to keep them hidden from me. They don't get like that in the ordinary course of things.'

'You want to mind your own business. You're not my old woman. I got no need to take notice of you.'

'Thank God I'm not or I'd tan your backside with a hairbrush, big as you are.'

'It's your dirty mind that's all.'

'It's your filthy dirty ways of carrying on.'

'I'm no worse than you were.'

'At least I stuck to one man, I wasn't up a back alley with all and sundry every night of the week. Besides I've paid for what I did, if there was any paying to be done.'

It happened at last of course and Gladys was caught on the hop.

'And I bet she doesn't even know who the father is,' my mother said, 'though she's pinned it on this Irish bloke and he's daft enough not to say no.'

It fell to her of course to manage the thing from beginning

95

to end. Gladys's swelling belly was kept within bounds and disguised as long as possible. Then she was packed off to an unmarried mothers' hostel and the whole business done quietly and effectively. At first they'd tried every possible way to get rid of it, gin and hot baths, emetics, laurel leaves, but it stuck to that womb wall like grim death and after three months my mother wouldn't try any more.

'Why didn't you come to me, Mrs. Willerton, straight away?' boomed Dr. Croombes, my mother's doctor. 'I might have done something. And now you're landed with another to look after. It might as well be your own. She'll do nothing, the lazy little slut.'

Peter when he was brought home was a fat, dribbly, smelly baby, given to colds on his chest. He slept downstairs and now we were eight.

Fortunately for the Irish boy, a building worker, who fell for Gladys's blowzy charm, she was just over seventeen by the time Peter was born or she would have summoned him for criminal assault.

'And what are you going to do now?' asked my mother.

'Do?'

'This is no place to bring up a baby in. There's no room. It's not fair on the child. D'you want to marry this boy?'

'Gawd no.'

'Right then. D'you want to keep the baby?'

'Not particularly.'

'I don't believe she cares for him at all,' my mother said to me later. 'It'd be best if he were adopted. I'll have to see what can be done. He'll have no chance in life if he stays with her. After all it's not his fault.'

'He's very fat.'

'That's not his fault either. It's because he's bottle-fed.'

'He smells.'

'And that's because she doesn't look after him properly. She's just a dirty little bitch.'

I disliked Peter right from the start. I never wanted to push him out. When my mother told us to take the pram it was Arthur who pushed it not me, though I wouldn't let the boys have rides in it as they wanted to and I saw they were careful

96

crossing the road. But I didn't want to nurse it or even hold it and the sight of the soiled nappies and the putty-coloured mess round his little balls made my stomach turn. I couldn't stand to see him fed, with the aftermath of wind and sick and the sour smell of half-digested milk. The whole house seemed to reek of him.

'Never mind he'll soon be gone,' my mother said. 'He's being adopted by some very nice people who're taking him right away. He can't help his mother. Not that I think he's very bright, mark you, just lies and looks, but maybe he'll improve in better surroundings. I believe they're pretty well off, he'll have every chance. Not like you. You'll have to fight for everything you want.'

When the time came I went to the adoption society in the county town to hand Peter over.

'Is she your sister?' the secretary asked.

'No,' I said. 'Only my step-sister.'

'That's all right then, you can be a witness, as long as the name's different.'

'Oh yes, quite different.' And so I witnessed Gladys's illegible signature.

'They must have thought I was much older than I am,' I told my mother excitedly later.

'That's because you were so sensible.'

'And then she just handed him over. He might have been a bundle of washing. There wasn't a flicker, not a sign.' Even I'd felt that something tremendous was being done but Gladys never mentioned the child again.

'I'm glad you weren't like that. I'm glad you kept me. You wouldn't have let me go like that, would you?'

'No, I wouldn't have let you go. You're mine. You're all I've got.'

But soon there was something else to worry about, something much more important than anything else. I was taking the scholarship.

12

'IF ONLY it weren't so cold it would be easier.' Or would it have been? I'm not so sure. I remember too many exams taken in broiling heat so you dripped mingled sweat and ink from your pen and your head buzzed fly-like at the window of memory. But then there was that other horrible time when we all sniffed and snivelled and blew our snotty noses and coughed over our papers til every word must have been crawling with minute life, and worst of all I'd forgotten my handkerchief, only by then they were nose-rags, old sheets torn up and hemmed, bits of shirt tail and faded summer dresses split under the arms, the tops that is, the skirts were remade into blouses. My mother had a splendid method of boiling the dressing out of flour-bags and hemming them up, and lovely soft to a sore nose they were too, only this day I hadn't got a thing, not a scrap of rag and my nose kept running, sitting in the chilly, stuffy room. But no one must know. How terrible to be seen with a runny nose. I cuffed it craftily, then, in desperation, I blotted it with my new square of pink examination blotting paper. I felt a miserable slum kid, though Mavis Cooper, the doctor's daughter, picked hers and worse. The whole idea made me retch; hastily I fixed my mind on the paper itself—anything was better than that.

This time it was cold and damp, grey and the lights were on. At ten o'clock we would pick up our pencils and start. It was two minutes to. On the far side of the hall the headmaster was still giving out papers. There were three to do, intelligence, English, arithmetic. This was the intelligence. 'If Cousin Gilly can do it,' I thought, 'so can I.'

The second hand swung through the last minute.

'Pick up your pencils and begin.'

I read the instructions very carefully, sure that I shouldn't be able to write at all. Time was important. If you didn't finish they couldn't give you marks for what you hadn't done. Mr. Evans had explained that again and again. All my class were there and lots of strange boys and girls from schools not big enough to be a centre.

'You're young,' my mother had said. 'Don't worry. If you don't pass you can try again next year.' But that wasn't it. If I didn't pass I was stupid. I was no different from everyone else, I'd be a slummocking trollop, like Gladys, living in one room, screwing and scraping in filth and ignorance for the rest of my life. There'd be nothing for me. I couldn't go to sea, round the world, cross the desert on a camel like my current hero Lawrence of Arabia—I sat in trees, on ant-hills, for what seemed hours on end, while I was stung or got hideous cramp, so I could be another blue-eyed Arab. I dressed in a sheet and painted my skin with my brown water-colour paint like Kim but I was just a girl and life offered only things I despised, houses, children, security, housework. I had to pass. I had to. I had to be different. There must be more to life than this or there wasn't any point in being born. And there had to be a point for her sake.

I began the questions.

'If you can't do one, leave it and go on to the next. Don't waste time,' Mr. Evans sang and roared in my head.

'*Branch* is to *tree* as *arm* is to: head, bone, body, leg.'

I underlined *body* and went on.

With ten minutes to spare I came to the end of eighty-nine questions and sat back. Just time to look them all through to see if I'd made a mistake. Then I saw the boy in front looking at the back page. I hadn't thought to turn over. It seemed so logical to end at the bottom on the second inside page. The boy turned back to the beginning and began to go all through. Terrified I turned over. There were eleven more questions and only nine minutes to go. Of course, how stupid, I knew there were a hundred questions, I knew, I knew. Shakily I began on them, the hardest, kept til last. I finished with a minute to spare. There was no time to look through the rest.

The headmaster called time, the papers were gathered, somehow we got up and went silently to the milk table. The milk had been warmed against the radiators and tasted slightly sour but it was probably the taste of fear. My legs felt weak and thin as if I had been in bed for a fortnight. Two more papers to go.

When I got to the front gate I held it right back against the fence and shot off as I let it go. If I could get to the bend in the lane before it crashed to it would be alright, good luck. I ran as if I would die; I made it.

Mum was waiting for me with a bright fire.

'How did it go?' I told her all about it. 'Don't worry it'll be alright. It's not the ones who finish first that do best. What's tomorrow?'

'Arithmetic.'

'Well it'll soon be over and then there's only English and you're alright at that.' I loved coming home to her like this. I was always first and we had about three quarters of an hour together before the rest began to come in, demanding food, their tea. She was usually sewing at the machine or reading by the fire, the place spotless and tidy, herself washed, always a good wash every day, and changed into something different, often her mustard silky blouse and black skirt, both made from remnants. But then I never saw her untidy, or the place, wherever it was, either. She would make a cup of tea and we would be quiet and talk. Sometimes there were biscuits when she had made them. Tea and biscuits seemed a bulwark of civilization.

The fire hissed and gurgled as we talked, her hands stroked the arm of her chair, or she prodded at the coal to make it flame and the rain fell stilly outside.

I don't remember the other two papers, my mind closed down on them and then it was all over. I couldn't draw back or change one mark on the three papers and there was nothing to do but wait.

When the forms had come round for her to fill in in the first place there had been anxious deliberation.

'You'll stay on til sixteen at least, so that's alright. Ten pounds if you leave but we won't worry about that.'

'What about the school?'

'The High School first, what then?'

'I don't know.'

'It had better be the Fitzjohn. It'd be a long way. You'd have to have a bike.'

'It's mixed. It's not half so good.'

'But it's better than the Alderman Cressley.'

'Oh yes!' The Alderman Cressley was the senior school where the boys went, it seemed, to throw ink pellets at the teacher and stick darts in the ceiling and to learn nothing. Cretia had gone there too the year before, her parents disagreeing to the last. She was top of the A stream of course, way out in front, and had managed to form an élite who took no notice of the rumbling from below. But I couldn't go to the same school as the Willerton boys. It would be the end of all her hopes.

Everyone who had put down Wortbridge High School first was called for interview. I was scrubbed, put into a clean summer dress, a nice white ribbon tied my hair. I shone almost to transparency. We sat in alphabetical order in the impressive hall, waiting our turn to go in to the headmistress. She was a strange woman with short wiry, greying hair. She wore a tweed brown costume and thrust two fingers into the plaquet of her skirt, leaning back from the hips at a curious angle. Her voice grated and purred as she questioned us in her Oxford drawl. We read, and answered one or two questions on the text and were then dismissed. It was impossible to draw any conclusion.

I just couldn't visualize failure, it was too terrible to be conceived. Sometimes I thought I'd passed, but mostly I didn't dare think consciously about it at all. It was always there though, as a layer of fear and suspense blanketing my mind. Then when I got to school one morning one or two had heard.

'What was it like?'

'A thick brown envelope with all the things about the uniform and a copy of the school rules and a letter from the headmistress.' The morning was terrible. Last lesson was singing with Old Ma Hayward who hit you on the head with a thimble if you were out of tune. Once she told me to stop singing altogether and I was so humiliated that I never sang again out loud, just mouthed the words and let the tune run silently through my head.

> 'Dark brown is the river,
> Golden is the sand,
> It flows along for ever
> With trees on either hand.
>
> Green leaves afloating,
> Castles of the foam,
> Boats of mine aboating,
> When will all come home?'

We sang, and the smell of the dinners being put out in the hall outside wafted through the door; stew and chocolate tapioca. That day I hardly cared. I wasn't hungry.

The afternoon was sewing, Mrs. Hayward again. I tried to seem occupied with the grubby square of grey stuff I was supposed to be hemming but sewing was always the slowest of lessons. When the bell finally went I was out of the building and running along the street in a flash. I held back the front gate and bolted up the lane. If it banged before I reached the turn my heart would stop. I rushed in the front door. Mum was standing waiting for me.

'It's come.'

'What does it say?'

'I waited til you came home to open it.' She took a knife out of the drawer and neatly slit the top, took out and unfolded the sheets of thick paper and glanced quickly through the top one.

'It's all right. You've won a free place!'

It was alright. I could go. Sometimes I'd wondered which would have been worse, to fail altogether or to get a place provided I paid fees. Either way I couldn't have gone.

She sat down by the fire and I stood beside her, reading over her shoulder. There was the letter from the headmistress, a small sheet with the rules on them—there seemed to be very few—and several sheets about uniform. I looked aghast. All those clothes! How would we ever afford it?

'Don't worry,' my mother said. 'We'll manage. Most of them I can make and some you needn't have just yet.'

The most expensive items, that I couldn't do without, were the tunic with its box pleats, the green fringed girdle, and navy velour hat. Everything had to be marked, including the purse worn on a string round the neck. All she could make she did, blouses, socks, gym-dress, a strange shapeless garment split up the sides, navy coat. Finally there was only the satchel. Anxiously we toured the shops looking at the prices. They were all quite beyond us. My heart went down to my boots. How silly I should look on the first day without one! And the paper had talked about homework, pens, pencils, books, how should I carry them about? She solved it of course, just when I was quite convinced I shouldn't be able to go after all. She bought a remnant of thick hard canvas and some webbing and made a satchel, banging down the seams with the scissors to get them under the machine foot and breaking a couple of needles in the process. Secretly I was a bit ashamed of it—it was so different from the glossy leather ones, like new conkers, that the others had but it was the only one I ever had and it lasted four years. Even then it didn't really wear out, just fell apart at the seams.

The first day I went with a tiny girl called Mary whose brother I often went swimming with—they said he was my boy friend, but he was sandy-haired and spotty; when he got cold after swimming, he lay out on the paving stones to dry, with his stick-like arms and legs, mottled blue and red, shivering and twitching. I had nothing in common with Mary except the new uniforms we both wore. Her hat was too big for her little body and made her look like a small black fungus. We were rapidly separated at school for she was older and in a different class.

I suppose everyone experiences the same bewilderment at a new school, milling girls, unknown corridors and routine, expanses of green playing field, but something strange happended to me almost at once; I changed, or maybe it would be truer to say a side of my character hidden at my various junior schools, perhaps because I was always new and at a disadvantage, came out in this different atmosphere. I'd always been quiet and unnoticeable at school but all that vanished overnight. Maybe for the first time I had confidence in me, perhaps because one day when I was standing at Mr. Evans' desk with something to be marked, the headmaster had walked into the room to ask him a question.

Seeing me there he suddenly put his hand on my head and said, 'D'you know, Mr. Evans, this child was top in the intelligence test for the whole county.' At the time I hardly understood what it meant, it was so terrible to be singled out in front of the whole class, but it must have gone in deep.

Anyway all at once I was a character, I was sure of myself, of me at the centre of all my attributes, feelings, actions; the hard core of the self. And my sphere of activity was school. I revelled in it, the work, the library, all the complex emotions and problems. It was my real world.

The difficulty came in dove-tailing it in with home life. There was homework to be done with seven of us crowded into one living-room. My stepfather's constant occupation was keeping the boots and shoes repaired. In the evenings the snobbing foot was put on one corner of the table and my books on the other. As I tried to write the table leapt up and down under the hammer blows that nailed the slices of rubber tyre to our soles and rammed them home secure with studs and blakeys.

The wireless blared with the latest pop-music, 'Johnny Zero' or Glen Miller's 'In the Mood', Arthur and Billy squabbled over the washing-up in the kitchen, Gladys sang as she ironed a blouse to go out on the town with her latest, my mother treadled away by the window. Somehow I always got enough done to get by with.

As soon as I was finished it was bed for Arthur, Billy and me. The gas in the bedroom was turned low and we were supposed to sleep, Fred was at the pictures, Gladys at a dance. Often we crept down the stairs and sat on the bottom step and listened to the wireless through the latched door, *Itma* or the Saturday-night play. Sometimes my mother and Ted went out in the evening for a drink at the pub next door, or to the pictures. Then it was high old jinks. With all my reading I had plenty of ideas for games—Mutiny on the Bounty for instance with me stripped to the waist in baggy pyjama trousers, lashing the mutinous Billy with a pyjama cord, or wrestling with Arthur. I could beat him as long as he didn't use his fists but if he punched me in the chest I was done, partly through fear that it would give me T.B. Or else we put coats over our pyjamas and went out into the garden where we played ghosts, lifting up our handless sleeves under the moon and frightening ourselves to death, or howling and hooting, hidden in the lane as people passed by our gate.

And the fascination of fire in all its forms, stubs of candle, matches, tapers we made with grease droppings and wool, bits of cotton set alight to watch the flame creep and climb up the thread. All this left a telltale smell.

'You've been playing with the gas again,' my mother would say when she was brought up by the suppressed giggles and thuds above her head, and her hand would fall again and again, clout, as we hid under the bedclothes.

In some kind of way I was still trying to copy her childhood but all this had to be kept apart from my life as a High School girl. Already the boys were beginning to call after me in the street. 'High Schoolite, High Schoolite! Mummy's pet!' and there was a new viciousness to Arthur's punches. Education was setting me apart from my step-family and we all knew it. The truth was that none of them could even read or write except Gladys. Fred didn't care. He had a job on a farm and came home stinking of manure. He kept his magnificent, lithe, muscular body clean to show off to his girls in the baths; he had no need to read. Billy was unteachable, everything he learnt one week had trickled through his sieve brain by the next. Only Arthur managed to struggle through a paragraph. Ted could barely sign his own name.

I'd never met anyone before who couldn't read and write as a matter of course and childlike I despised them. Arthur was the only one I had anything in common with and he and I, sleeping together as we did, made tentative experiments that came to nothing because we were too young. I envied him his ability to tie his little soft winkle into a knot at the end and blow it out like a balloon with unshed piddle.

Then, all at once, all games ceased and I wasn't a child any more. My mother was ill. She was going into hospital for an operation. She might die. I don't know how I knew. No one told me but I knew she might die.

13

TED went to fetch her home ten days later. I'd wanted to
go too but he said there wasn't enough money for both
of us. It was evening and dark before they got back. I
remember we were all doing something in the living-room;
Gladys was saying us three ought to go to bed, but we never
took any notice of her, and I was listening with my whole
body. And then I heard them coming up the tarmac path and I
stood still and waited, watching the door, holding my breath
tight. He opened the door for her and she came slowly through
into the living-room. The Willertons all stopped what they
were doing and stared. She was blue-white in the gas light, as if
the shilling was running out and the flame sinking lower. I
didn't move. I couldn't.

'Get a chair,' said Ted. 'Glad, put the kettle on. Give us your
coat,' to my mother.

'Leave me alone. I'll be alright in a minute.' She sat down in
the chair Arthur pushed forward and breathed shallowly,
raspingly, once or twice. Then she looked at me. 'Have you been
a good girl while I've been gone?' I nodded. 'It's high time you
three were in bed.'

'We waited up for you,' I said.

'Well up you go now. I shan't be far behind myself. Have
you done all your homework?'

'Yes.'

'Alright then, off you go. And mind I don't find the light
still on when I come up. Whose turn is it to turn it out?'

'I did it last night,' said Arthur.

'Right then, Billy, it's yours.'

'I'm always doing it.'

'Up you go all of you.'

She stayed in bed for most of the next day and only got up at tea-time. As soon as I came in I was sent out again shopping and then I had to lay the table and cut up a two-pound loaf into doorsteps of bread and marge and mix up some chocolate spread from cocoa, sugar and a little milk. The boys often ate fourteen slices of this each—after fourteen apiece Mum wouldn't cut any more. She said it was just eating for eating's sake. There was a big tin of golden syrup on the table too to alternate with the chocolate spread. Carefully I cut some thinner pieces and put real butter on them for my mother and myself. After all, as she said in justification, the others couldn't tell the difference after they'd coated it with syrup, while we ate ours just plain, savouring the butter itself.

Three ounces, the ration a week, went nowhere and sometimes by the end of the week I was down to plain bread with a scrape of chocolate spread. Marge I just couldn't stomach. There was something about the consistency of it in my mouth that made me heave.

I boiled a kettle and took a bowl of hot water, lifebuoy soap and a towel up so that she could wash and she was dressed and down in time to preside over the tea table and keep order there.

The Willertons ate like animals or starving savages, talking and spitting out of full mouths, arms planted on the table, nudging and kicking each other until there would be a real scrap. Young Fred hated Billy, who was always telling tales, and took every opportunity to cuff him or kick him. They all grabbed from the plate, slopped the syrup on the table, just as well there was no tablecloth to soil, and stuffed half slices into their mouths at once. None of them dared to get down though until she gave them permission.

After tea began the battle of washing-up which was divided into three sections: washing, wiping and putting away which was the easiest. We took these in strict rotation but Billy was continually trying to skive out of his turn. My mother was the final arbiter but sometimes even she forgot. Once I was putting away in the larder when a terrible commotion broke out in the kitchen. Mum dashed out to see what it was and found Arthur with the broom and Billy with the hatchet trying hard to split each other's heads. She seized the net curtains from the window, ripped them off the bamboo rod and pasted the two boys unmercifully until they dropped their weapons and fled into the corner by the copper.

'Why should I hurt my hands on you,' she said. 'Now come out, come on.' Sobbing with frustrated temper they charged out of the corner together trying to duck out of the way of her bony hand. But it was no good, though they covered their ears with their hands, she clouted them both smartly and sent them spinning out into the yard. Then she sank into a chair puffing and trying not to cough.

'They'd have killed each other if I'd have let them. I think I'll keep this down now,' indicating the stick. 'It'll come in handy. The curtains can go up on a piece of tape.'

This night however there was no rumpus, maybe even they were awed by her new frailty. She cooked Ted's tea for him, fried corned beef and chips and he soon came clomping up the path in his blue overalls and big boots, his face and arms grimy with ash and smoke from the boiler he now stoked in one of the mills. He sluiced in the sink and sat down to his tea. Arthur and Billy had gone off to find their mates in the town and the others were out after their own kind of pleasure. It was Friday night, pay night.

After tea Ted tipped his pay packet out on the table and began to tot it up. There was never enough there it seemed. They were trying to do him out of hard-earned cash. Laboriously my mother would go through the pay slip interpreting the strange signs that meant nothing to him. His actual money was about seven pound ten, not bad for then, but he worked twelve hours a day for it.

When he was finally satisfied that all was in order he would pass it all over to my mother and she would give him thirty shillings back for cigarettes. I settled in a chair with a book. Ted went out to the kitchen where he stripped to the waist and washed his white slack body and knotty arms. The sound of his cut-throat being stropped came through the door, my mother poured another cup of tea, cinders fell in the grate.

Next morning I did the shopping. I was the only one who

could read the items written on my mother's note so it had to be me. We queued for fish and chips for dinner which saved the washing-up.

That afternoon I went down the road to see Cretia. Already we were beginning to drift apart as different schools brought different interests. I went into the musty stale-smelling shop where Mrs. Smith nodded and sniffed behind the counter. Rumour had it that she drank on the quiet. She was brown-skinned and wrinkled with black-shot-silver plaits, tied up with a bootlace wound round her head.

'Is Cretia in, Mrs. Smith?' I asked. I didn't like the Smiths' shop and house much. Somewhere in my mind I had labelled them dirty.

'I'll give 'er a shout,' the old woman sniffed. 'Cretia! Cretia!'

Cretia appeared. She always wore the dingiest, draggle-tail clothes, shapeless and the colour of mouldy tobacco.

'They ought to dress the girl in something brighter. They don't encourage her to make the best of herself, and my goodness she needs to, poor little devil,' my mother said.

'You coming out?'

'No, you come in.'

'Alright.' I slipped under the counter flap. The Smiths' smelly dog ambled forward and lifted up his face with the doleful eyes that were always fassy at the corners.

'I've got to polish the floor,' Cretia said, leading the way upstairs. She leaned heavily on the banisters and dragged her unbending legs up from step to step. I trailed behind, trying not to seem as if I was dawdling on purpose.

'What floor?'

'The passage.' By now she was panting with the effort.

'But how?' I wondered. 'She can't kneel down and the passage is yards long.'

'Are you gonna help me?'

'Yeah, I'll help.'

She pointed out a tin of yellow polish and some rags.

'You start one end and I'll start the other and we'll slide the tin of polish up and down between us.'

We each took a rag, I knelt at one end and Cretia lowered

herself to the floor at the other and sat, with both legs stuck out in front of her, looking like a rag doll. We worked hard smearing the yellow wax on the lino; Cretia working all round her and then sliding back on her backside to get at the bit she was sitting on. Soon we bumped in the middle and sat like book-ends.

'I know, let's tie the dusters on our feet and slide up and down to polish it,' I said as I pulled Cretia to her feet. This made the polishing a game. We ran and slid, shouting and waving our arms. Then I hauled Cretia up and down the passage while she squatted on a pile of dusters. At last the passage gleamed in the gloomy house like a strip of water in the dark and we stopped for breath.

'I'll see if there's any tea made,' said Cretia and trundled laboriously downstairs. I sat in the darkening front room that was furnished mainly with boxes, a sofa losing its stuffing and a couple of hard wooden chairs. It began to rain, large drops trickling down the dirty panes. The houses up and down the street looked as if they were crying. The ruins on the waste ground opposite, where we played in summer, crumbled silently away under their wiry tangle of leafless brambles. A shrouded figure pedalled down the hill, water hissing under his tyres and leaving a tiny wake behind. The gas was being lit and curtains drawn. Cretia came back with a tray of tea and bread and jam, sweet chunky Australian pineapple out of a tin and sawdusty yellow cake.

'Why didn't you put the light on?'

'I forgot.' The Smiths had electric. Cretia put down the tray on a box and snapped on the light. I blinked and rubbed my eyes. There were no curtains to draw. We ate and drank, talking quietly and gravely. For a short time we had gone to the same gospel hall but I had given up because the preacher said the theatre was wicked and I loved acting. I was going to be Balder the sun god in the class play and be slain by a mistletoe shaft, because my hair was fair and I was tall.

Cretia still went to the gospel hall.

'I'm going to be baptized soon. Will you come and help me?'

'What do I have to do?'

'Just help me get dry and dressed afterwards.'

'What will you wear?'

'My swimming costume.'

I thought of Cretia in the cubicles at the baths, blue with cold, teeth chattering, pigeon's breast-bone sticking out between her small, round breasts that were just beginning to swell, and then Cretia swimming up the bath with a strange hinged movement at the knee and strong strokes of her arms.

'Alright I'll come.' But I was apprehensive. I knew they'd try to convert me again and something about their narrow fanatical happiness repelled me. I had decided to be an agnostic, and kept my eyes open during prayers at school and only sang those parts of the hymns which didn't seem to contradict reason and were in keeping with the pursuit of the good, the beautiful and the true.

'You need the Lord Jesus Christ,' said Cretia. I thought of the people at the meetings she went to: the man with no roof to his mouth, the pale, plain girl with feverish black eyes, a woman in a wheelchair, the very old man with white hair who was always moved by the spirit to loud extempore prayer.

'Yes,' I thought. 'Maybe they need Him, but I can't believe.'

'I must go,' I said aloud. 'Mum said we might go to the pictures tonight.'

'The pictures are evil.'

'I'll see you in the week,' I said, moving towards the door.

'Come on if you're coming,' my mother said as I ran in. She was dressed in a neat suit she had made herself and the mustard, shiny blouse. Her little feet twinkled in cleaned black shoes. Ted was wearing his navy-blue pin stripe with a clean handkerchief in the breast pocket, his thin hair slicked back with a hair cream he made himself. All three, arm-in-arm, we set off for the Regal. That night I slept sound.

No one got up early Sunday morning. Ted was cooking the dinner, he'd been a cook in the army, Gladys was washing some of her smalls and the rest of us were told to bugger off out. My mother stayed in bed.

'Dinner's at two,' said Ted.

We set off through the park; past the mill, over the Minny

Brook and out of the gates on the other side and then up the road. About a mile or so along we came to a disused camp, nissen huts with smashed windows that we peered through.

'I bet tramps come here and make fires,' said Arthur.

'Come on,' said Fred. 'I know a place.'

We followed him across fields to a road.

'Up here?' said Arthur.

'Yeah, there's walnut trees and apples. Scrumping,' answered Fred. 'Over that wall.' An impressive brick and wrought-iron gateway appeared in the wall and here there were foot and handholds.

'You keep look-out,' said Fred, 'and come up when I whistle.' He clambered up the wall and disappeared. Nothing moved on the damp road. There was a shrill whistle.

'Go on,' said Arthur to me.

'I want to go next,' Billy whined.

'She's going next. Go on.'

I began to clamber up the wall. It was no use saying no. At the top Fred reached down a hand and I hauled myself up flat on the top, heart thudding with fright.

'Jump,' said Fred.

'I can't.'

' 'Seasy.'

Slowly I lowered myself down the other side. Arthur came next and landed with a thump of heavy boots beside us. Billy was last, snivelling that we were going to leave him and he'd tell our mum, they all knew she was the only authority and it was no use saying anything to their father.

We were in a strange wood of exotic trees, great palms and papery bamboo-like plants with pale stripes through the leaves. A path led away from the gate and we followed this. It was awesomely quiet in the wood, no branch stirred.

'Listen,' said Fred. We stopped and held our breath. There wasn't a sound, no bird piped in the bushes. It might have been a dead world. Then faraway came the report of a gun. The birds held their song with fear.

'Suppose they think we're poachers and shoot us,' I thought.

'Come on,' said Fred. We continued down the damp path, pungent with the smell of growing fungus and rotting leaves.

Great white growths jutted out from the tree trunks like shelves; our feet trampled the crumbly layers of burnished copper leaves into loam. Billy was last, his nose ran, his feet stumbled in the heavy boots. We were going too fast, trying to leave him behind, he would tell.

'Look,' said Fred. He pointed to a bird lying in our path. It was quite big, the handsomest bird I had ever seen, pink and bright blue with a crested head. He picked it up and put it in my hand. There was a raw red hole and a smear of blood on its breast and the head lolled as if the neck were broken. It was still warm. I imagined it daredevil-flashing from tree to tree.

'What is it?' asked Arthur.

'A bird.' Fred took it by the head and threw it into the bushes.

'You shouldn't have done that,' said Arthur.

'Why not? It's only an old bird. You're soft. Come on.' We filed deeper and deeper into the silent woods.

'Look at my breath,' said Arthur. 'I'm smoking,' and he puffed clouds of steam. The visible breath hovered round all our faces. It had frozen hard overnight and our lips were blue, hands in our chilly pockets frozen. Our voices too were thin and sharp in the bitter air. Cold eyes seemed to glitter behind every grotesque trunk. Still we moved farther into the silence but the trees were thinning out now and becoming more familiar, although leafless and dead.

'Here,' called Fred at the fringe of the trees. We came up and stood beside him.

'Cor, look at that,' said Arthur.

Before us was a huge lake, frozen hard and clothed with small islands.

'D'you think it'll bear us?' asked Arthur.

' 'Course it will. Last one on's yeller.' We all advanced a step on to the ice.

'Look, it's hard as a rock,' said Fred going out farther. 'Makes a smashing slide,' he shouted and ran a few steps forward and skimmed across the lake. Arthur followed and Billy came up behind. I stood still and listened; they were far out now, their shouts coming thinly across the ice like voices blown by the wind along the sea-shore. I could hear the ice creaking beneath their weight.

'Back,' shouted Fred. 'This bit's not safe.' A flaw appeared suddenly beneath his feet and ran, like flame along a lit fuse, towards the shore. They turned and skated off in another direction. Something caught my attention at my feet. The dark shadows of trapped fish, imprisoned as in an aquarium, darted and flew under my boots. The soles of my feet tingled with fear. I went further looking for more, walking between the tufts of reeds that stuck, stiff with frost, through the ice in the shallow reaches.

By this time Arthur and Fred had broken branches from the trees and were skating along on them, riding them like hobby horses.

'Give us a pull, Fred?' called Billy.

'Come on then, hang on.' And Fred began to pull him round the lake. There was a sharp crack, a new flaw appeared and Billy screamed with fear. They were way out now. Fred turned towards the bank. New flaws appeared under his feet. The ice began to creak and snap as if it was suddenly all breaking up, as if it had lured them out there to drown them.

Arthur too began to head for the bank. The ice was cracked in all directions now like flawed crystal. All at once Bill let go of the stick.

'Come on, you twirp,' shouted Fred and dashed for the shore. His heavy boots went through the ice at the edge and he soaked himself to the knees.

'Sodding hell!' he swore. 'Round the other way young Billy. Go round the other way.' But Billy was too frightened to take any notice. He pounded across the ice after Fred and yelled as it gave way beneath him and he went in nearly up to his waist.

'I can't get out! I can't get out!'

'I've a good mind to leave the silly little bugger,' Fred said but he grabbed Arthur's branch and thrust it out over the ice.

'Hold on to that, and for Christ's sake hold on this time,' and he hauled Billy towards the bank.

'You won't arf get in a row and it'll be all my fault for leading you on. Come on.'

We turned back along the path. As we passed through the bamboo thickets again we heard firing quite close.

'Hurry up. They'll see us.' We began to run. Suddenly there was a shout behind and a man came in sight running after us. Fred reached the wall first.

'Over you go,' he said to Arthur. Arthur scrambled up and dropped down on the other side. 'Go on,' to me. I scrambled my way to the top. 'Now jump!' I thought desperately that I couldn't. Then I imagined myself had up for trespassing. HIGH-SCHOOL GIRL SUMMONED FOR TRESPASSING. I jumped. I jarred every bone in my body and nearly twisted an ankle but I was down. Billy appeared at the top of the wall and Fred beside him. He was down in a flash.

'Come on!' Billy clung to the top whimpering. 'Come on. Look, she's done it and she's younger'n you and a girl. Come on or we'll leave you. Let's get moving.'

'He'll tell on us if he's caught,' muttered Arthur.

There was a shout behind Billy, 'Come down, you boy.' He leapt in the air as if he'd been shot and fell down on our side. Crying he picked himself up and staggered towards us.

'Now run,' ordered Fred, and we pounded up the road. There was no sign of the man and we stopped when we reached the fields.

'I'm all wet,' moaned Billy.

'We'll light a fire in one of the huts in the camp,' said Fred.

It was four o'clock by the time we reached home dry, but cold and hungry. Fred had given us all a bunk up through a broken window. There had been plenty of old paper and cardboard boxes in the hut and we soon had a fire going. When it was time to go, Fred kicked the door open for us.

My mother had left a note on the table:

Your dinner is in the oven. We couldn't wait any longer. Fred's is the one with most pots. Billy washes, Arthur wipes, you put away and make some tea and bring it up at half past five.

'Where does it say I wash?' demanded Billy. 'It's not fair, I'm always doing it.'

'It says there,' said Arthur, who could read names and a few simple words. The dinner was a bit dried up but we were so starving we hardly noticed.

'Wherever have you been?' my mother asked when I took the tea up.

'For a walk,' I evaded. 'We didn't know the time.' Somehow I felt we had been doing something wrong, something she wouldn't have approved of, something I couldn't tell her but I wasn't quite sure exactly what bit of the adventure had been wrong. Or was it all wrong from the beginning? I didn't know, only that the silence of the strange thickets and the bright dead bird were somehow symbols. Why had they shot it when it was so beautiful?

On Monday when I got home from school with a satchel full of homework, Latin and French vocab, a poem to learn for English and three geometry problems, she was nowhere to be seen.

'Mu-um!'

'I'm upstairs. I'm just coming!' I went upstairs. She was standing by the bed in a pink knitted vest and her knickers.

'I don't know,' she said. 'It doesn't look right to me.'

'What doesn't look right?'

'Well you have a look and tell me what you think.' She lifted up her vest and pushed down the top of her knickers. A still angry scar ploughed its way down her belly from top to bottom as far as I could see. There were little pock marks on either side where the stitches had been. But the strange thing was the shape. Instead of lying flat, her little brown belly stuck out at the bottom in a pear shape as if at any moment it would burst through the scar again.

'What is it?' I asked.

'I don't know quite but it doesn't look right, does it?'

'No. It looks funny.'

'I'll go and see Dr. Croombes. Or, perhaps you could go round with a note after tea.'

'But what was it? Why did they make that big cut?' This had nothing to do with her chest.

'They took my womb away. Sterilization they call it. You see I was going to have a baby and they said it was either it or me.'

14

I'D NEVER thought about it before, never considered it in relation to her at all. I knew all about it of course; we'd had sex lectures at school and giggled silently in the dark when Miss Martin had got the picture upside down on the epidiascope and the visiting doctor had said coldly,

'I believe the little red dots should be in the bottom right-hand corner,' and I had seen Miss Martin blushing in the reflected light from the machine as she hastily took the slide out.

And suddenly it all fell into place, as the picture on the screen had taken on a new meaning when Miss Martin had dropped the slide into place the right way up.

'There can't be any more now, can there?'

'No, not now.'

'Supposing you'd had it. Would you have loved it as much as me?'

'You're my girl. The only one. Of course I wouldn't.'

Then desperately I thought, 'It might have been a boy.'

'What will you do? What do you think it is?' I asked.

'Don't know. Anyway you can slip round for me, can't you?'

It was already dark when I left the house with the note in my pocket. A cold wind blew dead leaves and grit down Clarence Street; the Williams's fish-and-chip shop glowed and reeked invitingly. I caught sight of Cretia in the queue and dawdled till she came out.

'Where you going?'

'Up the doctor's. Mum's not well. I'm taking a note for him to come and see her. Gi's a chip.'

'Go on then. Don't take the biggest.' We walked towards her house. Almost I wished she would offer to come with me but it was a long walk, all uphill and it was getting rapidly colder.

'See you then,' she said.

'See you.' I turned away into the dark. The cold stung my legs and pinched my nose and ears. Still, I'd have to stay up late to get my homework done when I got back. Why hadn't I gone out the back before I started? The cold wind blowing up my skirt was turning my stomach to water. I drew the muscles together tightly and turned my feet up Silver Hill. At the top was the surgery with a waiting-room in a draughty passage where half a dozen unfortunates hacked and wheezed and shivered. I sat down on the cold wooden chair that sent a spasm through me and began to wait. I tried crossing my legs. Maybe if I could get warm it would be better. But I was perished through and through and there was no relief.

A bell clattered harshly, rustily; the woman nearest the door stood up, dragging a child with a dirty bandage round his head after her, and pushed open the door marked surgery. The child immediately set up a wail. The door closed behind them mercifully. My mind began to run on the unknown tortures going on behind the dingy panels.

In there they poked things in you. They stuck needles up your bum and cotton wool down your throat until you retched. I shifted on the painful wooden seat that was now only one degree chiller than my bare legs. Another spasm shot through me. The bell croaked again and an old man pulled himself to his feet with the aid of a stick and tottered out of sight. Three more to go. A young chap with an arm in a splint and sling was next, soon in and out, only wanting a certificate signed, and then a middle-aged woman took his place. I could tell by her face that she would be a long time. She had come for a chat. Her mouth drooped and her thin hair was swept up in pitiful imitation of the current fashion, three rolls, at either side and on top of her head. The rest straggled behind in Medusan locks and the three sausages were flat and lustreless with grease.

By this time I was in a state of perpetual motion on my chair. When it came to my turn I wouldn't be able to move. But I had to; the passage had filled up with patients now. I couldn't just sit there. Once more the bell grated and the last woman between me and the ordeal of standing up disappeared inside. I tried to remember the last poem we had learned at school, but it was 'The Brook' and it was better not to think about that.

The bell gibbered. Somehow I got off my chair, I couldn't stand up completely, and walked into the surgery. He was bending over his desk writing. A great brown dog lay on a silky, black, long-furred mat in front of the hearth. The only light came from a small bendable desk lamp trained on the doctor's big hands.

'Well, what can I do for you?' He looked up over the top of little half-moon glasses. I took out the note and handed it to him. I stood on the rug, wondering if the big dog would bite, as he unfolded the note and looked at the signature.

'And who are you?' he demanded.

'I'm Paddy,' I said and he turned to his note again. Suddenly I felt something hot running down my cold leg like a sharp edge. I tried to stop it by contracting every muscle as hard as I could but it was no good. It was flowing quick and free and there was nothing I could do. The doctor read on and the stream continued its course. Then he looked up. I was paralysed. I didn't dare move.

'When did this happen?'

'The other day.'

'Tell your mother—no I'll write a note. She must rest as much as possible and I'll be in to see her tomorrow.' He took a piece of paper and began to write quickly.

Slowly it died to a trickle and stopped. My shoe was full and my sock sopping but I could move. I went forward and took the outstretched note. I moved towards the door. Thank God for the dim light.

'Good night, Paddy.'

'Good night.' Perhaps he would think it was the dog. Going home was even colder with harsh wind chapping my wet thigh.

We were late to bed that night. The boys wouldn't go til I'd gone because they were older than me, and I couldn't go til I'd finished my homework, so it didn't seem as if we'd been upstairs long before Mum and Ted came to bed—though the boys were asleep already, Billy in the middle and Arthur on the outside, breathing heavily. Sometimes he walked in his sleep and then my mother, who slept with an eye and ear open like a cat, would wake to find him at the top of the stairs and order him back to bed. He turned and went at her voice, without any fuss, like an automaton. My wet sock I'd secretly rinsed out and put under the bottom sheet to dry in the heat from my body during the night, and I lay there listening, making myself breathe deep and heavy as though I was asleep too.

I heard the fire being raked over and then the door opening downstairs and sensed the faint glow behind my eyelids as my mother came up with the candle. There was a soft pop as she lit the gas. I wanted to hold my breath but forced myself to breathe in and out regularly and keep my eyes shut. I heard her undress, and the creak of the springs as she got into bed though she was only seven stone nine. Ted came heavily up the stairs, undressed to his shirt, I knew he slept in his shirt, and then the light went out with another little pop. Ted felt his way towards the bed in the pitch black. I heard a stifled 'Sod!' as he stubbed his toe on the iron leg of the bed before he climbed heavily in. Fred and Gladys were still out.

I lay there in the breathing dark listening. Now I held my breath to hear better. I was almost relieved when the regular movements began.

Next afternoon I ran all the way home from school. The doctor had been and gone; Mum was up and dressed.

'What did he say? What is it?'

'It's a rupture, a hernia. I shall have to wear a belt. I'm going to get one fitted next week.'

'Won't it ever go back?'

'No, not now. But the belt'll keep it in place.'

'What'll it look like?'

'The belt? Like a corset I expect. Drink your tea up. It must be nearly cold.'

Mechanically I swallowed my tea. 'Mum.'

'Hmm?' She was reading *Rogue Herries*.

'I don't like sleeping with the boys.'

'Why not?' She laid down the book.

'Arthur's not nice to sleep with.'

'What d'you mean? What about Billy?'

'Oh, he's alright. He's not old enough to be a nuisance.'

'Arthur's a nuisance?'

'Yeah. I don't like sleeping with him.'

'Do you want to sleep with Gladys then? It's only a little bed.'

'Oh no! I don't want to sleep with her. Let me come in with you. Go on, let me.'

'We'll see. D'you want another cup of tea? Put some water on the leaves then.'

That night I tried to stay awake til they came to bed but my eyes were tired with reading and I couldn't keep them open.

I don't know what my mother said to Ted but the day after she told me I could sleep at the bottom of their bed. So I did, like a watchdog across the threshold. The boys didn't mind; it meant they had more room. My mother said the change was because they kicked and fought too much over the bedclothes, which was true as well. Yet in some way they resented my promotion and Arthur's secret punches became harder. And there was still Sunday afternoon.

Mum was fitted with a belt, a pad to push the stomach into place and a quantity of straps and lacings to keep it there. 'Holiday for Strings', she called it when she took it off. Gradually the scar faded until it was only a wrinkled white furrow in the brown skin, but the little pot remained.

'Anyway,' as she said, 'at least I get me corsets on the National Health.'

15

I T WAS Sunday afternoon. I had washed, Billy wiped and
Arthur put away. Ted and Mum had retired upstairs.
'Where shall we go?' said Arthur. 'There's nothing to
do here.'

'Come on up the park.' We put on our coats and went into
the perishing winter world. Running and sliding down the hill
over the railway bridge we warmed our fingers on our hot
blakeys. The Minny Brook tinkled icily as we chuffed past,
our breath flying wraith streamers over our shoulders. Frost still
curded the grass tussocks, the day had brought no thaw, and
the ground had set hard as cement. We stopped and pounded
over the footbridge and into the park proper. There was no
wind, only raw air that we sucked into our bodies and blew out
of pursed lips to warm our noses grown sharp with the cold.

No one, nothing moved in the park. The swings hung limp,
the roundabout seemed carved from immovable rock. The
iron bars and handles were like red-hot pokers on numb hands.

'I'm frozen,' Billy's teeth chattered.

'Let's go to the pictures,' suggested Arthur. 'How much we
got?' He pulled his money out of his pocket. We had recently
graduated to a shilling a week. Arthur had fourpence left, I had
ninepence but threepence of that was school fund on Monday,
Billy had eightpence. We needed a shilling each.

'We can't do it.'

'Come on, I know where we can get some. Off the Yanks.
We'll just ask them for a penny.' Arthur moved away.

'But where?'

'Up the Red Cross. You just stand outside and when they

go in or out you ask 'em. Sometimes they give you a tanner. Whitey Davis got half a crown once.'

'You done it before?'

'Yeah, me and Whitey we done it lots. Sometimes they give you gum instead. Come on cowardy, Mummy's pet.'

The building that had been made over to the American troops for their Red Cross—they were quartered in the barracks just outside the town, the local battalion not needing it since they were busy in the front line—was a little way off the street. We stopped at the entrance to the drive and waited, staring at the grey stone building with its classical entrance of two columns and a pediment. An American corporal ran down the steps, hands shoved in his pockets, drawing his trousers tight across his bum; his forage cap, dented in the middle, stuck up fore and aft, his jaws worked mechanically; he strutted towards us, his dark head bobbing like a moorhen. Nobody moved.

'Go on, thingy,' said Arthur. 'They like girls.' I shook my head.

'I will,' said Billy and ran after the soldier.

'All you gotta say is "Got a penny, mister?"' said Arthur. Billy came trotting back.

'He gimme a packet of gum,' he said.

'Come on, shairsie.' Billy handed us both a long flat strip of gum. Another American appeared down the street.

'I'll try this one,' Arthur said. 'You come with me.'

But this one brushed past with no answer.

'Supposing the police see us?'

'Let's go up the drive then they won't.'

It was a few minutes before any more game appeared, two soldiers together, warm and sleek in their light khaki. A blast of heat and laughter blew out every time the door swung to. They paused a moment on the steps.

'Gotta penny, mister?' said Arthur. One of them looked down.

'You kids oughta be home out of this cold.'

'Go on, mister, gi's a penny.'

'What d'you want a penny for, son?'

'Aw, come on, Sel, let's git.'

'Me and my sister wanna go to the pictures.'

'If I give you sixpence now you run along home?'

'Yeah.'

The American dug in his pocket and fished out a sixpence.

'There y'are. Now git along home.'

'Aw, come on,' and they swung off up the road. Now we felt we were getting somewhere.

'You try the next one,' said Arthur. 'Go on, it's easy.' He was a tall thick-set man with a dark face.

'Gotta penny, mister?' I repeated the formula almost stuttering with fright. The soldier fished in his pocket, drew out some coins and handed me a penny. Then he selected a shilling and held it up.

'You come round the back with me, I'll give you this white piece.'

'No thanks. I mustn't leave my brothers.' My heart thudded chokingly. The man muttered something and ran up the steps.

'How much more do we want?' Billy asked.

'Another elevenpence.'

'If we hang about long enough, we'll get it.'

Suddenly a little sash window to the right of the door was thrown up.

'Come here,' said a voice. We turned and looked. There was a great expanse of curling hair with the white flesh gleaming through. All together we turned and ran.

'The dirty old sod,' said Arthur when we stopped for breath.

'Now what are we gonna do?' Billy asked.

'I'm not going back there,' I said.

'It's too early for the pubs. They don't open til seven on Sunday else we could have tried the Lamb.'

'I know,' said Arthur. 'We'll go in the back.' He began to walk very fast down the street.

'What do you mean?' I said, trotting to keep up with him.

'You'll see when we get there.' And he hurried on. We stopped just before the gravel desert in front of the Regal. It was nearly dark now and a chill wind was beginning to stir out. The Regal glowed invitingly in a neon haze.

'Now Billy takes the shilling and goes in normal. You and me goes round the back to where you come out. When Billy's been in there a little while he goes to the lavatory only he doesn't really, he lets us in the back. And if you don't come, young Billy, I'll bash your face in. Go on and wait til no usherettes are about before you come for us.' Billy walked off towards the bright entrance.

'Let's go round the back.'

'But it's stealing, Arthur.'

'No it ain't. We're not taking nothing.'

'I'm going home. I don't want to go.'

'No you're not going home. You're not gonna split on us so you're coming too or I'll bash you. I'll punch you right in the chest. So come on and don't be so soft.' He pushed me along in front of him until we reached the back exit. It was cold and creepy waiting for Billy to come. We needed him to push the bar from the other side. Then we heard him thrusting against it and the big door ground open.

'Sh,' said Arthur. 'Where's the seats, Billy?'

'There's three up the side by the door.'

'Right. Paddy's first, so's you can't hop off. If they catch you don't give your real name and address.' He shoved me down the steps towards the darkened cinema. It was alright for them but I had to look as if I'd been to the gents. Cautiously I opened the door, everyone seemed to be busy with the screen. I made up a false name and address quickly, slipped out of the door and into the nearest seat in the front row. My ears drummed and I stared fixedly at the screen though I saw nothing for a few minutes. When I did get it in focus Charlie Chan was advising his number two son of the foolishness of haste when pursuing a criminal.

At the interval I joined the boys. I had seen them come in and walk openly to the seats Billy had chosen. No one had noticed that where one went out two came in. The second film was a Bowery Boys classic. We roared with laughter when the little stubby one hit the lanky one round the head with his hat, but every time an usherette pointed her torch in our direction the stabbing finger of light pinned me to my seat like a spitted pig for roasting. When the end came we walked boldly out in the surge of happy patrons.

Outside, the moon, refusing to be blacked out, had got up early and shone grinningly down on the huge bulk of the county offices, trying to hide under a trailing camouflage, a netful of brown and green seaweed. A small group of children posted outside the Lamb was demanding chewing gum and pennies from the American soldiers as we had done earlier.

'Wotcher, Arthur,' called Whitey Davis. 'Where you been?'

'Pictures.'

'Any good?'

'Flipping good, mate. We was up the Red Cross this afternoon,' he boasted.

'Go on! How'd you do?'

'More'n you.'

'How much then?'

'How much you?'

'Elevenpence and two packets of gum.'

'Ah we had more'n that.'

'Where you going now?' Whitey asked defeated.

'Home. We 'ent had our tea yet.'

'Cor, 'ent you had you tea?'

'No. Our mum won't half give us a clout,' said Arthur with pride; Whitey's mum didn't care enough to clout him. The phrase stuck in my throat.

'Come on,' said Billy. 'It's cold.'

'Coming out after?' asked Whitey.

'Reckon we'll have to go straight to bed,' said Arthur. 'See you tomorrow in the playground.'

'See you.'

They were all ready to go out when we did get home. For once I was glad; there was no time for questions.

'Have your tea, wash up and up to bed at eight,' said my mother. She didn't clout us. Ted was in a hurry to get some cigarettes from the Lamb before the soldiers bought them all up. There might even be a drop of whisky if they were lucky, since the landlord knew them. I wondered if she would recognize Whitey in the group outside the pub. I hoped not but I doubted if her quick eyes would miss his pale straw hair and almost colourless eyes. He sometimes came to call for Arthur.

'At least he's clean,' my mother would say. 'Though I reckon he leads Arthur on, makes him too big for his boots. It's alright for him, but Arthur's still on probation. If he does something silly they'll put him away. I've told him but it doesn't seem to sink in. Just thinks I'm nagging at him I suppose.'

'It's your turn to wash,' said Billy, when they'd gone.

'No it isn't. I did it dinner-time.'

'It's my turn,' said Arthur surprisingly. Secretly I was rather sorry.

'I can always tell when Arthur's done the washing-up,' Mum said once, 'because he's the only one of you who wipes the bowl and the draining-board after.' I watched him pour the boiling water on to the lumps of soda at the bottom of the bowl and saw them shrink away like ice in a warm hand and the water discoloured like thin milk, Whitey Davis's eyes.

When we were finished I took a book out of my satchel and began to read. It was *Ivanhoe*. Last week I had put my hand up to read at the beginning of the great battle scene and I'd read on and on, through page after page, while metal clashed and rang all round me, feet slipped on the bloody pavement, stroke, counter-stroke; weak from a great gash in my side I had summoned all my strength for the last mighty blow that would bring my enemy crashing low; then I too had sunk down senseless. Miss Martin had let me read on and the class had listened. At the end I paused and looked around dazed. She had laughed a little and complimented me by saying it had seemed a pity to spoil it. This week I was going to be prepared.

'What are you reading?' asked Billy.

'*Ivanhoe*,' I said. 'It's all about fighting,' hoping this would excuse it.

'You're always reading.'

'Well it's better than not even knowing what picture you've seen.'

'I do know.'

'I bet you don't.'

'It was the Bowery Boys and Charlie Chan.'

'But you don't know what the pictures were called.'

'Who wants to know? What difference does it make?'

'You might go and see them again by mistake.'

' 'Ere, Billy, it's your turn. Stop gassing.' They were playing rummy.

'No I wouldn't cos I'd look at the pictures outside see.'

'Supposing there wasn't any pictures?'

'There would be.'

'Yeah but you'd have to go all the way there first to find out, you couldn't look it up in the paper and see.'

'Who cares . . .'

'Oh shut up, for Christ's sake, or I won't play with you.'

'Well she just shows off cos she can read. Reading's nothing. Our dad gets on alright and he can't read.'

'Yeah but he don't know how much he's got in his pay packet every week. He doesn't know what they've taken away or why.'

'Who cares? He's alright.' Arthur threw down his hand.

'Will you shut up and play. And you shut up keeping on about reading. And leave off about our dad. Mummy's pet, Mummy's pet, Mummy's pet.' Bill joined in the chant. I read on in a superior silence and soon they were arguing because Billy had cheated. Billy always tried to cheat.

'You rotten cheater,' said Arthur and punched him hard.

'If you're going to fight I'm going to bed.' I made for the door, clutching *Ivanhoe*. 'Mum said you weren't to be late.'

'Shut up!' said Billy. 'She's a silly old cow.'

'Don't you call my mother a cow,' I shouted.

'Yeah, shut up, Billy,' said Arthur. 'She's not bad.'

'I'll hit you, you call my mother a cow.' I turned and ran upstairs. I put on the gas, undressed quickly in the shivering room and climbed into the end of the bed and lay for a few minutes looking up at the cracked ceiling. Then I picked up *Ivanhoe* and read on, the hand holding the book growing number with the cold and one eye squinting at the page, the other closed, as I lay on my side. Rummy continued noisily below.

Sounds of feet on the path put a sudden end to it; there was a scuffle, a pop of gas light and the boys crept up the stairs, scuffed off their boots, shirts and trousers and leapt into bed, dragging their pyjamas with them to put on under the bed-clothes.

We all lay breathing heavily like pigs in a pen when Mum came up. She turned out the gas and went downstairs saying:

'Don't worry, I know you're not asleep.' The door closed behind her and I heard Billy gurgling in the dark.

16

'GO ON,' said Arthur, 'or I'll bash you.' And he would have done too. Don't run away with the idea that underneath it all we were nice kids pretending to be tough and that just because he was three years older than me he wouldn't have put all he had into it, or that deep down in me there was a hidden spring of courage and decency that would well up at the last minute like *Eric or Little by Little* and I'd stand up to Arthur and say, 'Go on hit me. I don't care.'

It was Saturday morning. We stood in the alley next door to Woolies, a warm wet, muggy morning with the moist breath of wind puckering the surface of the puddles in the gutter and the shopping women muckying the backs of their bare legs as their platform soles and wedge heels carried them from window to window anxiously looking for something off points to eke out the carefully hoarded meat ration, sacred to Sunday dinner, but you have to eat on Saturday too.

'You whip it,' said Arthur. 'And pass it to me. Let's go.' We pushed through the swing doors. Inside was stifling, glaring with heat and light, crowded, the floor trampled and muddy. We wormed our way towards the toy counter and stood staring avidly. There were so many things I would have liked: pencils, books, rubbers, soldiers, although Cretia and I were past playing with them now but just to fill some past emptiness.

'Paint-brush,' muttered Arthur. We moved a little further along the counter.

'Look,' I said loudly, pointing at the back of the ranked goods. ''Ent that a stunning pencil case?' At the same time I slipped my left hand over the glass barrier, rested it on the camel-hair paint-brushes and began to feed one delicately up my sleeve. I let my hand lie still for a moment, the fingers innocently open and then withdrew it, letting it hang at my side where it met Arthur's hot, damp palm and transferred the paint-brush. We lingered a little; haste was suspicious we knew from the pictures.

Our next call was the electrical counter where I managed a torch bulb and battery before we slipped away. Automatically we made for the park, the only place we could be sure to be unobserevd, and stopped behind the big open reservoir marked 'Stagnant water'.

And all this time I was scared to death, don't think I wasn't, yet excited too, my heart going bomp, bomp, throat dry, ears singing. I suppose this is one of the things we lose soonest, this intensity of physical feeling, so that, as a child, I was always aware of my body's demands and manifestations and every emotion had its counterpart in the quickened blood, sick surge of the stomach or weakening of the calf muscles so I felt I'd fall down if anyone asked me to stand up or move.

'Got a pin?' asked Arthur. I fished in my pockets, cluttered as any boy's, and brought out a big safety pin.

'See a pin and pick it up,
All the day you'll have good luck.'

Arthur unwound the pin, stuck one end under the battery, the other on the terminal at the top and pressed the bulb against it. It glowed faintly in the daylight.

'That's alright. Here you can have this,' he passed over the paint-brush.

'I don't want it.' The reservoir was green with scum and the water stank putridly. Vaguely I wondered what might be stirring in the slime at the bottom. We had been doing pond dipping in nature study and dredged up all shapes of monstrous life. I had watched with sick fascination while the gristly shadow of a hydra, magnified to the size of a human head, had devoured a water flea on the blank wall of the biology lab. Amoeba might be painfully dividing to multiply, slipper animals paddling with hair-thin cilia in search of prey.

'You've got to have it.'

'But it's no use to me. I can't use it without everyone wanting to know where I got it.'

'That's your look-out. Anyway you're gonna have it.'

So that was that. Every time I put my hand in my pocket it was there, straight and thin like a knife blade yet somehow I couldn't just throw it away.

When I got home on Monday afternoon she was juggling with some pieces of parachute silk she had been given, trying to shape them to a pair of cami-knickers. I spread my cold hands to the fire, the backs cleared of the little red cracks that winter had chapped there, before I put on the kettle for our ritual cup of tea.

'How did you get on today?' she asked.

'Oh alright. I got A minus for English.'

'What was it?'

'A poem.'

'Read it to me.'

'I dunno if I got me English book.' I ferreted in my satchel. I knew it was there; I'd brought it home to gloat over, carried it around all day, the remembrance of it glowing through dull periods of algebra and domestic science. I pulled out the brown-paper-covered exercise book.

'Make the tea first and then I can stop this and listen properly.' I hurried with the tea.

We sat on either side of the scrubbed wood table, littered with pins, newspaper pattern and pinned pieces of white silk, two steaming cups at our elbows, the fire burning contentedly, and suddenly I was embarrassed. I didn't think I'd be able to read without choking.

'Go on,' she said. I breathed deep and began, my own voice as I listened to it sounding thin and high, the words falling meaninglessly into the dead, dud air.

'It's called "Vanished".' I felt myself going pink.

> 'The grey sea breaking on the rocks,
>   And echoing along the cove,
>   Beneath the green weeds' hanging trails,
>   Lies the empty treasure trove.

Gone are the golden doubloons,
The glittering pieces of eight,
The pirate's rusted sword belt,
The tarnished coppery plate.

Each has found a resting place
Far from the lonely shore,
The sand and silt now keep them—
Safe for evermore.'

It was always the same; when you'd written it it all seemed dull
and pointless, though at the time it was wildly exciting so you
hardly dared breathe or look up from the dry twigs of letters
you were scratching on the page in case you lost it before you'd
finished. My mother stretched out her hand.

'Let me see.' I gave her the book, taking a quick look at the
expression on her face. Was she disappointed, or laughing even?
But her face had only a serious concentration as her eyes moved
down the page.

'It's not bad, not bad at all but your writing's terrible.'

'Oh, writing! I can't write.' Only dull people who liked
maths were tidy and wrote neatly. My writing had character.

She looked back through the past work.

'This isn't very good, B.'

'I didn't like any of the subjects.'

'Still you usually manage to get B plus or A minus.' I waited
anxiously while she read through one or two pieces.

'You seem to be quite good at English. You'll have to work
hard at maths and things you don't like so much if you're going
to get to college. There's a new bread pudding in the cupboard.
It's right at the back out of sight. I'm keeping it hidden or the
boys'll scoff the lot.' I cut myself a long wedge across the baking
tin.

'While you're up let's have some more coal on the fire.' I
took the shovel and piled it with the slatey coal, looking at each
lump carefully in case it should hold a find, the bones of a leaf
aeons dead and me the first ever to see it, or a gleam of gold
thread to make our fortunes forever.

'We saw that Davis boy again last night, outside the Lamb,

begging off the Americans.' I took up the poker and began to prod out the little pockets of ash silted in front of the grate, so they fell to the hearth in small clouds. 'It's disgraceful, kids out begging in the street, and goodness knows what Gladys gets up to, out with the Yanks every night. Before we know where we are there'll be another little bundle on the way. It's no good my telling her, she takes not a scrap of notice, but let me hear either Billy or Arthur have been out cadging off the Americans and I'll give them the pasting of their lives.' Methodically I poked the dead cinders through the bars til the fire burned clear and fierce.

'Their father's like putty with them, they do just what they like with him. Leave that fire alone now, you're poking the coal off. The thing is they just don't seem to see anything wrong in what they do. I know we were mischievous when we were kids, what with Dick and his acrobatics, but we were never in trouble with the police.' Her fingers tacked the pieces of white silk together, but it was rather like trying to hold down an eel while you lopped its head, it slithered and tugged at the binding cotton.

'How d'you think I'll look in these?' She held up the garment, pieced together but so light it seemed it would blow away. 'They're very fashionable but I reckon they'll be draughty too with these wide legs and just a couple of buttons in the middle. Still, spring's coming.'

I put the brown English book away in my satchel.

'Have you got much to do tonight?'

'We've got tons of biology, three diagrams and masses of notes.'

'Well get on with it now while there's some peace before the ravening horde comes pounding in.'

' "The Assyrian came down like a wolf on the fold." '

She laughed delightedly, clattering the cups together into a precarious pyramid. 'I don't know what I'd do sometimes if I didn't have you to talk to. I did it all for the best but it doesn't seem to have worked out very well. Still you work hard and you'll be alright. We'll be alright. It'll all come right in the end.'

I didn't go straight home next day or at least I did but I

didn't stop, I kept on going past the gate, past Cretia's, hoping she wouldn't see me, down the hill to the low stone bridge that carried the road over the Minny Brook and up into the town. I leaned over the parapet and stared into the gurgling waters. It was a shallow, rapid stream, swollen now with February rain —February filldyke, Granny had called it so Mum said. The rough cold stone struck in a damp hard ridge through my coat across my diaphragm.

I'd fished under this bridge, wading in my wellingtons wet-shiny as a seal's back. Cretia and me had once made match-box boats and put two celluloid bears, hers pink and jocular, mine blue and sinister, afloat on the rapids and they'd whirled away out of sight, spinning like falling ashkeys. Just here I'd gaped fascinated while a thick, brown leech had sucked down a worm that'd been unlucky enough to fall in, and the strangely animated piece of rubber tube had absorbed it, straightening the desperate kinks and knots with its persistent mouth. Upstream I could see the stepping stones used by generations of children to cross to the island, their wild kingdom; the mill where Ted and Gladys were busy at work and the swimming pool. The coins in my hand were hot and sticky with the acid smell of sweaty copper.

A weak sun lit my reflection in the water where it ran clear over pebbles. I wavered and danced before my eyes as I stared at myself. What did I really look like? My thick pale hair was cut short under the green beret, my cheeks tinged the same colour. I was taller than Arthur and Billy, angular and long-faced. With an effort I might even be interesting but the face seemed un-real. This year I'd be thirteen. I'd never fish or sail match-box boats again.

The paint-brush had cost one-and-eight. I would drop in sixpence for two weeks and eightpence on the third. I wondered who would find them—maybe one of the kids fishing. And who'd be appeased by this sacrifice, some watery river god, justice? I wasn't sure, only I knew it was the right thing to do somehow to even things up, but I felt bloody silly. More people were passing now as it got towards tea-time. What would they think if they saw me chucking money into the river? I leaned over the edge and let my hand dangle as far down as my long arm would let it. Then I let the coins slip out as surreptitiously as I'd drawn the paint-brush and the other things in. The coppers sank heavily through the water. I could see them lying beside a flat oval stone like regular brown pebbles. One, two, three, four, five I let them drop and then my fingers closed on the sixth. With that I could buy a bar of chocolate peppermint cream that she liked so much. I drew back my hand with the sixth coin and put it back in my pocket.

For a minute I stood looking down into the water growing misty now, then across at the island fading into the evening. Next week I would put in an extra penny. I turned away up the hill, feeling easier yet as if I hadn't done the thing quite properly. I should have dropped the other coin in. I thought of turning back to the bridge but the sweetshop glowed enticingly just ahead.

'You've got a lot left,' said the shopkeeper, a little man with gold-rimmed glasses, as he snipped half a coupon from the end of the row. Mum always gave us our own coupons to spend when the new ration books came in. I took the bar of chocolate and hurried out of the shop and up the hill.

At the gate I nearly ran into a tall, smart-looking man coming out.

'Who was that?' I asked as soon as I was inside the door. I could see she was pleased, exultant almost.

'A man from the Town Hall, the sanitary inspector. They're going to give us a new house. I wrote to them last week. After all why should we have to live like this? I didn't say anything before in case it didn't come off but I showed him everything this afternoon and he said he didn't know how we'd managed so long.'

'Where will it be?'

'One of the council houses up near the gas-works.'

'Chinatown!'

'Is that what they call it? Oh well, what does it matter, it's a house with three bedrooms.'

When they said to me at school, 'Where do you live?' I should have to say Chinatown. Even Clarence Street was better than Chinatown. They were all the scrapings up there from the town's slum clearance before the war.

'When will we be going?'

'As soon as possible, the first one vacant he said. We'll have to rustle up a few more sticks of furniture and the move'll cost us something. I'll have to see if old Dearlove'll take the machine again for twenty.' She pronounced it Mac-Hine to show she wasn't worried; it was a game we played mispronouncing words. There was a standing arrangement between my mother and the old junk man, who lived in a dirty caravan with his gipsy wife and litter of tumbling children in the middle of his scrap yard, that when an emergency arose he took my mother's machine for twenty pounds and she bought it back again by instalments. It was our only security, that and the sale of our clothing coupons.

'I made the inspector a cup of tea while he was here and he said he didn't know how I kept it so clean and tidy. So I said soap and water were cheap enough and he said, "You wouldn't think so if you saw some of the things I see." '

'Is there any tea left?'

'Try and see. You're late tonight.'

'I had some things to do.' She never pried into my private affairs. 'I bought you this.' I gave her the bar of chocolate. I wanted to see her eat it but she popped open the front drawer of the machine that was divided into little compartments for spools and needles and had a key to it.

'I'll eat it later. I mustn't spoil my tea.'

'It's for you; you're to eat it. You won't give it away will you? You'll eat it all yourself?'

'If you want me to. I'll have it tomorrow afternoon.'

I stirred the thick tepid tea. 'Mum, am I ugly?'

'Ugly? Whoever says so? And even if you were as ugly as a toad I'd still love you best in the world.'

'You do love me best, don't you?'

'Of course I do. There's no one else.'

'Will it cost much more, the house?'

'A bit more I expect. There'll be more work and more stairs. Everyone'll have to help.'

'One day, when I'm older, I'll buy you a bungalow so you'll never have to go upstairs again. And you'll have fresh air by the sea, and you'll get better. There'll be just you and me.'

'When our ship comes home. What about the Willertons?' she laughed.

'We don't need them. I can take care of you and earn enough to keep you. I'll go to college and then we'll go away together. There'll just be you and me.'

17

THE patriarch was on his feet again now, his white hair flopping round his shoulders, eyes tight closed, arms thrown wide, wrestling with the Lord.

'O Lord, we pray you for, for our brethren who are about to be immersed in the healing waters of Jordan, that they may indeed be washed in the blood, the blood of the Lamb and free from every stain of sin become indeed thy children. Amen.'

His congregation, heads bowed in their hands, threw out a handful of scattered amens and one elderly woman rocked to and fro crying allelujah. It was draughty in the little passageway where I waited to rub Cretia down. I peered out again. Sitting in the front row were the two candidates for admission, Cretia, blue and shivering in a maroon swimming costume with a navy mac draped about her, and a thin, stooped man about forty, very self-conscious in a pale blue costume that looked as if his wife had lent it for the occasion.

The floorboards had been taken up in the front part of the hall and a vast cement sink exposed with steps leading down, half full of chilly water. The initial ducking was to be done by a visiting brother, sinister in black oilskins, more diabolic than divine.

He came forward now and entered the water, as the harmonium gave an introductory wheeze and the brethren rustled the leaves of their hymn-books.

'Come forward, Sister Lucretia, and be received into the family of the Lord, by the blood of the Lord Jesus Christ who alone can save you from the fire of hell and bring you into everlasting life.'

Cretia slipped off the mac and began to lower herself down the steps, her face radiant. The harmonium coughed and swelled, hoarsely but triumphantly, the congregation sang with rapt fervour. Watching from the wings I felt cold and excluded by my own complexity. 'If this is what she wants, if it will make her happy then may it bring her peace,' I thought incoherently.

The baptizing brother caught her by one arm and placed a hand behind her back.

'Do you believe in the Lord Jesus Christ that He alone can save you from sin, the world, the flesh and the devil?'

'I do!'

'Then be washed in the Blood of the Lamb.' He gave a heave, her legs shot from under her, she sank under the water and was expertly hoisted to the surface again.

'Saved by Grace, saved by Grace!' roared the congregation. Cretia tottered up the steps and out of the hall towards me. I ran forward with my towel at the ready. She was trembling violently.

'Are you alright?'

'Yes, yes. Oh, Paddy, it was wonderful. When he pushed me under I 'it me 'ead on the side and I nearly fainted.' I rubbed vigorously. She was still dazed but whether from conviction or concussion I couldn't be sure. From the hall came another howl from the congregation.

'Saved by Grace, saved by Grace.'

I rubbed harder and then helped Cretia almost roughly into her clothes. Adornment and beauty were vanity, the brethren said, making a virtue out of necessity.

'I'm going back for the last hymn,' she said. 'You coming?'

'No thanks. I'll have to get home. We're moving this week, there's a lot to do.' I crossed my fingers in my pocket. 'You know the address?'

'Yeah. I'll come and call for you one evening.'

'So long then.'

'God bless you, Paddy. I'm so happy.' I hurried out into the dark, windy streets before I could be caught by the pale girl with the feverish eyes who would ask me if I had found the Lord yet.

In fact there was little to pack. Our few possessions fitted easily into a small van and looked pitiful when unloaded in their new quarters. The machine, with its polished walnut and gleaming metal, was the only piece of furniture worth moving, my mother said. She had decided not to let Mr. Dearlove have it this time but to try to make some money by doing alterations instead, so it stood in pride of place under the window for the best light.

There were three bedrooms, a living-room, a scullery, a bathroom, with a stone copper for heating the water and a fixed bath, and an indoor lavatory opposite the coal cellar. The boys were put in the big front bedroom, Gladys in the boxroom, Ted, Mum and me in the back room which was shaped like a squashed L. Never had so much been outlayed in beds and bedding, lino for the floor and even a small dressing table and chest of drawers. In the evenings my mother treadled away making a rug, while I wound the wool on the steel frame for her to stitch down. Ted dug vigorously in the clayey soil of the back garden, getting it ready for beetroot, cabbages and beans.

Arthur and Billy were greeted with delight by Whitey Davis and the rest of the Chinatown gang. Fred was too old for such kid's stuff and seemed to be following Glady's example of spreading the family face round the town.

With the instinctive knowledge that attack is the best form of defence I informed my friends at school that I was going to live in Chinatown and cut short all discussion with a superior smile. My real problem was the journey to and fro. When I'd been late three times in a week and earned myself a detention my mother became worried too. I just couldn't seem to judge the journey right. The estate stood on the very fringe of town with only fields beyond the back garden, at the top of the hill leading up from the gas-works, a killer of a hill that.

'One day I shall drop dead going up that hill,' Mum had said, sizing up the enemy when she had first set eyes on it. I'd long known the knack of adjusting my steps to hers, talking to save her pride, chatter that needed no answer, pausing at strategic moments to point out some interest so she could stop and draw breath, giving her my arm at the steepest parts specially since I'd out-topped her, but this was an ascent, alright if you were St. John in the picture, young and nimble, driven like a goat by the spirit and leaping up and up from crag to crag, but a daily ordeal to her.

I ran down the hill in the morning, my satchel bumping on my hip, down, down, down into town, drew breath on the bridge over the big river, not our swift little Minny Brook but the slow brown coils that undulated across country til they dropped the great slack body in the sea. Then on again uphill over the railway, past the station, down to Trinity Church and the last, long, slow pull nearly half a mile up Radley Road to the school gates, a gentle slope all the way that cracked the calf muscles and gave no chance to make up for lost time. And somehow time was always lost somewhere along the route. I never knew where either, the only clock being that on Trinity Church, permanently stopped at ten to twelve. Only when I reached Radley Road and saw the moving green figures jogging up the road I knew I was safe. But too often the street was deserted and the bell jangling for assembly as I panted through the gates.

'If I had a bike it'd be alright,' I moaned. 'After all Cretia's got one. If she can ride I bet I can.'

'We'll have to see. I'll look next time I'm in town. Maybe they do them on the H.P.'

The results were encouraging, a quarter down and the rest weekly over eighteen months.

'A lady's costs about twelve pounds. It's no good getting you a child's one, you'll soon have outgrown it.' Twelve pounds seemed a fantastic sum that made me gasp. 'It'll be worth it in the long run. You'll be able to take it shopping on Saturdays and hang the bags on the handlebars. I don't like you carrying those heavy weights.' Saturday shopping always began with seven pounds of potatoes at the bottom of the bag.

'It's alright, I can carry them.' But sometimes it seemed as if my arms would drag from their sockets.

It took a month to get the deposit. My mother treadled and stitched at alterations that would bring in a few more shillings; I put my pocket money aside and the remains of the Christmas money Aunt Lyddy and Uncle Dick had sent me, and at last three pounds had been gathered. The cycle shop was a fabulous place of shining steel and glossy paintwork. We chose an up-right model, very solid, last for years, with dynamo to save the expense of batteries. It cost two-and-tenpence a week and I would pay it myself every Saturday morning, collecting the round rubber stamps in a book.

I spent that weekend learning to ride, Ted holding me up at first and then off on my own. Stopping was the difficulty: my feet just reached the pedals and the effort to get them to the ground before the heavy bike heeled over was almost beyond me at first. Monday morning I back pedalled down the hill, whirled over the bridge and halfway up Station Road with hardly any effort. Then I stood up on the pedals and drove it to the top, sank on the saddle for the run down, made a shaky right turn and pedalled exultantly up Radley Road, fell off at the gates and wheeled the bike down into the half-empty shed where I propped the front wheel in the rack. Looking back down the road I saw the little green figures toiling towards me, breaking into a burdened run as the first bell went and the pre-fects on late duty sauntered towards the gate with notebook and pencil.

So began the bicycle era. In the summer evenings, when I'd finished my homework, I cycled the five miles to Hillbury where Janice lived, my best friend at school, in a small, neat semi-detached—her father was a clerk—and we would talk school-talk or I listened while she played the piano. She had a plump mother who always gave us great teas, with home-made cakes on a white tablecloth instead of the newspaper we used at home. Then I rode home in the long summer twilight through waves of warm and cold air that washed over me as I pedalled in a green trance along the blue-grey tarmac, past fields, under trees, thinking huge thoughts of poems I would write and the meaning of sorrow and how much greater Keats was than Shelley.

'Mum, d'you think people really go to hell like Cretia believes? I can't believe a God of Mercy would really send people to hell for eternity.' She was sitting up in bed. She'd had one or two bad days recently, days when she hadn't been able to drag herself up in the morning and the least exertion had made her cough. The tin of Nippits had rattled unceasingly and the little covered pot sat constantly by the bed. It was hot and airless. I put down the tray of tea and extra-thin bread and butter.

'I think heaven and hell are here and now. This is my hell. If it was wrong to have you I've paid for it. You pay in this life. You can't go on paying forever. That's what I think. This life is heaven and hell.' Outside the window a bird chirped lustily for a moment then was silent. Sunlight lay across her legs that made hardly any hump in the bed; her restless fingers puckered the sheet into tiny regular gathers.

18

'AVE 'er come yet?' asked the tall woman who had just arrived, in a loud whisper.

'No, not yet,' my mother answered.

'Us are to be yer by ten but they do come when they do like. I 'opes 'er ent late. Last time I comed 'twer young Dr. Salter and 'er didn't get yer til nighly eleven.'

'We shall all die of pneumonia if we have to wait that long, or be choked to death by the fumes from that stove. It doesn't throw out a scrap of heat.' We sat in a row on a bench against the wall, facing the pot-bellied, cast–iron monstrosity; Sister's table and the weighing machine stood close by.

'Next,' called Sister sharply. 'Is that you, Mrs. Stace? Come along now. Have you brought your card and a sputum test?'

'Ah!' Sister busily filled in the card.

'Take off your coat and get on the scales.' The woman un-wrapped herself from yards of dirty tweed. Sister adjusted the weights and then wrote the result on the card.

' 'Ave I gone up or down then, Sister?'

'You've gained two pounds since last time. Put your coat on and go and sit down.'

The woman grinned triumphantly and rolled herself in her vast coat again. My mother's fingers knitted busily. I tried to concentrate on my book. Sister took a file from a cabinet and put it with the others on the table.

'We shall have to have a special cabinet soon just for you, Mrs. Willerton,' she joked wryly. Everyone gazed with interest at my mother and the bulging folder that was hers on the table.

'Yes, you will won't you,' my mother smiled back. 'She's a dry old stick but she's alright as long as you speak up for yourself,' she always told the others. 'Like the doctors, don't be frightened of them. They're only human like anyone else. Give 'em as good as they give you and they'll have to respect you for it. One of 'em said to me years ago, an old man he was, about seventy, and he said to me, "You ought to have been dead years ago," he said. An' you know what I said, oh I was very cross that time, I said, "Don't worry I'll outlast you," and I did.'

A pale young woman had come in, her face taut with worry. She sat nervously on the farthest edge of the bench near the door as if at any moment she would start up and rush away, like a frightened animal.

'Next,' barked Sister making furious notes on someone's card. No one moved. She looked up. 'You're next aren't you?' Everyone stared. The young woman stood up as if it were a great effort and walked uncertainly over to the table.

'Card?' She held out an envelope.

'My doctor sent me with this.' Sister sighed, took a new card from a drawer and began to fill it in with name, address, previous illnesses. Then she asked,

'Any T.B. in the family?'

A look of absolute terror came over the young woman's face. 'No, no, none!'

'Right. Take off your coat and your shoes and step on to the scales. Heels together, stand up straight.' The measuring arm was brought down on her head; she stood there trapped and trembling.

'Right, sit down. Take your letter in to Doctor when you go in.'

The young woman huddled into her coat and turned to the row of inquisitive faces along the bench. My mother moved up and patted the space beside her.

'It's draughty by the door,' she said.

'You'm after I,' said Mrs. Stace from the other side.

It was a wide stone-flagged passage in which we sat. From time to time a caretaker would amble up with a bucket of coke, open the mouth of the stove in a yawn and throw the coke inside, closing it with a clang. It seemed to burn for some ritual

145

purpose to itself alone. Whenever anyone came in we shivered in the howling draught that accompanied them.

I nudged my mother's arm and nodded out of the window. A new car had drawn up. My mother stared for a moment then whispered: 'It's Dr. Fathers. Good, he's got more experience. You get more sense out of him than out of Salter. It'll mean X-rays for us all.'

A young workman was blown through the swing doors. He gazed calmly around then walked up to Sister's desk.

'Yes?' she snapped. Silently he passed an open letter for her to read. 'It's no good you're coming today; this is the women's day. Who sent you?'

'Dr. Bond.'

'Dear, dear. You really shouldn't have come today. Oh well, perhaps I'd better take your particulars, possibly Doctor will see you.' He was indexed and stamped like the rest of us and dismissed to the bench where he sat apart and took out a comic to read.

A buzzer sounded above Sister's head and she gathered up an armful of papers and disappeared.

'She's rather sharp isn't she?' the young woman turned to my mother.

'Oh take no notice of her. She doesn't mean any harm. This is your first time isn't it?'

'Yes. I'm so worried. You look so calm. I don't know how you do it. There's never been anything like this in the family before.'

'Maybe there isn't now. It may be all a false alarm. He'll examine you, send you for an X-ray and find there's nothing there. And even if there is, it doesn't mean you're finished. I know lots of people think it does. Look at me. I've had it twenty years and I'm still here. The great thing is not to let it get you down.'

'I've got two little boys, I worry about them.'

'This is my daughter. She's at the High School. She's never had anything wrong with her and she's been with me all the time. I suppose one day they'll find a cure for it like they do for most things in time. Then it'll be no worse than having the measles. But don't you worry, my dear, you'll probably find there's nothing wrong with you.'

'I do hope so. I don't know how you do it.'

'I just keep pegging along. I've been coming here so long even Sister knows me. They say it's the old creaking gate that hangs on longest.' She laughed up into the young woman's strained face. 'Time I put me knitting away. They'll be sending for us in a minute. You go in there and strip to the waist. I should keep your vest on and just slip it down when you get in to the Doctor. And if he sends you for an X-ray, as he probably will, don't you worry. It doesn't hurt, and if there is anything, they can see it and catch it in time, and even cure it.' She folded her knitting and put it away.

Sister returned with an empty arm.

'First one in and strip to the waist,' she said. We got up and went into the tiny cubicle. We were always first.

'You have to get back to school and I have work to do,' my mother said. 'We can't waste a whole morning.' So we got up early and strip-washed to the waist.

' 'Cos I shouldn't like to be a doctor and have to examine dirty bodies,' said my mother.

When the buzzer whirred above our heads we went in. The doctors all knew my mother well. To them she was a kind of walking miracle, a living example of mind over matter. Dr. Fathers was kind and civil. They exchanged a little conversation, about the weather and how little difference the end of the war had made to rationing, while he looked through our papers.

'And how's Paddy?'

'Very well thank you.' I had learnt that from my mother; she was always 'very well' too.

'No cough?'

'No.'

'Breathe in, out. Again. Cough. Cough. Now just turn round. Breathe in, out, cough, cough. Again, cough. That's fine. Right, you can put your vest on now.' He scratched something on a large green card from my folder. Thankfully I put on my vest. I had reached the stage where I hated to be seen naked by any-one. I was conscious of the sweaty prickings of fear under my armpits.

'Does she eat and sleep well?'

'She's a bit fussy about food, doesn't always eat the things that would do her good, fat and greens.'

'You must try to eat these things; you need all the vitamins and calories you can get.'

Now it was my mother's turn. I knew she dreaded it. She spent all her days trying desperately not to cough and here was someone asking her to do just that. Inevitably, she would begin to cough in earnest, her hand over her mouth, her eyes apologizing, pleading. I felt the cold end of the stethoscope leaving its firm points on the shrinking flesh of her back and chest, as it had on mine.

'I see you've lost a pound since last time. I think it's time you had another X-ray and Paddy can have one too, just to make sure.' And that was that. On our way out Sister issued us with cards to attend for X-ray next Wednesday, which meant missing maths and French. My mother smiled at the young woman as we passed.

Westerton Sanatorium was fifteen miles from Wortbridge. The bus bumped along the country road; sodden branches, bent low, lashed the steamy windows although it was only a single-decker. I clung to the rail, swaying wildly on every bend, there were never enough seats, and almost suffocated with the smell of hot damp bodies, mackintoshes, rubber, sweat.

'Westerton Hospital,' the conductor shouted and we fought our way to the front of the bus, clambered down the muddy metal steps and on to the rain-swept road. The hospital was a quarter of a mile up a gravelled drive, under tall elms that moaned and tossed, scattering fresh showers from their thin, broad leaves. I gave her my arm and we began our slow progress to the hospital buildings.

By the time we reached the X-ray department we were soaked through on the shoulders and my white ankle socks were spattered with mud. When we took our coats off, our skirts too were dark with damp. The ritual presentation of our cards was made to a starched staff-nurse and we were directed to cubicles and told to strip to the waist.

'Keep your cardigan on,' my mother muttered to me. 'Talk out of the side of your mouth like a convict,' and she winked a big brown eye. That made it easier as she knew it would. I was rigid with apprehension.

'When you're ready, go straight in,' called the nurse who had directed us. Quickly I pulled off my cardigan and unbuttoned my gym slip at the shoulders so that it fell to the waist, then my blouse and vest so they lay in a roll caught by my green girdle. Then I put my cardigan back on again and buttoned it right up.

'Ready?' asked my mother. I drew the curtain and stepped out. 'In there, I suppose.' She pushed open a door marked 'X-ray dept.'. I drew a deep breath and followed her.

It was a large room, almost in darkness except for the radiance from the huge machines. A young nurse took our cards, examined them, and motioned us to a row of chairs along one wall. The frightening equipment, and the strange light, in which the white coats of the two radiographer gleamed ghostly, had taken all my attention before. I'd hardly noticed the huddled shapes slumped on the hard chairs. Now, eyes accustomed to the unnatural twilight, I stared fascinated. They were women of all ages, stripped to the waist, their clothing hanging dishevelled about them, hair awry. None of them had covered themselves as we had. They sat with sagging breasts, their faces distorted with caverns of shadow under high-lighted out-crops of nose, cheek-bone and jaw, like the pictures of waiting prostitutes in the big art books of French painters we had studied at school: the same listless postures, the lumpy bodies that gave me a shock of compassionate horror. We sat beside them at the end of the row.

As their names were called they went forward, stepped into the machine and the plate lowered. Then, as the radiographer pressed a button, we saw into them, the dark rib cage, the linked spine, the shadowy organs filled the screen before us. Every five minutes the young nurse came back, called a name and dismissed the owner to get dressed; she could leave. Rarely she came to tell someone that the first plate hadn't taken and she would have to be done again. I prayed this wouldn't happen to me.

My name was called first.

'Slip off your cardigan,' my mother whispered—I had been

149

gradually undoing the buttons as we had moved up the row. I went forward. The radiographer guided me to the machine and stood me in position, shoulders hunched, arms pulled forward and resting in metal sockets, chin thrust up, propped awkwardly on the top of the ice-cold plate flat against my chest.

'Now take a deep breath and hold it.'

Suppose I sneezed or didn't breathe deep enough? Now they could all see inside me. The machine purred massively. 'That'll do.'

I went back to my seat buttoning my cardigan over the chilled flesh. It was Mum's turn but I was still shaking and nothing registered. If only the nurse would tell us we could go. Soon she was back beside me.

'How did I look?' she asked anxiously.

'I couldn't see, someone was standing in front.'

'Mrs. Willerton and Miss Mahoney can go!'

The ride home was much quicker. The rain stopped and although there was no sun, the sky lightened a shade or two.

'We'll treat ourselves. We'll have a little something in the Court Hall café. We need it.' Even the hill home seemed less grinding and it was only two o'clock, too late for me to go back to school, I argued, and won for once.

'I'd like to go to the library this afternoon if it weren't so far,' she said. 'I feel like a good read.'

'I'll take you.'

'Take me?'

'Yeah, I've thought about it a lot. You sit on the saddle of my bike and I'll push you.'

'You couldn't, you're not strong enough.'

'Yes I am. Honest.'

'Suppose you let me fall?'

'I wouldn't. You know I wouldn't.'

'Whatever will people think? "Look at that wicked woman letting her daughter push her."'

'I don't care what they think. Neither do you really. Let me try. Oh go on!'

'Alright then, just a little try. I could walk part of the way and then try when I'm tired.'

'You wouldn't ever have to go up that hill again. I'd always take you. When we went to the pictures I could take the bike and bring you back.'

I wheeled the bike down to the front and propped it against the kerb. Then I gripped the handlebars as she mounted. She put her hands on my shoulders and I pushed off. I wheeled her steadily along.

'Don't try to pedal.'

'I want to help.'

'No, just sit still.' Together they were heavy, she and the bike, but I kept on. I wouldn't give in. I'd get stronger with practice. I must. These days she hardly went out at all. The hill defeated her, imprisoned her. There was an alternative, a long, slow climb that was just as bad for her but possible for me with my new burden. I took this way.

When we reached home again I was exhausted; sweat had poured from me under my coat but I'd done it. At the kerb outside our house I braked, the bike fouled the pavement edge and nearly toppled; my arms were weak but I made a last effort and dragged it upright.

'You nearly let me fall,' she had grazed an ankle. 'I said it was too much for you.'

'It isn't, it isn't. I can do it.' I was on the edge of tears. 'I want to do it. You will let me, won't you?'

'We'll see. Come on in now. Don't get upset, you're a good girl. You're all I've got. We'll see. Next time I'll walk there and you can push me back.'

'I'll get more used to it. You'll see.'

She never had to climb the hill again as long as I was there.

Next week we went back to the clinic for the X-ray results.

'I don't think you need worry about Paddy, Mrs. Willerton. The X-ray was quite negative. She stands very well, no round shoulders there.' I drew myself up. 'You'll be able to look after your mother now you're older. See she doesn't do too much. I know what you ladies are like. You still need plenty of sleep and fresh air, and good food. Come and see us again next year.' He turned to my mother as I began to dress. 'There's very little we can do for you, Mrs. Willerton, you know that. Rest as much as you can, try not to do too much and don't worry. I know that's difficult with all that family. You should never have married again, you know.'

My mother's head went up. 'I did what I thought was best. You should try living on National Assistance for years. Alright perhaps I made a mistake.'

'I'm sorry, I shouldn't have said anything, it's none of my business. But do take things as easy as you can. We don't want to lose you, you've been with us a long time.'

Going home she leant on my arm, not heavily, there wasn't enough of her.

'You heard what he said. You've got to take things easy.'

'Easier said than done.'

'He doesn't care.' I no longer called my step-father by his Christian name as I'd done at first. I'd never called him Dad. 'He ought to try and control them more. They just think he's soft and laugh at him behind his back.'

It was true too. She exerted the only influence to curb the mad storms that sometimes broke through the house. Once, before we moved, she'd gone out in the garden, brought by shouting and screaming. Fred, Arthur and Billy were over by the shed, Fred holding Billy off the ground with one hand, shaking him like a scruffy rat and punching him hard.

'Leave him alone.'

'I'll hit him if I want to. You're not our mum. You can't tell me what to do.'

'If you hit him again I'll hit you, big as you are.' He towered above her, dark and heavily muscled. Suddenly he stretched out a hand and tore a two-foot length of joist from the rotten shed and lifted it high over her head. She looked up at him un-blinking, holding him to the small flames deep in her brown eyes.

'You dare, just you dare, go on.' He stood for a moment staring at her undecided, then, slowly, his arm went slack.

'Well . . .'

'Now put it down and leave him alone.' She turned her back and walked calmly back to the scullery. With one blow he could have killed her but she held him with her eyes.

'Ted doesn't understand. They're used to that way of life. It doesn't worry them.'

'Barbarians!'

'Never mind it won't be forever. They leave school at the end of this year—at least Arthur does. Maybe he'll be better when he's at work and got money of his own. Not that he's the worst. I'd rather have him than Billy. He's more honest somehow. He's the sort who'd get caught and take the can back for the rest.'

'You wait til I'm older, I'll take you away. It'll all be different.'

Some weeks later when we were shopping one Saturday morning a young woman with two children caught her by the arm.

'Excuse me, you are the lady who was at the clinic aren't you? I've wanted to tell you so much, it was alright just like you said it would be. There wasn't anything wrong after all and I wanted to thank you. You cheered me up no end. I was so frightened. I went home that night and I said to my hubby I said, "There was such a nice lady there and she told me not to worry and I felt much better about it all, as if I could face it." ' One of the children began to grizzle and tug at her coat.

'I'm so glad you're alright. I thought you would be. You look better already.' Her face had filled out, colour tinged her cheeks, her hair was freshly permed. The child whimpered again.

'Well, I'd better get along. I hope you'll be well again soon. Goodbye,' and she was absorbed by the shopping tide.

'That was nice of her to stop and thank me. I wondered if she would.'

'You saw her first?'

'Oh yes, but I looked away so she wouldn't have to stop. Lots of them don't like to acknowledge you in the street if they met you there.'

'Why not?'

'They don't want people to know. They like to keep it quiet, like madness in the family.'

'I suppose you ought to go round like a leper with a bell, shouting "Unclean".'

'I've known people ask me not to visit them in case I gave it to their children.'

'What a cheek!'

'Oh you can't blame them in a way, they're not very bright, but I've known it. That's why it was good of her to stop.' That day she seemed a little stronger herself.

19

'Look,' she said and put aside the top layer of clothes.

'Crikey!' I stared in amazement. The bottom of the drawer was filled two layers deep with boxes of milk chocolates. 'Where on earth did they come from?'

'The boys.'

'They stole them?' I'd known at once of course. There weren't enough sweet coupons in the whole street to buy that many chocolates, let alone the money. 'But where from?'

'I don't know and I don't want to.'

'How did you find out?'

'I noticed Fred's jacket bulging and Billy was eating when he had no business to be, so I watched and saw them making a lot of trips down the bottom of the garden. I had a little search yesterday and I found them. I got Ted to bring them up last night.'

'But what are we going to do with them? Supposing the police come and search?'

'I know. I'd bury the lot but it seems such a wicked waste with people so short of food. I'll send some to Aunt Lyddy, not telling her where they came from, and the rest we'll have to eat ourselves. I daren't give any away here, they'd suspect at once, and I daren't let the boys have any, they're so daft they'd be dropping the boxes all over the place.'

'You can't leave them in that drawer.'

'No, I've had an idea about that, besides I don't want them to find them again. I thought if we took all the drawers out and laid the boxes on the floor underneath no one'd look there. That's why I need your help. I can't lift the drawers by myself.'

Night after night we sat around solemnly stuffing ourselves with chocolates, and they were all the poisoned chocolates I'd ever read about, the ultimate symbol of cloying worldly pleasures, great sickly cups of cream, over-rich to stomachs used to three ounces of butter a week and a quarter of sugar. And every day we waited for the police to come. The robbery of a sweet factory was reported in the local papers but the case remained unsolved, the work of hooligans.

Even Ted himself was worried and threatened them with a belt if they got into trouble.

'What he means is if they get caught,' she said to me afterwards, 'and then they know he wouldn't. I swear I saw Arthur grinning to himself.' The trouble was that thievery was the order of the day. Anything brought home from work was regarded as only what was due in compensation for long hours and low pay. Both Ted and Gladys would come home with yards of cloth wrapped round them under their coats. True the cloth snagged on the loom was regarded as fair game by both management and workers, and the girls used it as aprons.

'And the old man expects me to burn up all the dogs his son runs over in his sports car, in my stoke hole,' Ted said, 'so I'd call it quits.' But where did you draw the line that would stop the boys pilfering, breaking in and beating up their rivals?

'Sooner or later they're going to get nabbed and that'll look nice all over the *Wortbridge Express*. They're not smart enough to keep it up for long. I shouldn't be surprised if the p'lice haven't got their eyes on them already.'

It was a great relief when the last of the chocolates had been safely disposed of, but now we lived on the edge, expecting some new problem every day. ' "Rest," he said, "and don't worry." Don't make me laugh!'

She read about it first in the paper and knew at once what had happened. 'Hooligans' had broken into a store and stolen some knives, a hatchet and one wellington boot. Finding nothing else they had smashed the place up and left.

Tea was late that night. She waited til Ted came clomping up the path, before we sat down to our spam fritters and chips. Gladys had already gone upstairs to take out her dozens of tight curlers she wore all day at the factory, under a headscarf. There was the usual shuffling and digging before Arthur and Billy came to a working arrangement about their elbow room. We were well settled in to our plates, not a word being spoken, only the clash of cutlery on china, the scrape of a chair and the dogged champing of jaws, when suddenly she put down her knife and fork, looked straight at Arthur and Billy and said:

'Well, where've you hidden them this time?' Arthur went white, Billy choked on a chip, Ted stared in amazement. Only Fred and me went on eating as if nothing was happening, me hoping I wouldn't be noticed. I always felt guilty at these moments as if I were involved or as if I ought to be and someone might turn with a derisive snarl and call me yellow—and Fred because he was in a hurry and didn't care anyway.

'What? What's this then?' demanded Ted.

'If I have to waste my time looking for them it'll be the worse for you,' she went on.

'I haven't got nothing,' said Arthur.

'Don't tell me lies. I can't stand liars.' Arthur was ash-faced and shaking now. 'Where are they? Go and get them.' Arthur got up slowly then punched Billy between the shoulder-blades.

'Come on you too.' Billy got up and followed him upstairs.

'What the bloody hell's going on?'

'You'll see in a minute. I wanted you to be here.'

Sullenly the boys returned and put a knife and hatchet on the table.

'Where's the other knives?'

'See,' said Arthur. 'I told you she'd know.' Billy took a smaller knife from his pocket and laid it by the hatchet.

'Whitey Davis had one,' he said.

'Shut up!' said Arthur. 'You didn't have to split, you dafty.'

At last it was beginning to dawn on Ted what was going on.

'You silly bloody sods,' he roared. 'I'll smash your bleeding heads together.'

'You're mad, Arthur,' said Fred, 'pinching things like that, not worth taking. I told you you'd make a mess of it if you tried a job by yourselves.' And he wiped his last chip round his plate and took it outside.

'What happened to the wellington boot?' asked my mother with grim humour.

'We bunged it away,' Arthur muttered. Billy sniggered. It was a mistake. Ted lifted up his dinner-plate in one hand and was just about to hurl it at him when my mother jumped up and took it from his hand.

'I'll bloody kill him!'

'Alright but don't waste your dinner, it's not worth it.' He subsided grumbling, rumbling, into his chair.

'Don't want no bloody dinner.'

'Sit down you two and finish.' Billy was snivelling with fright—it was rarely Ted was so roused.

'They'll have to be got rid of somehow. We can't swallow them like chocolates. The best place is the river but they can't take them out of here in case they're stopped.' She picked thoughtfully at her tea.

No more was said that night. When Arthur asked if he could go out he was smartly put right, so we sat in a sullen circle round the table, my mother knitting, me trying to keep a straying mind on a French translation about firemen. . . . '*Les hommes braves risqueront la vie pour sauver vos bagages* . . .' Ted took out his soldering iron, paste jar of spirits of salts and thin silver bar of solder. He thrust the iron into the fire, then hissing viciously into the jar and tried to fix the molten quicksilver solder to the bottom of the bowl he was mending. Arthur and Billy stared vacantly into the fire, scuffed their boots, fidgeted.

'Oh get something to do for goodness' sake,' my mother said. They got the cards and gradually became absorbed in rummy, but the air throbbed and twanged with unspoken words and the taste of unshed violence tainted the atmosphere.

Next day my mother was waiting for me when I got home.

'You'll have to do it,' she said. 'I've been thinking about it all day and there's nobody else. But it's quite safe. No one would suspect you.'

'It's alright,' I said. 'I'll go.'

'You'd better take them now. I'm worried that they'll find where I've hidden them and pinch them back again.' I followed her upstairs and watched while she unwrapped them from a towel in her drawer. I hadn't really looked at them last night but now I saw they were vicious weapons, straight and shining butcher's tools.

158

'They're dangerous. God knows what they might get up to with those in their hands. You'll have to walk. You can't cycle with those things on you; if there was an accident you'd run yourself through.' I felt the cold blades in my guts and sickened. 'I'll wrap them up a bit.' She took some newspaper and covered their brightness. 'How will you carry them?'

'The knives up me sleeves and the hatchet in the front of me coat. I'll drop them in in different places.'

'I don't know what I'd do without you. You'd better go before they come in. I'll say I've sent you shopping.'

I began to arrange my armoury. The hatchet was easy in the front of my coat; it lodged quite firmly against a button. The knives were more difficult. I shoved the hilts up my sleeves, and my hands, holding the pointed blades, into my pockets. My arms felt stiff like a scarecrow's but when I looked in the mirror I thought no one would notice.

Going down the hill I met Arthur and Billy coming home.

'Where you going?'

'Sainsbury's.'

'Our mum in?'

'Yeah.'

'We'll eat all your tea, won't us, Arthur?'

'Yeah.' I walked on, refusing to rise. I knew Mum always doled the tea out fairly. My share would be kept.

'Stuck up, stuck up! High Schoolite!' they shouted after me.

I had listened to a dozen plays of suspense where the hero walked with death in the shape of an unexploded bomb, a cargo of dynamite, a poisoned foil, and now I was one with them. Again and again in my mind's eye I stumbled and pierced my hands, or fell with the edge of the hatchet against my breast-bone and this fear made my feet less sure than usual, ready to falter at every uneven paving stone. A cold wind pushed me in the face. Dusk was falling, people hurrying home. Good, the park would be empty. I avoided the main streets with their crowds and walked quickly through the turnings into the park. It wasn't closed at dusk. There was no point since it petered out beyond the children's playground into fields and the river. It was the same river where I had dropped my offerings in what seemed so long ago, when I was young. Tonight I was old and the knife points stuck through their wrappings into the palms of my hands.

Once inside the park I was easier. There was no one about. Only the shadows of the tall trees strode over the grass towards me out of the falling dark. The swings hung straight in their gibbet chains, the slide was a looming scaffold. I walked quickly, whistling to show I wasn't afraid, clumping my heavy shoes like a grown man, thinking how I would slip the shorter knife from my sleeve and run my attacker through when he stepped from the clump of bushes fringing the grounds. There was the river ahead of me, gleaming faintly through the shadows.

I dropped the first knife from the little footbridge. It sank quickly under the muddy water and I hurried on, leaving the path, to where the river joined the Minny Brook. Here it flowed sullen and dense; the hatchet went next. Looking round carefully I pulled it from my coat and whirled it like a boomerang out over the water. It threw up a shower of great dark drops before it sank.

Now there was only the little knife, settled comfortably in my pocket. I'd grown used to it, had the knack of it. Why shouldn't it stay there? I began to walk along the bank under the pollard willows towards the lights of Clarence Street. The dark was my friend now, I saw through it clearly, the people coming and going, up and down the lighted road, who couldn't see me even if they turned their thoughts from home for a moment and peered across the dim fields. I watched them like God the scientist, staring one-eyed into a microscope.

I touched the point with my finger; I was a wild thing on the edge of civilization. I would keep it. I'd always wanted a knife, a heavy blade for throwing—I'd tried with kitchen knives but they weren't properly balanced—a smart edge for hacking bits of wood into imagined shapes—I bought razor blades and sliced my fingers on them but didn't dare complain. The urge to kill, to thrust and stab rose up in me with a cold thrill. As a child I had wreaked it on small creatures, mutilating all crawling things in my power when the mood was on me.

I'd nearly reached the street. The bridge carrying it over the river gloomed solidly above me. I didn't want to go back. I stood for a moment staring up at the heads and shoulders sliding along it. 'Puppets,' I thought. Then I shrugged my shoulders and turned towards the path that would lead me up to join them. The smell of the river and the damp fields clung round me like a mist as I hunched my way on to the street.

At the second span of the bridge where it crossed the river proper I stopped and hung over the parapet gazing out across the dark I had come from, like the people I'd watched. Only I was different. I held the dank world inside me. Here the mill where Ted and Gladys worked discharged its waste into the river. He was a fool, a stupid brute. He would destroy her with his tribe of savages who sucked her vital energy. And he gave her no comfort and security, only the continual fear of losing those fiercely kept standards of intelligence and human pride under the rush of violence and senselessness.

'I don't know what I'd do without you.' I eased the knife up my sleeve, took my hand out of my pocket and let it hang over the bridge. Then I opened my fingers and the knife plunged straight down. Its wrapping blew away and the blade pierced the dark skin of the water without a sound. I turned away and walked quickly up the hill.

My mother was looking out for me and met me at the door.

'You've been a long time.' She slipped a packet of tea into my hand.

'I met Cretia.'

'Did you get it?'

'Yes.' I gave her the packet of tea but no one took any notice, they were too busy eating, thrusting wedges of bread and golden syrup into their mouths and swilling them down with tea.

Next day Arthur, Billy and Whitey Davis were picked up at school.

20

'THERE they stood as if butter wouldn't melt in their mouths, saying, "Yes, sir; no, sir." ' Impatiently she dug the bread-knife into the tablecloth as her hand raked the crumbs into a pile, like the terminal moraine of a glacier deposited on the white snowfield they were I thought, having just learnt about such things in geography.

'What did the magistrate say?'

'Oh he asked them if they were sorry, so of course they said they were. Then he said Arthur was obviously the ring-leader, which shows how much he knew, but since they'd confessed he'd be lenient.'

'So?'

'He put Billy and Whitey Davis on probation and Arthur's to be sent away for two years since he's on probation already.'

'Where is he now?' The house was very quiet.

'He's at the remand home waiting to be sent away. Billy went back to school this afternoon and Ted went back to work. We can't afford to miss a whole day's pay.'

'Poor old Arthur!'

'He's the best of the lot really.'

'I wish it'd been Billy, he's such a whiner.' There didn't seem to be much sense to it and all for a couple of knives and an old boot.

'I said I'd done my best. I spoke up for Arthur, said he wasn't a bad boy just easily led but I'm sure they were thinking I was a wicked step-mother who didn't look after them properly. But what can you do when you can't get through to people, when they don't know what you're talking about?' Her lower jaw trembled a little, her lips were very blue and moist.

'You've done all you could.'

'I've tried but it just doesn't seem to be any good.'

'It's his fault, he doesn't help. You shouldn't have to do all this. Did you have to come back yourself?' She nodded. 'You should have let me stay home and bring you back on the bike.'

'No, I couldn't. You mustn't miss school. You must get on. Besides I don't want you mixed up in it. There's no need for anyone to connect you with it—the names are different. You needn't say they're your brothers.'

'They're not anyway. They're no relation to me, any of them.' She coughed quietly into her hand, her thin fist clenched defensively in front of her mouth.

'Get me my little pot.' I moved quickly, sick with apprehension. She always knew when it was coming. There wasn't time to argue, and every time could have been the last. I handed it to her and she turned her back to me, but I could still see the long threads of spit that she wiped from her mouth, and I couldn't turn away, though my stomach retched, because I loved her and she must never know how my inside turned to bile every time. I waited in terror wondering what I should do if it happened: leave her and go for the doctor, I couldn't leave her alone, call Mrs. Nextdoor? But it was alright, she put back the cloth and smiled at me. I smiled back with relief.

'Pour us out another cup of tea.'

It was Friday night, pay night. We were already having our tea when Ted came in, Billy rather pale and subdued saying nothing. Gladys was hardly in the house at all these days. Mum had given up trying to keep track of her comings and goings. It was rumoured, by Gladys herself, that she was going to get married but, as my mother said, who wanted second-hand goods.

'He doesn't seem to care what happens to her, so why should I?' Fred was sluicing in the kitchen.

Ted took out his wage packet and began his usual Friday complaint.

'They done me, took off a whole day instead of a half.' I

sighed ostentatiously. It would mean a whole evening of argument before he could be convinced that his right money was there and for once I didn't see the point of it.

'Not again!' He took my statement literally.

'Yeah. Come on, you're supposed to be clever. You work it out. See if I'm not right.'

'You never are so why should you be this time?'

'That's enough of that!'

'Well you asked me. Of course it's right. It always is. That's what they employ a wages clerk for.' Inside I wondered at myself. The words seemed to be coming out of their own volition. In a minute he'd get mad and begin to shout, but I didn't seem to be able to stop.

'Don't be so bloody cheeky!'

'It's not cheek, it's just the truth. We have this every week and every week it's right.'

'You shut your mouth.'

I sighed again and went on with my tea. My mother brought his plate in and he fell to. For the moment the money was forgotten.

As soon as he was finished Billy asked if he could go out.

'Yes,' my mother said. 'But mind you're not to go near that Whitey Davis. You've been lucky this time but you're on probation now and you'll be put away like Arthur.' Billy kicked his boots sullenly; this was nagging and they hated it, preferring a good clump on the ear. He escaped as soon as he could. I took the crocks out and began to wash up. The table was cleared except for Ted's last cup of tea.

'Let's go to the pictures,' he said suddenly to my mother. She hesitated.

'She's too tired,' I said, coming through from the kitchen. 'She's been down and up once today. Anyway there's nothing good on.'

'Who asked you? In any case she can go on the bike.'

'They're nothing but a load of tripe, the pictures this week.'

'Well it won't worry you. You don't have to come. We only need your bike.'

'That's my bike, you can't take it.'

'Who bought it for you?'

'Not you.'

'Well I'm buggered!'

'It's just as much her money as yours. She works just as hard at home.'

'You're getting too big for your boots, that's your trouble, think you're so bloody clever.'

'You couldn't push her anyway, you don't know how. You'd let her fall and there's no need to start swearing just because you know you're beaten.' I was like someone possessed; now I'd started I couldn't seem to stop. My mother looked on in amazement.

'I'll give you such a clout in a minute.'

'You can't hit me, I'm too old for that.' With a roar he leapt out of his chair towards me, caught me round the waist and swung me upside down, my hair brushing the floor. He shook me. The blood rushed to my face.

'I've just washed my hair if you don't mind.'

'Put her down, Ted,' said my mother calmly. He shook me again and swung me up.

'You had to resort to brute force because you knew I was right,' I said when I was the right way up again. I was trying hard to keep my dignity but I was angry and humiliated.

'That'll do, Paddy,' said my mother. 'Go and get your things on and we'll all go to the pictures.'

'You mustn't let him do things like that,' I said on the way home as I wheeled her along, her arms round my neck. Ted was a few steps behind. 'I'm too old for that.'

'Try not to make him annoyed, for my sake.'

'Alright, I'll try.'

The following week was my half-term, and on Wednesday we went to visit Arthur in the remand home. It was a grey cheerless building with long passages. We were shown into the headmaster's study when we arrived. He was a tall, just man, who shook hands with us both.

'He's not a bad boy, Mrs. Willerton, we have a lot worse but I think he's weak.' My mother agreed. 'He'll only be here for six weeks and then he'll go to an approved school. He'll get a proper training for a job there. He's not of a very high educational standard but he'll probably improve. We make them work hard and they have less chance to think up mischief. You're not his mother?'

'No, his step-mother. I've tried but I'm not used to children like this. I don't really know how to deal with them.'

'What about their father?'

'He's either too lenient with them or too harsh. They've never had a chance really.'

'I can see you've done your best. Now we'll see what we can do.' Arthur was brought in and the headmaster left us.

Arthur looked very grey and quiet, which was partly because of the uniform flannel shirt and trousers. The food wasn't bad. He slept in a dormitory. They did all the housework. He'd had to polish the corridor. They did lessons. And then there was nothing more to say. There would be no visiting once he was in the approved school.

'Be a good boy and do what they tell you and the time'll soon pass. Don't try running away—you'll only make it worse for yourself. They'll teach you a trade. Try and write some-times and let us know how you're getting on.'

Arthur hardly answered, only when we were ready to leave he suddenly said: 'It's not fair. I'm taking the can back for every-one. I wasn't no worse than the others. I'll get our Billy and Whitey Davis when I get out.'

'Don't be so silly,' my mother said. 'I know they were as much to blame but it's no good looking at it like that. Maybe you'll learn you can't go around doing just what you like. You've got more sense than Billy. Try and make something out of yourself.' And he was silent again.

'What can you do with people like that?' she said as we went home. 'They just get caught again and again, because they haven't got the sense to get away with it. And in a way he's right, he's taking the can back for the others. I'm tired, tired of it all. I'd like to go away and leave them all to get on with it.'

That evening was a difficult one. Ted was in a belligerent mood. Why were his boys victimized? We dragged our way through swamps of argument and resentment while my mother tried to explain why they were being punished and how it would happen again if they didn't learn. I was sick of the whole business and when I looked at my mother under the harsh electric light her skin was thin as tissue paper over the high cheek-bones and the veins were stiff blue ridges on the backs of her hands.

'She won't be able to go on much longer,' I realized with a shock.

PART THREE

Because I must not come to you I haunt
The streets, seeing you in the turn of a stranger's head,
The way a glass is raised but the mouth
Is different . . .

21

Two months later she was back in hospital. It was a two months' hell, when I knew what was happening and I couldn't do anything to stop it. In fact I made it worse and I couldn't do anything to stop that either. I grew to hate his demands on her time, his insensitivity, how he couldn't seem to see that it was all too much for her. So we tore her to pieces between us.

When people called her Mrs. Willerton in the street I was bitter.

'That's not your name. Your name's Mahoney.' Willerton was a daft name. She was my Louey, I no longer called her Mum. And he was Sir Edward or His Lordship in our private talk, nameless to his face.

At night, feigning bad dreams, I crept into the bottom of their bed or even beside her. I no longer cared what I said to him and delighted in goading him like a terrier at a chained blind bear, picking on his ignorance, his mispronunciation of even the simplest words.

She charged me with jealousy and I gloried in it. I sang songs of envy and desire, made us private jokes and a language of our own that shut him out. But he was still there, I couldn't ignore him completely only torment and enrage.

And not understanding he fought back blindly, laying himself open repeatedly to my scorn and sharp thrusts. She stood between us, puzzled and divided. In the end she was glad to go I think, for the peace, though she worried about us left alone together.

So I shopped and cleaned while he cooked and saw to the

garden. At night we slept in the same bed. He tried to call truce, and put his arm round me in comfort, but I turned my back and moved away from him in the dark, til he gave up. How could he understand, I didn't myself.

Every Sunday almost we went to see her, though sometimes when money was short he went alone while I fumed and sulked and sometimes wept that it should be his right not mine. Thirty miles on the bus, through Hillbury and Carminster where Polish soldiers got on from the camp nearby, for the rest of the ride into Sarnford with its great green cathedral, pointing out of the plain. I remember noticing the short bull neck and straight back of the head the Poles had, and reflecting on racial differences.

At Sarnford we ate in a little upstairs café behind the market square, then caught the bus to the hospital, where it stood high up on a pine hill outside the city. At first she was in a ward, but, as soon as possible, she asked to be moved outside into a hut. Some people preferred the company indoors, but she found the dying depressed her—especially after Tilly.

Always she made a friend in hospital and together they would joke and laugh, driving away the terrible descent of apathy that clouded the high hill air. Tilly and Willy they called themselves, a kind of Gert and Daisy. When young Mr. Swan the curate came visiting, with his loose collar circling his skinny neck and his nervous hands, she would listen gravely to his words and when he bent his head to pray, wink wickedly, convulsing the rest though her own face stayed as straight as his. And he was so grateful that anyone should listen to him.

'Ah well if it makes him happy. He's only doing his job.' She knew nothing of the clergy, they'd never bothered her with embarrassing attentions. Then Tilly took it into her head that her husband Bill was getting tired waiting for her to come home and nothing would shift the idea. Gradually she faded until she lay hardly stirring the air with her breath and slipped away like water through the fingers. Then Mum moved out.

Herself she grew fatter, colour came into her brown face, determinedly she grew well. When we arrived she would be

172

sitting up in bed, hair combed, face powdered, a touch of lip-stick, bright as a robin, her eyes shining. We took it turn about. I went away to pick the little trembling harebells and fresh fir-cones in the piney woods while she talked to Ted. Then it would be my turn.

It was a blazing summer and below the hill lay the city and the plain beyond, stretching for miles to the biscuit-coloured line of the heaving downs. Once my form-mistress took me to see her on a Saturday with the junior maths mistress, a dry old stick who was really quite funny away from the blackboard and I rowed them on the river.

Aunt Lyddy came down to stay, bringing her family, and we took photographs in the grounds, Cousin Gilly, all bosom in the strong sunlight, and me with great gleaming calf muscles in a dress much too small. The others were all slightly drunk, except my mother of course, and dozed in the heat. I wandered about the kitchen garden picking half-ripe fruit.

That day we were all mates together but when Aunt Lyddy went home we returned to our underground war. It was a struggle that no one understood. My mother had discussed it with Aunt Lyddy, I know now, but she was just as baffled. It rumbled all the time below the surface but sometimes there were violent eruptions.

Apart from Sunday my real world was at school. The annual play competition had come round. I'd been in every play, always the male lead since my first year. This time I was a young man suffering from claustrophobia who is caught in a tube train, stuck between stations, on his way to the theatre with his girl friend. Janice was my girl friend and I had to give a performance of mounting hysteria. I borrowed Ted's suit for the part. He had two—a navy pin-stripe and a light grey which he felt was only for secondary occasions.

In the excitement of the play I forgot to bring home the dark suit on Friday when I'd finished with it. He wouldn't go on Sunday, he swore; how could he go in a light suit. Secretly neither my mother nor I liked the light suit—it made him look too much like a coster on the street outing, and we were too close to that life not to despise it. But he had to go. She wasn't to be upset. If he didn't go she would worry. I begged and argued. In the end he went but I was left at home, a punishment I didn't mind. I sent her a note instead.

Dear Invalid,

> *I am entrusting this to Sir Edward in the hope that he will deliver it intact. You are lucky to see him at all (in light suit or not) for, having borrowed his navy blue for our form play and having also forgotten to bring it back from school, I had great difficulty in making him come at all because he said that he couldn't come in a light suit which I said was 'balderdash, piffle and poppy cock'.*
>
> *I'm longing to see you alone on Sunday for a change (jealousy!).*
>
> *So will say cheerio for now, lots and lots of love,*

Paddy

All week I was on the peak of excitement. At school we began exams with all their attendant anxieties. When Sunday came he said there was no money to take me. I argued and wept until it seemed as if I'd be ill. I even threatened to walk there and in the end he gave in. I said nothing during the ride and hardly ate my dinner. One kind word from her and my hysteria broke. She sent him away while I sobbed without power to stop.

'What is it? What's the matter?'

'I love you. I love you.'

'I love you too, you know I do. Tell me what's the matter.'

'I can't tell you. I can't.'

'But if you don't tell me I can't help.'

'You must help me.'

'I'm trying to. Tell me.'

'I can't. You must understand.'

'How can I if you won't tell me? Go to Cissie in the next hut. You'll like her; she's got daughters of her own, maybe she'll understand you.'

I sobbed uncontrollably. 'You're my mother. You must understand.'

She put her arms round me and stroked my hair.

'I'll try. Don't upset yourself any more.' So she soothed me and I became calmer. But she hadn't understood, I knew she hadn't and a chill despair crept through me.

Any attempt at discipline had vanished as soon as she left. Billy was out til ten o'clock every night; Gladys we hardly saw; Fred was having his last fling with a girl in a hut in the woods, before he was called up in September. I took to riding the streets in the evenings rather than staying alone in the house with Ted.

One evening, in my circuit of the town, I came across Stella Lee and her fat friend June. Stella was in my class. Everyone knew she was boy-mad and not interested in school; June followed her everywhere. They were laughing shrilly on a corner. I stopped to talk. Without thinking I knew they were waiting for boys. It was hard to know what to say, we'd hardly spoken to each other before, though we'd sat in the same room nearly every day for three years. Two boys cycled slowly by, wheeled and came back. Stella giggled loudly. They passed us at crawling speed, turned, came towards us and drew up. Stella teased and nagged them provocatively. They gazed at her in admiration. She was already pretty in a showy way, her fair hair touched up with peroxide, and permed.

I felt a suppressed excitement watching her lead them on. The elder was dark and flashy; he began to give her back, crack for crack. The brown-haired boy was quieter and he attached himself to me. June seemed unlucky. Together we wandered through the town and the boys bought packets of chips. I realized it was getting dark.

'I'll have to go now.'

'I'll see you home.' The brown-haired boy and I walked off together, Stella's laugh following us shrilly.

He told me his name was Stan. He was an apprentice butcher. He was going to work hard and have a shop of his own. He spoke with a strong Wortbridge accent and he wore the local uniform sports coat and grey flannels. He was what Aunt Lyddy would have called 'a decent lad'.

We stopped at the end of my road under a gas lamp.

'I live up there,' I said. I didn't want him to come any further.

'When can I see you again?'

'I don't know. I have a lot of homework to do.'

'This time next week. We'll go to the pictures. I'll meet you outside the Regal at seven.' I was about to turn away when he put his arms round me and kissed me with his lips slightly apart, a hard passionate kiss he'd seen at the pictures. I'd never been kissed by a boy before. I didn't struggle—it would be too undignified—but I hoped that no one would come along. My arms had gone automatically round his neck, my head tilted at the right angle. I'd always wondered where the noses went but they seemed to fit in alright.

Then it was over and I escaped down the road, wheeling the bike quickly beside me like a mobile shield. I'd felt nothing. Nothing at all. Not dislike, disgust, excitement, 'the deep tender throb of a first kiss' as they called it, nothing at all. It all seemed a waste of time. I knew I wouldn't be there next week.

Stella looked at me meaningly for the next few days. Janice was puzzled.

'I met her in the town one night. She was out with some boys,' I explained. Janice was carrying on a mild flirtation with one of the boys in Hillbury church choir whose father was a director of something.

Next Wednesday I stayed in, terrified that he might come to call for me, but no one came. I thought about it a lot. After all, Juliet was married at my age. Physically I was mature enough for having children though my chest had hardly developed at all, like my mother's; Stella obviously got something out of it or she wouldn't have spent night after night in draughty shop doorways. I gave it up.

The next morning Stella sidled up to me as I bent over my desk between lessons.

'Stan was ever so mad you didn't turn up. He likes you. He said would you come next week.'

'Tell him I can't. My mum's coming out of hospital and I shan't be able to come out.' That was true anyway, the six months was up.

'There'll have to be some changes. Goodness knows what you've all been up to. I hope you've remembered to pay for your bike every week and Billy's been to see the probation officer regularly.' She was her old self again, eager to take up the reins of our crazy trap.

That Sunday morning, I shooed everyone into the kitchen

and shut the door. I took up the bas-matting, disclosing the piles of dirt underneath. I swept them up in great clouds and washed the dusty lino. Even Gladys was goaded to a fever of energy and cleaned the boys' bedroom. Then I set to on the mound of washing, even doing Ted's thick sweaty socks that discoloured the water to gravy. My mother's own demon of cleanliness possessed us all.

She stayed in bed the first day, to let herself down lightly, as she said, but when I got home from school on the second day she was up and treadling away for dear life turning sheets. Order and discipline were back.

Fred was carried off by the army to an even stricter regime. Actually, though he grumbled like all soldiers, he rather enjoyed the life, with no responsibility and a uniform that made him even more irresistible to the girls. He was so keen in fact, that Billy caught the fever and wanted to join as a boy soldier. This seemed a good idea and my mother took him for an interview. He was given a short test to do and told to go and sit at a small table. He sat for a while looking at it abstractedly. Eventually the officer leant over his shoulder to see how he was getting on. When it became obvious that Billy couldn't even read the questions he shook his head. Apologizing my mother took him away.

'But I've never felt such a fool in my life,' she told Aunt Lyddy later. Billy was finally found a job in Slater's mill.

Arthur wrote occasionally and came home for a few days on parole. He was taller and better dressed than any of us and said he'd passed up his turn on the escape rota.

'It's a mug's game. They always catch them.'

It was Gladys who felt the tightening of the rope most and she took the quickest way out.

'She wants to get married,' my mother said. 'I say good riddance, then she's someone else's responsibility, but she needs her father's permission first. I pity the poor bloke.' It was difficult to think of Gladys being under twenty-one. She'd been a grown woman and a rule to herself since she was fifteen. Ted signed the form laboriously and a week later she came home saying she'd taken the morning off, got married and had come for her things.

'Now you can have a room to yourself,' said my mother. 'We'll get you a tall-boy for your clothes. You'll be able to do just what you like and no one'll be able to interfere.' The days of sleeping in their room, creeping in beside her in the dark, were over. But I didn't care; I was in love.

22

I SAT at the back of the class and waited. Any moment she might call out my name and I'd get up and say it, the poem I'd chosen. Janice was reading now. What had she picked?

> 'Now more than ever seems it rich to die,
> To cease upon the midnight with no pain.'

Poor Janice, she had to hurry home tonight, and couldn't wait for Miss Tyson and walk down the road with her, like we did most days, Janice almost running by her side, Miss Tyson trotting along swinging her little brief-case, me wheeling my bike along the gutter, glancing up to see if she was looking and then hurriedly down at the handlebars as the large grey eyes turned full on me and the low voice asked:

'What do you think, Paddy?'

She was the only one of the staff who called me Paddy, to the rest I was Patricia. I thought of Light-the-long-handed, Lleu-Llaw-gyffes who'd had no soul til he had a name. Nouns— names were the most powerful words. They strike home like the pin through the butterfly—liar, cheat, girl, bastard, king and you're caught wriggling, staked through the heart by an identity, and no matter how much you squirm and protest, 'No it isn't like that,' the noun holds you down till you set fast in the pose it nails you to.

'And what have you chosen, Paddy?'

I stood up a bit dazed.

'Shakespeare, Miss Tyson.'

'Good. A speech from a play?'

'No. A sonnet.' Miss Tyson had given me the little red book of sonnets for my birthday. No one knew, except Janice of course and my mother. I knew many of them by heart already and, in the evening, when I went upstairs to bed, I sat at the window in the room that was mine now, watching the sky turn apple-green behind the red-brick council houses and the fields beyond blur into the horizon, and repeated them softly into the twilight, lips hardly moving, the whispered syllables dropping into the stilled air, gentle as the brush of bats' wings against the sky.

> 'Being your slave, what should I do but tend
> Upon the hours and times of your desire?'

The words moved over the hushed room, over the other girls' faces upturned towards me as I spoke. I didn't look at the book in my hands but towards Miss Tyson who sat listening, her head slightly bent.

> 'Nor dare I question with my jealous thought,
> Where you may be, or your affairs suppose,
> But, like a sad slave, stay and think of nought
> Save where you are how happy you make those.'

'How could she understand?' I thought. No one understood. There were so many ways of loving. I felt my voice beginning to break and dug my nails into the palms of my hands; I crushed my bare knee against the underneath of the desk where the splinters were. The quick pain brought relief and I managed to finish the last couplet in a clear full voice:

> 'So true a fool is love that in your will'

Miss Tyson raised her head. Was there the ghost of a smile on her face? Maybe she was laughing at me all the time.

> 'Though you do anything he thinks no ill!'

I ended with head held high.

'Thank you, Paddy. A very good choice.' There was no trace of a smile now.

I sat down dazed. Had she understood? The rest of the lesson passed; I was scarcely conscious of the other voices reading, only of her every movement, every word.

I think I was in love with Evelyn Tyson as soon as I saw her come into the room on that first day at the High School, and three years later I was still in love with her. It hadn't faded as these things are supposed to do, in fact it had grown in intensity until now it was like a fever that occupied my every thought, sleeping and waking, and raged in my blood. Far off I heard the bell ringing. She gathered up her books, I stood up with the rest of the class while she left the room.

After school I hung about in the cloakroom until the prefects turned me out, then in the bicycle shed, ducking when Granny Wright, the senior mistress, and Sergeant-Major came past on their way home, my two worst subjects maths and games. When they were safely by I heaved my bike out of its stand and trundled it up out of the shed into the sun. I propped the front wheel against the gatepost, wandered back along the path and picked a big ox-eye daisy from the tall bouquets of weeds and feathery grasses decorating the door of the shed.

'She loves me, she loves me not.' I stripped off the flat white petals. There was a sound of footsteps, light swinging steps on gravel. I knew the rules of the *amour courtois*, the lady must never be embarrassed. I dropped on one knee beside the bike and fiddled with the back brake-block which could always be relied on to be slightly at fault. The footsteps were nearly up to me; I could hear her breathing and the soft guttural sound as she cleared her throat. Would she speak or just pass on?

'Hallo, Paddy, trouble with the bike?' Anyone else would have said bicycle. I straightened up, feeling pink in the face from stooping.

'The brakes, but they're alright now.'

'Good.' She began to move away. I took hold of the handlebars and wheeled the bike along beside her.

'I thought you read very well this afternoon.'

'I used your book, the one you gave me.'

'I'm glad it was useful. I thought you'd appreciate it.'

'I understand now why he's considered the greatest poet. I used to think Keats was but he seems sickly sometimes.'

'What did you think of the Koestler?'

'It's wonderful. I've nearly finished it, but it raises so many questions, things I've thought about myself but never seen discussed in a book.'

'Yes. I think I know. What exactly were you thinking of?'

'Well, religion. What do you think about God?'

She laughed. 'An immense subject; we haven't time to go into all that now.'

I looked up. It was true, in a few yards our ways divided. It was always the same: waiting for her, walking beside her, time no longer existed, until we were nearly at the corner and it sprang out on us, wolfing down the last few seconds, tainting the final moments with the sourness of its breath.

'It would need a whole evening for a subject like that and then we should hardly have started.' I held myself still inside for a second, willing her to go on.

'Please God let her say it.' And then the sudden thought, 'You're not sure there is a God any more.'

'Why not come round one evening to tea, and then we can talk it over?' I was willing her so fiercely to say the words that when they came I barely heard them. Perhaps I'd dreamt them. I looked down at her. Her eyes were like grey sea; I felt myself drowning.

'Could I? That'd be marvellous. When could I come?'

'What about tomorrow?'

'Oh yes!'

'You're sure your mother won't mind?'

'Oh no, I'm sure she won't.' But my heart hesitated for a moment. 'What time shall I come?'

'About six, then we'll get tea out of the way early and have plenty of time to talk.'

'I'll bring back the Koestler.' I paused. There was something else I ought to say. 'You're sure it's alright? I'm not taking up your time, not being a nuisance?'

'I don't think so, do you?' She looked at me straight and full. I looked down. I wanted to bother her but I knew the rules. 'Tomorrow then,' she said.

'Until tomorrow.' She turned up the road towards the terrace house where she had rooms. I got on the bike, thrust at the pedals and whirled down the road and over the bridge in wild exultation. At the killer hill I stood up on the pedals and forced my way, foot by foot, up to the top and over the brow.

My mother was standing at the front gate. 'We're out of jam,' she said as I pulled up. 'I've been waiting for you. You'll have to go down to the stores.'

I was exhausted by the effort to beat the hill and cross at everyday concerns intruding on my mood. I'd wanted to go upstairs to my bedroom hugging the thought of tomorrow to myself.

'Oh Lord can't we do without it?'

'No we can't, there's nothing for tea.'

I took the money. 'I wish you'd think of these things in the morning, then I could get them on the way home. I'm tired by the time I get up here.'

'I can't think of everything, and anyway you'd forget all about it during the day. You're too full of other things.' She turned away up the path.

I let the bike take me down the hill. Why bother to brake? Let it run on gathering speed until it collided with one of the big brewer's drays coming out of the bottling store. I sat back on the saddle steering mechanically. That would be that. All problems solved. But the bike seemed to know its own way and reached the bottom safely, slowing gradually as the road flattened. I bought the tin of over-sweet pineapple mush and pedalled wearily home. This time I got off at the bottom of the hill and pushed my way to the top.

The table was all laid when I got in. She came to meet me at the door, hearing the scrape of the bike against the outside wall.

'You got it? Good. I was afraid they might be shut.' She opened the tin and spooned gleaming yellow dollops of jam into a jar.

'If you sit down now you can have some butter before the others get in.' She poured the tea and gave me a plate with three thin pieces of bread and butter. I ate slowly, savouring the taste while she told me about her day. The Red Cross had been with a parcel.

'Don't worry, Mrs. Willerton,' the lady had said as she delivered it. 'I've seen their curtains twitching as I came in. I know who deserves a parcel. You take no notice of anything they say. They don't know what you have to put up with, just because you're always clean and decent.' And she stamped on the clutch with her heavy brogue and rattled away.

'I thought we could all go to the pictures tomorrow,' she said.

I took a deep breath and said casually: 'I can't. Miss Tyson's invited me to tea.'

'Oh!' I went on eating slowly. 'Oh well, Ted and I can go to the Horseshoe then.' Without me to take her and bring her back she wouldn't go down to the town.

'I can't really refuse now I've said I'll go, can I?'

'No, of course you can't.' But the accent fell on the wrong word somehow. I finished my tea.

'I've got a lot of homework to do.'

'Yes, you'll have to get ahead won't you, for tomorrow.'

I went heavily upstairs, the bread and butter seemed indigestible. They would sit in the pub on the corner, which she disliked because it was modern and characterless, full of the Chinatown neighbours, the Wortbridge swedes we called them.

Sitting on my bed I took out my diary and wrote rather shakily.

Tomorrow I am going to tea with Evelyn. We shall talk about God and Arthur Koestler, philosophy and art. I shall take her my poems to read. It can never be the same again.

Then I sat looking at it for a moment, prodding the page with my pencil.

I put the diary away in my drawer and took out my books. I'd have to get stuck into it to finish tomorrow's quota as well. Firmly I kept my mind on the job, only when Venus rose in the opaque sky I opened the window and let the evening in.

'Bright star, would I were steadfast as thou art'

The words moved out into the calm twilight.

'Pillow'd upon my fair love's ripening breast,
    To feel forever it's soft fall and swell
    Awake forever in a sweet unrest.'

I scarcely saw her the next day, just a glimpse at the end of the dining-room, then a smile and a thank you as I served her with shepherd's pie. I was afraid she might have changed her mind but, if so, surely she would have told me. I said nothing to Janice; it would have seemed like triumphing.

'I don't need any tea,' I said when I got home. 'I'm having it there.'

'Mind you behave yourself.'

I didn't answer. The imputation made me angry. The house seemed stifling. I couldn't breathe. I washed my hands and face in the sink and went upstairs. I rolled my tie into a short sausage to straighten some of the creases. The cuffs of my blouse were beginning to grey with grime, it was nearly the end of the week, but if I pulled my cardigan well down and kept it on all the time they wouldn't show. I put on my tie and knotted it in the thick part to look less stringy, then combed my hair. I went downstairs.

'I'll have to go now.' She looked up from her book.

'Have a nice time. Mind you're in by ten. Are you taking the bike?'

'Yes.' Every word seemed double-edged.

'Go on then. Don't keep her waiting.' She looked back at the page in front of her. I rode off dispiritedly.

It was a bit early I knew. I circled the block once or twice then drew up outside the house, propped the bike against the kerb and rang the bell. I smoothed my hair nervously while I waited. She was hovering in the doorway behind as her landlady opened the door.

'Come in.'

'Shall I bring supper in now, Miss Tyson?'

'Yes please, if it's ready.' She urged me into her room.

For ten minutes I was lost. I could hardly breathe or speak for my heart, which was like a mad thing in my body, pounding to get out, but she spoke of this and that, easing me into the situation until I was calmer. I sat on the edge of the armchair, clenching and unclenching my hands, while she moved about the room, tidying away books, the letter she'd been writing. Finally she gave me a thick volume and sat down in the opposite chair, draping a cardigan around her shoulders and drawing it close with a characteristic gesture.

'That has a lot of sane answers.' It was the *History of Western Philosophy*. 'Or at least it asks the right questions.'

'And God?'

'He is there or here, we agree on that don't we, but . . .'

'How is He to be worshipped?'

'Yes, that's it exactly.'

There was a knock on the door. She opened it quickly and ushered in the landlady with a loaded tray. We were both a little constrained in front of her waiting for her to go, while she chatted of the weather and the iniquities of the ginger cat stretched on the rug in front of the hearth. She seemed an intruder.

'The wind's getting up. It'll rain before long. If there's anything else you want, Miss Tyson, just let me know.' She closed the door behind her.

'May I call you Evelyn?' Somehow I'd started the sentence before I'd decided to say it and halfway through I realized I had to go on.

'If this is going to happen very often you'd better I think.' It was more than I'd dared hope for.

We ate, me trembling for an errant fork or a clumsy gesture —we never had a tea table so full of hazards at home—Evelyn calm, and accustomed to the galaxy of cutlery. Between forkfuls of smoked haddock she told me something about her home.

'The country is very fine. You must come and see it one day.' And about her childhood. 'I hated school but then there wasn't much at home either. Parents very rarely understand, at least mine didn't. It's a closed world to them, this sort of thing,' she waved her fork towards the wireless that was playing Mozart's 39th Symphony and the open copy of *The Faber Book of Modern Verse* beside it.

I agreed guiltily, thinking of my mother's efforts to keep up with me against the hopeless odds of the Willertons and the circumstances of her life. Outside the wind had risen to a howl and rain thudded against the taut window panes. Inside was a cell of sweetness and light and civilized humanity, that made the rest of my life seem a shrieking chaos.

'If it gets too rough you'll have to stay the night,' she said when the evening was nearly over. What could I say? Desire was so great it became a pain that brought fear.

'I expect it'll stop soon,' I said, matter-of-factly, and we left it like that. I showed her the poems I'd brought with me.

'They're in chronological order starting with the last so you needn't plough all the way through.' Some she'd set herself as homework exercises, mostly the earlier stuff, but the most recent I'd written to her rather than for her. They were copied as neatly as I could, I was never a tidy writer, into an exercise book with stiff maroon covers. While she read I watched. The light fell straight down on to her face, reflecting from the soft down on her cheeks, the full lips and almost cleft chin.

'She isn't even beautiful,' I told myself but my hand longed to go out and trace the curve of cheek and lip.

The concert had finished long ago. I looked at the clock.

'I must go. I have to be in by ten.'

Outside the wind still blew but the sound of rain had stopped.

'I'll lend you a coat.' I wanted to accept but felt I must refuse.

'No it's alright. It's stopped raining I think.' She went to the window and looked out.

'Yes it has.' I was grateful that she didn't insist.

'Good night,' I said at the door. 'And thank you; it's been a wonderful evening.'

'Goodness, don't mention it.' And I laughed inside at the familiar phrase, laughed tenderly because it was her only verbal concession to convention. 'Good night then,' she said. 'Let me know when you want to come again, when you need a change.' Her hand touched mine by accident, just a touch but it seared into the flesh. I turned into the wind and rode off into the dark.

'She might have had the sense to lend you a mac,' my mother said when I got in. The room seemed bare and comfortless. 'Did you have a nice time?'

'Yes thanks.' I knew I was expected to say something, to explain, but my tongue wouldn't say the words.

'D'you want a cup of tea? We had a nice time in the Horse-shoe.'

'No thanks. I won't bother.' Everything seemed to be coming from a long way away.

'Up to bed then.' I realized I was exhausted, my legs would hardly drag themselves up the stairs.

'God, wherever and whoever you are, I thank you for to-night,' I thought as I lay in my narrow single bed, staring at the dark. Then I began to run through all the mistakes I'd made, the awkward silences, my importunity in showing her my poems, sheep-faced foolishnesses leaping the bounds of sense, until I fell asleep.

23

AND now all sense of time left me completely. There were no months, no changing seasons, only an endless procession of days when I imagined myself repulsed, scorned, restored with a smile, in the bliss of favour, cast out again and worst of all ignored.

'You think more of her than you do of anyone,' my mother said bitterly one evening when I announced that I was going to see her on the following day. Home became intolerable. Now there were fewer of us we seemed to exasperate each other even more. My battles with Ted grew more and more bitter as I neglected my mother in my obsession. There didn't seem to be anything I could do, circumstances and my age stopped me from taking her away as I wanted to and so I fought him and myself, Janice for Evelyn's favour, even Evelyn and my love for her, while my mother watched bewildered, until she too was drawn into the turmoil I spread around me.

Dog-tired of this conflict and uncertainty I began to search desperately for peace and security. I was haunted by my father; every fair-haired Irish labourer in his forties I made him. I met him on buses, in cafés and when he said, 'You must be my daughter,' I answered: 'I'm not your daughter. We've got on alright without you so far and we don't need you now. You're nothing to us.' But the idea of him was still there.

Then I found the foot-high crucifix in the trunk. I began to stare fascinated at the young history mistress who was a Catholic. She was beautiful with long, dark, wavy hair, grey eyes, a sinuous white throat and a gliding walk. I took to cycling past the small grey Catholic church set beside its presbytery.

One evening, out with Cretia on one of our rare meetings, I pointed it out to her.

'I wonder what it's like inside,' I said.

'If you set foot in there you're damned for ever,' she said firmly.

I laughed and we cycled on but her suspicions were aroused. Next week she brought me a collection of pamphlets, little stories about scheming priests and monks who kept a dying woman from the Bible, or spirited a child away to bring it up in their faith. But these only whetted my appetite. 'At least,' I thought, 'I ought to see what they say. After all it was my father's religion. I ought to give it a fair trial.'

The first time I didn't manage to get inside the church. I walked up and down past it a couple of times but didn't have the guts to go in. Then the light in the window went out and there was a sound of doors being locked from the inside. Next week I was back again. This time I took myself firmly in hand. It was a very dark night, the path to the porch was heavily shadowed with overhanging trees as if Cretia's devil was lurking there, waiting to pounce with outstretched arms, but I pushed this idea away as superstition, and walked up to the big wooden door.

I wrestled with the cold iron handle before I got it to open and then I was inside. The smell was the first thing I noticed, I'd never smelt anything like it before, and then the great wooden Christ on a cross that overshadowed the whole interior like a doom. The thick atmosphere took hold of me at once. It was all the sadness, the mystery, the romance I'd ever experienced, distilled into this overpowering perfume of incense and damp stone, guilt and forgiveness, the reek of heavy emotions and human flesh.

I went forward and knelt down in a pew, praying for enlightenment, a sign. For a long time nothing happened but I could have stayed there all night in the safety and comfort of the holy dusk. A small door in the chancel was flung open and a young priest hurried into the church dowsing the candles on one side of the altar, bobbing hastily on one knee, snuffing the rest. He bustled energetically about the altar, the long skirts adding to the housewifely effect. Then he trotted down the church to the porch door. I took it as a sign for me to leave, got up a bit stiffly, I'd been there a long time, and walked slowly down the aisle towards him.

'There's no need to go if you want to stay.'

'It's alright. I shouldn't be here at all really. I'm not a Catholic, my father was, I've never been baptized. I just wanted to see what it was like.' My little speech was carefully rehearsed for just this kind of chance.

'I see. You say your father was a Catholic and you were never baptized.' The voice was young, pleasant and burred with brogue. It seemed to suggest that an important bit of business had been sadly neglected. 'Well now, would you like to know more about it?'

'Yes please.'

'I tell you what now, take this little book home with you and have a look at it and you come along to mass next week and I'll speak to the sisters. I'm Father Carroll.'

I put the little red book in my pocket.

'What's your name?'

'Patricia Mahoney.'

'Well now, Pat, that's a good Irish name.' He was very young and attractive with dark-brown, crinkly hair, bright eyes and a fresh skin. In another minute I was out under the trees again, feeling slightly weak at the knees, his voice singing through my head.

'Don't forget now. I'll see you after mass next week.'

And so I passed into that world, of sombre, glowing colour and ritual chanting, filled with heart-breaking sorrow that made me weep while it lifted me up, that Newman and Lionel Johnson had entered before me.

The nun provided for my instruction was Sister Theodore, still quite young, her face shining pallidly with hard scrubbing, lack of fresh air, and inner conviction. She was kind and patient and explained the catechism to me point by point, without evasion. I bought a rosary and missal and set up an altar to the Virgin on my tall-boy, with jam-jars of heavy-scented May lilac. I wanted desperately to belong.

But the beautiful, black-haired Kitty Doyle, my sweet Kate, I hardly ever saw. She went to an earlier mass than I could manage and showed no interest in my pilgrim's progress. Still I followed her about, knowing though that this was only an infatuation and that I was really in love with Evelyn. All through my mother wisely said nothing to antagonize me. Sometimes she asked me what we'd talked about in instruction and we discussed a particular point. Once I asked Sister Theodore about my mother.

'Oh,' she said confidently, 'she's suffered a lot; she'll go straight to heaven.' I wondered what she would have thought of my mother's version of it.

I was so anxious to fit myself in that I joined the church youth club. There was old-fashioned dancing; mildly supervised by Father Carroll, all the girls were smitten with him, and the Canon, who stood at the side, hands in pockets, joking over the racing results. During the Christmas holidays a newcomer turned up at the club. His name was Christopher, he was fifteen, a year older than me, a serious handsome boy who wanted to be a composer. I'd never got on with the other boys at the club, they were all from good, sometimes even well-off homes, and we seemed to have no interests in common. But with Christopher I could talk about art, books, religion. He borrowed a bike from the aunt he was staying with and we went for long rides to all the places of interest round about, in spite of the cold. I had a boy friend.

At Easter I went to stay with his family in their house at the seaside. His mother I loved at once. She was lively and smart and we talked for hours, she telling me about her dead husband and the offers she'd had since and me advising from my mother's experience, until Chris came to drag me away to the beach. I knew what was expected of me and held his hand and let him kiss me but as we lay together on the wind-scoured beach, sand settling at the roots of our hair and pocking our skins, and he begged me to tell him I loved him, I knew I couldn't. It wasn't true. There was no response in my body. Yet I knew all about the body and its demands, and how to satisfy them while images of the rape of the Italian princess and her ladies by the German commander, or the story of the Sabine women passed through my head. I was glad when it was too wet to go out and we sat in the front room, overlooking the empty streets and boarding houses, while Christopher put on side after side of the Scheherazade music or we played chess together.

There were other doubts too. Sister Theodore could give no answer except faith to many of my questions, my mind wasn't satisfied, much as I wanted to believe and I knew I must accept everything or nothing. Back home again I struggled and prayed, wallowing deeper in the emotional satisfaction of the services and trying to drown my nagging reason, like biting an aspirin on a niggling tooth. And still Evelyn smiled at me, a little indulgently I imagined.

I'd come home early one day, we'd had a half-day off for something or other, and my mother and I were sitting reading when suddenly she looked up from her book and said:

'I'd love a bath.'

'Why not?'

'There's such a lot of paraphernalia to it.'

'I'll get it ready for you.'

'Would you? And would you wash my back for me? I don't think I could manage that and I'll need a bit of help getting out I expect.'

I went into the bathroom and lit the copper, a stone monster that crouched in the corner. Then I filled its belly with cold water from the tap above. It took a couple of hours to heat and then had to be bailed out with a saucepan into the bath, there was no outlet tap.

'When I call you come and wash my back,' she said as she went into the bathroom. I sat on, reading *Guy Mannering*, my mind miles away; I heard her call.

The air was full of steam that made me blink as I opened the door. It swirled above the big white bath in which the tiny figure sat, not taking up a quarter of the room. I'd never seen her completely stripped before, not even to the waist for months, and now it seemed as if with her clothes she'd taken off flesh and muscle as well, leaving only the bones loosely wrapped in the brown skin. She was like a little rickety waif with the great eyes in the sunken face and the little pot belly slung between the stick arms and legs. My silence must have penetrated her thoughts and she looked up with a smile, a soapy flannel in her hand, and she read my shock on my face.

'I look like something out of Belsen,' she laughed. 'I've soaped the flannel.' I took it from her and bent over the thin shoulders. Gently I washed the pitiful back, afraid to rub too hard in case she fell to pieces under my heavy hand. Then I rinsed it and patted it dry with the towel.

'I'm done now. Help me up.' I put my arms round her and lifted her to her feet, holding her there while she found her footing. I draped a towel round her and when she'd dried herself I handed her her clothes and sent her back to the fire while I cleaned the bath, my head in a wild confusion, thought chasing thought til it seemed the brain couldn't hold them all and must burst. Cleaning the bath I made a thorough job. She mustn't see what I was thinking. I must think of something cheerful to say when I went in.

'But he must have known for months,' that was the idea I couldn't get rid of. He must have known and he'd done nothing. He'd gone on just the same as if there was nothing wrong. That night I pounded on the doors of heaven with my prayers, I beseiged the calmly smiling Madonna. She was a woman, she would understand my love with this other woman who'd suffered too. It was enlightenment I asked for, that he'd have his eyes opened and leave her alone, try to make things easier for her instead of expecting her to carry all the burdens of his animal brood that sapped her strength, like dogs worrying a sick deer. And there was nothing I could do.

'Only a few more years,' I told her, 'and I'll be earning enough to take you away from all this.'

A few weeks later while I was still harassed by doubts and unanswered prayers, the headmistress announced that there would be no school that afternoon. A travelling company would present *Arms and the Man*, the whole school would watch.

The play was half done, the air in the hall thick with three-hundred-odd breathing bodies and the glaring lights. We sat in the dark, Janice was beside me, following a competent production, Shaw's sharp half-truths slicing at the conventional and sentimental, when suddenly the thought cut right into me.

'I can't do it. I don't believe it.' The comforting emotions I'd wrapped myself in for the last few months blew away on a gust

194

of cold reason and I was left strong and upright like Adam before the fall.

I heard nothing more of the play as a clear stream rushed through my head washing away the clutter of religiosity. Man was a lonely god climbing his evolutionary ladder to the stars. The pursuit of the good, the true and the beautiful, all manifestations of the one virtue, was his destiny, ever since he stood up on his two legs and looked straight ahead.

This mood of curious exaltation lasted til I went to bed. Lying staring up at the ceiling loneliness hit me. I had put away the smiling picture and the jam-jars, the room was ascetically bare, the ceiling very white.

The cleansing, purging, had left me a dry stalk standing by a frozen shore for every cold wind to sigh through. Eventually I fell into a haunted sleep.

In the morning I was out early, waiting at the end of Evelyn's road. She came at last and looked up at me questioningly, one eyebrow lifted humorously. I told her of my sudden conversion. She nodded.

'I didn't think it wasn't the right thing for you.'

'You didn't say anything.'

'No. I thought if it was right you'd find out for yourself in time.'

'But I might have got in too far to get out again.'

'Yes, once or twice I was a bit worried.'

'I thought I'd found peace.'

'Not your sort of peace, too much like complacency. You can't muzzle the intellect, it snaps back at you if you try.'

The rosary I sent to Sister Theodore with a rather pompous letter of explanation. I was glad we had someone else for history now, I was cured of Kitty Doyle but I didn't want to answer questions. I needn't have worried, I had never existed for her. Now there was only Christopher. I backed out of that one by forgetting to answer his letters. The episode was all over, leaving me with a taste for Gregorian chant and Siennese painting.

24

'I WANT to talk to you a minute. Shove those things out of the way.' She patted the bed and I moved the balls of crochet silk, patterns and knitting bag and sat down on the edge. It was Saturday morning, Ted had gone out for a haircut and she was sitting up in bed, spinning the intricate snow crystals of doyleys and silk collars, the bright steel hook stabbing in and out so fast I could watch the chain grow. And then, when I was settled, she started to talk and she talked on softly for a long time. Some of it I hardly heard, her voice came and went like the tick of a watch, but only because I couldn't make myself listen all the time.

'You mustn't be upset by what I'm going to say. I've thought it all out and it's all for the best and maybe it won't be necessary but this is just in case. I know I shall never be any better, there's nothing they can do for me, they've told me as much. And I shan't mind once I've seen you able to look after yourself. That's all I want. That's what's kept me going all these years, you, and you'll soon be old enough to look after me instead. I know it'll get me in the end. I've always prayed I'd have a haemorrhage and go off quickly but I mightn't be so lucky. And I can't face it the other way. I've seen too many of them lying there, just the decaying body left, the spirit almost gone and yet not able to die. It's not a pretty death. I don't want that. I couldn't bear that. I suppose it's pride. So you mustn't mind what I'm saying now, I've made up my mind, when I feel I'm beginning to slip I shall take an overdose of aspirins and just not wake up any more. Is it wrong d'you think? Would you blame me? I couldn't bear it if I thought you'd blame me.'

'How could anyone blame you? You must do whatever you think is best. I shall understand.'

'And if I fail I don't want you to stand by the bed holding my hand. Just let me go. Don't take any notice of what anyone else says. You're all I've got. You'll help me. And I don't want you to come to the funeral. I want you to remember me alive. And don't waste money on flowers and things like that, you keep it, you'll need it and you know I'd rather you had it. You think of me and what a laugh we'd have about it together. The machine'll be yours, you keep it. I know it's not much to leave you.... Now I've said what I wanted to say and I won't mention it again. I just wanted you to know. Maybe it won't be necessary, the doctor says I could go on like this for years yet.'

She never spoke about it again but I know it was there in her mind and I prayed that it wouldn't be necessary though I was sure there couldn't be any blame to it. I pushed it as far back in my mind as I could, it was too terrible a thought to have to live with every day, and she seemed to get better from that day on, as if a weight had been lifted from mind and body.

There were only four of us living permanently at home now but there was no more peace than there had ever been. Gladys had produced one child and was expecting another. One evening, at home, Ted made some succinct comments on the subject. I wasn't listening having long ago formed a protective sound blanket against the din of wireless, loud voices and heavy boots that was our daily background music, but Billy was. Next day he told his sister, who waylaid Ted outside the mill and gave him the rough side of her tongue in the open street, in full sight and hearing of the other workers streaming out of the gates. Ted arrived home, blind angry, and muttering he waited for Billy. He hardly got a foot in the door before his father was on him. I'd never seen such unleashed animal fury. He punched him savagely. The boy fled for the stairs door and was halfway up before Ted caught him by a leg and dragged him down, howling. He shoved him into the couch and began a systematic beating up until my mother managed to drag him off, shouting at him to stop before he killed the kid. Billy ran out into the street, to creep home when everyone was in bed.

I spent more and more time with Evelyn. Every few weeks I

would invite myself to supper with her, when I was desperate enough, or force her to ask me when I thought time enough had passed since our last evening together, and as I sat in her room and the talk ran on, I watched her subtle hands, with their blunt fingers and rounded nails, smoothing and ruffling the ginger cat, while he unsheathed and flexed his claws in an ecstasy that was pure blood. I knew how he felt; she played on me in the same way.

Every morning I escorted her to school and in the evening I was waiting at the gate, usually with Janice beside me. We followed her about all day for a chance to hold a door open or for one glance of recognition. The others laughed at us, Stella and her group were deeply immersed in their own affairs of what he said and so I said and then he—but half the time he didn't. We were love's fools and happy to be so. Everything we read convinced us we were right.

Sarnford had a theatre, not just a provincial rep, but a proper outpost of the London stage, a cultural Hadrian's Wall. Evelyn and Miss Parris, the senior English mistress, took parties of examinees there, to see their Shakespeare set-books step off the printed page and behave like human beings instead of aggregates of characteristics. By some lucky fluke there were two tickets not sold in a set of reservations. At the end of a lesson Miss Parris, who took us for English now we were in the Lower Fifth, called me into the corridor.

'There are two spare seats for *Hamlet*. I thought you and Janice might like them. They're half a crown each. I imagine your mother might find it rather difficult to find it at such short notice so I'll pay for your ticket because I think you would appreciate the play. You'll have to find your fare and bring sandwiches or something for lunch. Perhaps Janice would let me know if she wants the other ticket,' and she hurried away before I could say thank you.

My mother was delighted; Janice had said yes at once.

'We'll make up the fare somehow. What a good thing we've just finished paying for the bike.' She always found the money and the time for anything connected with my education. She came to every parent-teacher meeting. They were held in the afternoon, with tea provided by one of the domestic science classes at sixpence a head, and I would see her from my seat by the window, walking slowly, yet somehow briskly up the drive, among the first of the mothers to arrive, very erect and always smartly dressed in her tailored costume and a dash of make-up; never stopping to wave and laugh as some of the mums did, only a quick smile and wink with no turn of the head, that no one else but me could see. She thoroughly enjoyed those afternoons, talking to the staff, impressing them with her quickness and courage so that old Pussyfoot, the French mistress, once told me she was one of the most intelligent women she knew, eating scones and jam and drinking thin tea, her voice bright and alien among the thick Wortbridge burrs and the middle-class drawls of the higher-income mothers.

'I hear you're coming to *Hamlet* with us on Saturday,' Evelyn said as we walked her down the road, 'perhaps you'd like to have tea with me afterwards.' That was all we'd need to make a perfect day. 'You'd better read the play first if you haven't already done so,' but we both had.

I'd never been inside a theatre before, I don't know if Janice had. The first shock was the reversal of the proper cinema order with the cheap seats where the dear ones ought to be; had those people down in the front there really paid nearly a pound to see every fake wrinkle drawn on the face and the globules of sweat starting up under the grease paint, as I knew from experience they did, under the heightened emotion and the heat of the footlights? The furnishings and upholstery seemed tawdry after the picture palaces but on the other hand there was an intimacy of faded splendour that future generations may find in old cinemas, an atmosphere of nostalgia.

It was very dark when the lights went down. The curtain rose slowly to a sentry pacing the battlements. I leaned forward. Everything I'd seen on the screen was a flat fiction compared with this flesh-and-blood reality. For the first ten minutes I understood nothing of what was said, it was rattled off at such a pace as I'd never dreamed of, savouring the words to myself. Then gradually a phrase here and there, and then whole sentences, began to detach themselves from the morass of melodious sounds and as I concentrated the speeches became meaningful. I knew all about Hamlet of course—his problem was my daily bread. Ophelia I hadn't much patience with, but she was a splendid excuse for the gravediggers' scene. Hamlet himself was played by a young actor at the beginning of his career, in elegant black tights and spotless shirt, with verve and energy. His melancholy was alternately harsh and wistful. It was an interpretation completely in tune with my own feelings; as the mood took him he leapt about the stage like a young ram or drooped in a corner like a bird in moult. Janice thought he was beautiful.

I resented the intervals sharply; they broke a spell that had to be cast all over again, each time the houselights dimmed. Listening to the conversations around me I realized that other people regarded the whole thing as a diversion, as nothing to do with the reality of work and home, yet to me what was happening down there was more real than they were, opening and shutting their mouths around me in the half-light of the auditorium bowl. I knew why Hamlet couldn't kill his stepfather even though he wanted to and how his own struggle spread destruction around him. The last act was terrible in its implications and when the curtain fell on the sombre march, the dead beat of the drum re-echoed hollowly inside me. I knew now the meaning of catharsis. The applause seemed sacrilegious. I left the theatre in a daze, the light outside was a physical blow as I stumbled along beside Evelyn, half in, half out of the gutter in an effort to keep up with her in the crowded streets.

'No need to ask what you thought of it,' she said as we sat in the café. Janice enthused intelligently, saying all the things I couldn't.

By the time I got home I'd found words to describe the experience to my mother, words that showed nothing of my real feelings. Next time I stayed with Aunt Lyddy for my annual summer holiday in London, I would get Cousin Gilly to take me to the Old Vic I thought.

'Second marriages are always a mistake,' she said when I told her the plot. 'Why did she marry him?'

'She was in love with him I suppose.'

'I don't understand all this lovey-dovey nonsense. I think people make too much fuss about it. I know I was in love with your father but I could never see why he was so keen on that side of it. I didn't mind because it was him, and I was very fond of him but I really don't see what all the fuss is about. I remember once coming home from the Lamb, before I married Ted, some Yank following me home and getting me up in a corner. "Go on," he said, "can't you give a feller what he wants?" "No, I won't," I said. "Not any bloody feller," and when I got home you should have seen the back of me coat.'

'You didn't tell me.'

'No, of course I didn't tell you. Dilys now, she was a one. The things she used to tell me they used to get up to when he came home on leave. That's why she's got so many children. I met her in town the other day on her bike. "I thought you were expecting another baby," I said. "So I am," she said. "It's due in ten days!" And you wouldn't have known.'

'What sort of things did they do?'

'Oh piddling all over each other and so on. Seems more like animals than human beings. I don't understand it. It's like this,' she pulled the local paper towards her and put on her glasses. She ran her eyes over the double page devoted to the county's tally of indecent exposures, more lurid adulteries and assaults. Then her long fore-finger tapped the head of a paragraph. I read it quickly.

'What does it mean?'

'I don't know exactly, men going with men.'

'Oh.'

'What I'd like to know is what do they do. I suppose it's just mutual masturbation. I don't know, it all seems a lot of fuss about nothing.'

I nodded in agreement. The words meant nothing to me. Even when I looked them up in the big dictionary at school they seemed to have no connection with anything I knew.

The sound of Ted's boots on the iron scraper outside the back door sounded dully through the kitchen. In the morning the curls of mud would have dried and shrunk from the blade, and littered the ground as if some huge bird of prey had rested there leaving its droppings. He came through into the living-room wiping his hands on the towel. He'd been turning the soil ready for the runner beans, that would make a green curtain woven with red flames, between the patch of lawn and the rows of potatoes.

'Are you coming to the pictures with us tonight?' my mother asked quietly.

'No, I've got work to do.' I wanted to keep my impressions clear as long as possible, perhaps put them down in the exercise book that had replaced the diary.

'Work, you don't know the meaning of the word,' Ted said. 'Wait til you've got hands like that,' he took a penknife out of his pocket and began to pare the black soil from under his nails, 'then you'll know what work is.'

'There's more than one kind of work,' I said. 'There's mental as well as physical work that's just as tiring.' Deliberately I used long words knowing they were beyond him.

'Pushing a pen, that isn't work. You want to get out with a pick and shovel, that's real work.'

'Using your brain is as hard as manual labour. Look at Cousin Gilly, she's exhausted after teaching all day, just sits in a chair and falls asleep.'

'Dah, nothing to it! Shouting at a lot of kids all day, could do it standing on me head.'

'That's what you think, you've never tried.'

'Never done a day's work in your lives you people.'

'Oh for goodness' sake stop arguing you two.'

'Well, why should he have it all his own way just because he doesn't know any better? I've as much right to my opinion as he has.'

'That's enough from both of you. I'm tired of your arguments, they wear me out.'

Yet there were times when she too argued fiercely, darting in and out with her sharp wit while he stood like an obstinate boar, head lowered in the face of logic. I went upstairs to cosset the fading remnants of my day. Soon I heard the back door shut as they went out but I was restless when they'd gone, the mood was broken and I almost wished I'd gone with them. I tried to write but the words wouldn't come, I was trying the sonnet for discipline. In the end I gave it up, got my bike and let it carry me downhill into the town. I needed movement to still this strange restlessness. I turned towards Evelyn's and for a long time I rode the streets passing and repassing her lighted window. It seemed to do the trick, the feeling of calm resignation that had followed the play returned. When the pictures turned out I was waiting on the other side of the road to push her home.

'You're never in except to do your homework,' my mother said a few weeks later.

'Well, it's hardly the most sympathetic of atmospheres is it?'

'It's just as bad for me. Anyway you won't have to put up with it much longer.'

'What d'you mean?'

'I've written to Aunt Lyddy to ask if she'll have you there. You've always enjoyed yourself there, wanted to get away from Wortbridge and here, well now's your chance.'

London! 'But what about you?'

'I'll be alright and as soon as you're independent we'll be together again. It'll be something for you to work for. You'll be better there. The Willertons would only drag you down and I couldn't stand that.' She spoke quite calmly and I was calm too. It all seemed so unlikely, so remote.

It was only on Monday that I realized what it would mean. In a panic I invited myself to supper with Evelyn on Wednesday. Once there in the sanity of her room I wondered how I could tell her. Suddenly she said:

'I'm leaving in the summer.'

'Leaving, why?'

'I've been here five years. That's long enough I think.'

'It's strange isn't it? I'm leaving too.'

'Well! Where are you going?'

'London. It'll mean a new school in my school certificate year, still . . .'

'Oh, you'll be alright there. It's always been your Mecca. You'll soon forget us all there.'

I wanted to protest but the words wouldn't come. I felt detached, as if I'd already gone and was watching it all from a great distance.

25

And yet I'd never been so deeply involved with Evelyn. And this feeling two things at once I've always had, so I'm forever trying to decide what my real attitude is, what I really want, and while I'm still deciding, or so I think, I've already started down one way or the other; somewhere the decision's been made, only then of course I wonder if it was what I really wanted after all. So I'd started all this business of going away by my desire to escape and now I couldn't stop it.

Surely there never was a brighter summer, after a brutal winter that had kept us huddled by the radiators and piled snow in the open corridors, the sun blazed every day, the light had the mystical quality of a Stanley Spencer landscape, seen from eternity. Even Wortbridge was invested with a glow; I realized I should miss the country and got up at seven one morning to cycle out along the Hillbury road. I left the bike by the roadside and wandered into a field. The long grass stems tickled my bare legs and the short ones stuck their little dry arrow heads in my ankle socks: wild oat, foxtail, darnel mixed with bitter sorrel. I stripped some of the leaves to chew, vetches and clovers all tangled together. The hedge was thorny may, seed pearled with the heavy dew. Cupping my hands I shook some into them and rinsed my hot face in the liquid coolness. I watched a sparrow flick her way into a bush. She flew out as I parted the branches to find the nest with its blotchy eggs. The shells would break, for a time she would bring them food in her bill thrusting it down their stretched red gullets, then they would all fly away and that would be that.

My socks and shoes were soaking. I got on the bike and rode

home, ate a quick breakfast and got to school before anyone else. Wandering about the deserted fields and building I thought:

'This is how it will be when we're gone. It'll continue just the same but it won't exist for me any more and it'll never look the same to anyone else's eyes. It'll be deserted like it is now. I can carry all its life away in my head.'

But I couldn't tell Janice. As I sat in Evelyn's room I tried to learn by heart every square of buff wallpaper and every trite ornament that the landlady had perpetrated there, the ducks—or were they geese—in perpetual flight above the fireplace, the china mouse scrambling into its cold nest, the stags peering questioningly at each other across the room from their painted glade, as if they were a magic formula to materialize that room whenever I wished, and I would recite them to myself as I lay in bed like the last owner of the tribal mysteries that would provoke the gods to send the rain.

'I will remember, I will.'

I was standing by the pond, where we dipped for biology specimens, one break when I saw Janice tearing across the field towards me, her long plaits swinging round her head. 'She's found out,' I thought.

'She's leaving!' she gasped before she reached me.

'I know,' I said and turned away. 'I've known for a long time.'

'And you never told me!'

'I'm sorry. I couldn't. I'm leaving too.'

'It's not fair. I'll be the only one left. Well I won't stay either. I'll leave and get a job.' I scarcely heard her, again her voice seemed to come from far away.

And now time began to rush away under my feet so that it seemed as if I'd hardly got up before I was back in bed again. Everything I knew was slipping away from me. Janice and I had the leading parts of the blind beggar Martin Dhoul and his wife in *The Well of the Saints*, the revelation scene, where their sight is restored and they see themselves, the world and each other, as old and ugly, and pray for their eyes to be darkened again. The play carried us along on a wave of poetry and passion right up to the last week, rehearsing every night and every dinner hour until I even caught myself dreaming in the brogue. And then it was all over, leaving us stranded, high and dry on the mud flats knowing we would never act together again.

The last day refused to be held up any longer, I went round the school saying my goodbyes, giving in my books.

'I hope we shan't completely lose sight of you—I think you're probably someone worth watching,' the headmistress said as she held out her hand and I realized, as if I could see right through her, that she was really terribly shy instead of brusque and awesome as we had all thought.

I collected autographs from all the Lower Fifth and they signed themselves self-consciously with a flourish—even those I had despised as stupid rising to the occasion. Finally the whole school gathered together for the last assembly.

'Lord dismiss us with Thy Blessing . . .' rang out in the hall, everyone singing lustily at the thought of the six weeks' freedom ahead. The leaving staff were presented with appropriate gifts and each one made a short speech of thanks and benediction. The head said goodbye to the Sixth Form and wished them luck on their journey, now beginning, in the world. Then came the climax, the singing of the school song which I had always despised and derided along with the national anthem and 'Land of Hope and Glory', but now it brought a lump to my throat while Janice wept openly, and rather proudly, beside me.

'Three cheers for Miss Cane and the staff!' cried the retiring head girl, ludicrous in a long outgrown gym tunic that no longer even reached her knees. The school roared three times and it was all over.

Dazed and feeling a little sick I left the hall, half carrying Janice who was nearly hysterical. We lingered for a long while in the cloakroom until the school was nearly deserted but still Evelyn hadn't left. Janice looked up at me, her sad kitten's face smudged and swollen with crying.

'I can't go, Paddy. I must see her again. I must!' she whispered and half ran, half stumbled along the corridor towards the staff-room. Should I follow her? I looked at my face in the washroom. It was white and dead, the eyes empty. My lips moved but nothing came out. I shrugged my satchel up on my shoulder and went slowly out to the bicycle shed.

I waited a long while before they came, Evelyn grave and calm, Janice still red-eyed with her tears. We walked down the road together in silence. There was nothing to say.

'Goodbye, Miss Tyson,' said Janice when we paused at the corner, her voice close to breaking again. 'You will come, won't you? You promised.'

'Yes, of course I'll come. Goodbye, dear. Goodbye, Paddy. . . .'

'Goodbye,' I said, the sound falling flat in the empty street and for a moment I looked down at her. Then she turned and walked away.

'She's coming to stay with me,' Janice babbled as we walked on towards the station. I didn't answer. Sensing my withdrawal: 'Don't you want to know what happened? I sat on her lap and she kissed me and stroked my hair, and I told her I loved her and she said she was very fond of me too. "I'm very fond of you too, Janice," she said.'

'But she didn't say she loved you,' I thought. 'No, she wouldn't say that.'

'Oh, Paddy, it's all over; life will never be so bitter or so sweet again. I hate it. I don't want to grow up. I want to be like this always.' A train whistled dismally in the station. 'Cripes that's my train. I must go. We'll write often won't we? There'll be heaps to tell. We'll never forget, will we?' Her eyes were filling with tears again.

'No,' I said, 'we won't forget. We'll write to each other every week.' But I knew we never would.

26

THE bus jolted and swayed along the Solminster road. It was September; August had passed it seemed almost overnight, waiting for letters from Evelyn, making new clothes, sorting the things to take with me. Now the day was so near I could lean forward and touch it. But first there was this day. We were going to Solminster, she'd saved up a pound for the trip, and it was September. The bus was packed, I'd just managed to ease her into the last seat and now I hung above her, bending low to catch what she was saying or wink and smile knowingly and I felt so tall and strong, my arms long and supple, I could have straddled the little single-decker bus.

The heat of summer had lightened a little but the drought was unbroken. Already the trees were beginning to turn their foliage in an effort to preserve the precious moisture, and single yellow leaves dropped slow, sauntering down in the still air. We ran through tunnels of green, flecked gold, a slight haze over the distant fields, a gentle Indian summer warmth everywhere. The bus climbed and plunged, locals said you couldn't run double-deckers on this route, and looking back at each passed hillside the eye ran through every tint of green and I knew how soon they would blaze and glow with all the violence of decay, each tree as a tall flame consuming itself. We'd seen them so often; we always took this ride before I went back to school at the end of summer holidays. Our bus ground up the last hill, hung a moment on the top as if it would drop back again, then began the long run down into the city.

It lay in a deep basin, not like Sarnford which sprang out of the plain, a mediaeval city of narrow streets at the foot of the cathedral. Solminster was classical, gracious and well planned. We both felt different in Solminster, the Willertons were a different race in a far-off barbarous place, civilization re-clothed us. We walked more slowly with all the day in front of us, admiring, commenting on the people and the window displays, the tall houses with their elegant façades infecting us with the manners of their designers, til the day became a stately progress as I fitted my steps to hers and she leant on my arm.

Our trips to Solminster followed an approved ritual, morning coffee first in the Swiss Café with its great black bear and rough hewn wood, where the coffee and milk poured from separate spouts to your own specifications and the pastries, pastries, not cakes, were brought on a silver tray for your selection—we both had éclairs—then out into the warm sunshine to appraise the shops, not that we had money to buy anything but it was enough to look.

And this brought us down to the part of the city near the station and the Cliffview Restaurant. The dining-room was on the first floor, the stairs always made her wheeze a bit, but once up there we could have a table for two by the window, with white tablecloth, flowers in a vase and three-course lunch for two-and-nine. In the Cliffview I'd learnt to eat like a civilized being. The first time I'd looked at the table I'd been appalled at all I was expected to manage, dinner knife and fork, fish knife and fork, butter knife, spoon and fork for the sweet, that diabolical weapon the soup spoon and all flanked by a glass for water, just placed to catch a hand lifted a bit too much, and a plate for bread. She broke me in gradually, a course at a time, so that my alimentary education was spread over years. Finally one day I worked through soup, spoon brought sideways to the mouth, plate tilted away; grilled plaice, squeeze slice of lemon gently to avoid spurting, select correct implements, do not turn over, remove central bone; pour water for two; roll and butter, break into small pieces, do not cut; apple tart and custard, spoon and fork; coffee, black or white, stir gently, do not leave spoon in cup; all implements to be laid side by side, upwards and vertical at the end of a course; blot lips, screw up paper serviette. By the time I finished I was exhausted but triumphant; I could see by her face that I'd graduated. The

Swiss Café completed it with its strange pastry forks. What I never discovered was how she knew all this lore.

We looked about at the other people eating, we spotted a ridiculous hat below in the street, we laughed and were clever together. She was in her best form, grimacing, perking up her little nose in mock snobbery, the Willertons forgotten.

'What shall we do this afternoon?'

'I don't know. What d'you want to do?'

'The pictures?'

'We can do that any time. Let's be different today.'

'We'll go down into the town and see what we can find.' We paid the bill and magnificently left sixpence tip. 'You see,' she said as we went downstairs, 'if you've got the money you're alright. You can eat out all the week and save your rations til the weekend. One day you'll have lots of money and we won't have to worry any more. You'll have to work hard at your new school. They may be further ahead than you, coming from the country. You'll have to do well in school cert and carry on in the sixth form if you can.'

I thought how it was like a long-distance run I'd started on, with people dropping out all along the way at the higher and higher examination hurdles, until out of the sixty-odd children who'd started with me in the infants maybe only two would ever get all the way to university. And what happened after that? I didn't know. Perhaps you wouldn't know til you got there, or was it an end in itself to have run that far? I was too busy running to decide.

We passed the baths, where Roman generals had come to soothe their gout and Cretia had learned to swim in her long stay in the hospital that had left her no better and no worse than before, and I had once seen an old lady slip on the green slimy steps into the bright rust water, while the goldfish she was after with her cupped hands darted away quick as molten metal.

'What about that?' she said. 'I've never been to an exhibition. You can tell me all about it.' 'The paintings of Vincent Van Gogh—admission free', the notice she was pointing to said.

'You sure you want to? It won't be too much for you

walking round?' I was worried. What would she think of them? Suppose she didn't like them?

'We'll take it very easily and I expect there'll be a seat I can sit on.' We went inside.

It was only a small exhibition, not of the pictures themselves but of reproductions, sponsored by the adult education committee. We were given a printed catalogue with a brief life at the top and ushered into a beautifully proportioned Georgian room, the paintings burning against the cream-painted walls. There was a bench in the centre. I took her to this.

'You go round and look at them and I'll sit here and see what I think I'd like to look at more closely.' I left her there and began to pass from one to the other. They were very good reproductions, well hung and just enough to take in at one session. Some I knew very well already. *Man Going To Work* with its warm green sky I'd bought for Evelyn's Christmas present last year as a large calendar, and she'd kept it when all the months had been torn off.

'What d'you think of them?' I asked when I came back from my round.

'They're strange aren't they? Different but I like them. Give me your arm.' We began to move from one to the other, me explaining when I could and she questioned me hard, thirsty to know, to get at the meaning of this new experience.

'Why did he paint them like that?' She pointed to the heaving black sea of cypresses.

'Because that's how he felt them. That's how he felt inside and he saw it reflected in the things around him.'

'Is that why they said he was mad?'

'I suppose so, though he did some strange things. Once he cut off his ear and sent it to someone in a box, one of the girls from the town.'

'Sometimes when I'm looking up at the sky I see all kinds of queer shapes in the clouds. Look at those lights. He must have been drunk when he painted them.'

'I expect he was. He drank a lot.'

'Absinthe?'

'That's right.' I was full of admiration. I told her how he put his paint on and why it was a new idea; how he loved the sun and tried to get it down in flower and yellow chairs, whirling stars and naked light bulbs. And she listened and nodded.

'Which d'you like best?'

She considered a moment. 'That one.' It was the picture of the chestnuts in bloom painted in the spring of the year he died.

'Why?'

'It's beautiful. It's alive and yet more peaceful than some of the others. You can see them growing, almost moving.' The candles of the chestnuts were all alight, red and white burning softly. 'How old was he when he died? Thirty-seven. I'm not doing so bad.'

Outside in the sun we looked about.

'Let's go to the gardens.' We'd never afforded the gardens before, threepence for a deck-chair had always seemed prohibitive but today was different, we bought a chair between us. I carried it down the slope to the grass sward, still lush, it was watered every night, planted it firmly and sat down at her feet. The afternoon trickled away to the sound of the water falling over the shallow weir where the fishermen stood, thigh-booted, casting long lines into the dark pool below the cream and spume of the fall, and children's voices came to us thin and clear. The houses on the bridge, like old London Bridge falling down, falling down, were caught in the broad river under the span. Not far away a woman with braided hair sat knitting placidly.

'You won't forget to write?'

'You know I won't. You'll be careful won't you and not try to do too much?'

'Yes I will. And it won't be long. You'll be home at Christmas or half-term. But it's better for you to be there. I'll feel I've done my best for you. I shan't come to the station. You'll understand won't you? Ted can carry your case. We won't say goodbye because it isn't really, not for you and me, is it?'

When she was rested and the warmth was dying from the sunlight we went for our tea. It was part of the ritual that we ate three meals on these days. We caught the five o'clock bus home from the parade, a little wind beginning to stir as we queued.

'Are you warm enough? Put your collar up if it's draughty.' The ride home was too short, the hills falling away under the wheels and the streets of Wortbridge soon closing down on us. I was going away tomorrow.

27

THE alarm went off at quarter past six. I lay quite still for a few moments more, although I'd been awake on and off all night, before I got up and dressed. It was a grey morning with a look of rain, almost dark enough to have the light on. Summer was over. I went downstairs and put the kettle on. There were sounds of movement above; Ted was getting up. I washed quickly, feeling sick, knowing I ought to eat but not fancying anything. The usual breakfast before a journey was a plate of porridge but the thought of it this morning made me heave. I did some dry toast. Ted appeared, dressed already in his light suit. I poured the tea.

'Is she awake?'

'Yeah.'

'I'll take her up a cup of tea.'

'You ready then?'

'Yeah.'

'I'll put the cases by the back door.'

Mechanically I got myself into the green school-coat she'd made me out of a piece from the mill. I'd need a navy gaberdine for the new school, they'd said in the letter accepting me as a transfer.

I went upstairs with the cup of tea. She was sitting up in bed waiting for me.

'All ready then?'

'Yes.'

'You'll be alright with the cases?'

'I'll be alright.'

'Now remember give my love to Aunt Lyddy and everyone.

I'll send the pound to you every week and you can give it to her, so you'll be paying your own keep.'

'Alright.' There was nothing more to say. I looked at the blue plastic unicorn still watching from her dressing-table.

'Well, you'd better be getting along, you don't want to miss the train and there's the ticket to get.' I went up to the side of the bed. 'Ta-ta then.' I bent over and kissed her soft thin cheek as she turned her mouth away.

'Ta-ta.'

'It won't be long. The time'll soon go. We won't make a lot of fuss, you and I. Go on now.' I couldn't look at her again.

The first taste of autumn was in the damp air we sucked into our lungs as we stepped out of the back door, Ted carrying the cases. What was he thinking? Was he glad to see me go, feeling he'd won if only for the moment? I turned my head at the corner to look back at the house. The street was swept clean by the grey morning breeze, making the houses look hunched and pitiful on the hill-top. We walked steadily down, past the gas-works and the brewery. The few people about hurried with bent heads. Mostly we walked in silence with only an occasional remark.

'You got plenty of time.'

'It goes at seven-thirty.'

'What times does it get in?'

'Quarter past ten.' What was she doing now? Drinking her tea? Or maybe she'd finished and was lying down again or'd picked up her book to read. I couldn't know for sure.

We took the short cut past the pie factory, up the muddy back lane and all the time I was trying to print it all in my mind, this town I'd hated and was leaving at last, but somehow I couldn't seem to fix it, I couldn't take any of it in. And I felt a kind of cold despair because you can't ever keep anything, not even when you've packed it safe in your head. Oh I know they say it's all in there somewhere and nothing's ever forgotten, but you try thinking of that when you're fighting to remember something and it'll drive you mad.

We crossed the station yard to the entrance where I'd stood day after day with Janice, talking endlessly while she waited for me to come home. I got my ticket; the train was already in on the first platform, hissing and puffing gently. We got in. Ted swung the cases up on the rack. There weren't many travellers from Wortbridge that early in the morning.

'You alright?' Ted asked.

'Yes thanks.'

'I'd better get out then. I'll wait til the train goes, I said I'd see you off.' He kissed me rather wetly. He always kissed on the lips, not like our family. Then he got out of the train and stood on the platform for the last few minutes, looking up. I opened the window and leaned out. The train shrieked. The wind flicked up a strand of his thin hair.

'In another year or two he'll be completely bald,' I thought. With a jolt the train began to pull away, slipping a little on the rails and puffing throatily.

'Ta-ta. Look after yourself.'

'Give her my love. Ta-ta.' We both began to wave. I watched him growing smaller, a little man in a light suit, with receding hair and a big nose. I shut the window and sat down. The train steamed under Clarence Street and out into the country. I was tired but I couldn't sleep because of the emptiness inside, so I watched the telegraph wires looping past, the big black and white Frisians, like the cows in the Stanley Spencer postcard on Evelyn's mantelpiece—only it wasn't there any more. I was between responsibilities. Briefly I felt the old sensation of freedom that a journey always brought but it quickly faded. I knew every station, every halt on that line. Always before they'd been rungs on a mounting ladder to the start of my summer holidays in London.

Gradually, as the train drew towards the suburbs, to the tall houses that seem to be trying to elbow their way on to the line until they form a grimy cutting into the heart of the city, I began to feel better. In any case no one must guess how I felt.

The train plunged into a dark tunnel, slowed down and slid out into the gloom of Paddington Station. I struggled off with my cases, stood still a second and looked up. There they were, flying about among the steel rafters and broken glass of the bomb-damaged roof, the pigeons. I took a deep breath of thick

London air, expelling the past, and began to walk up the ramp towards the Underground.

The journey East was long and slow but the names of the stations were magic the further I went. At Liverpool Street Uncle Dick might get in, in his driver's shiny-topped cap and blue overalls. At Bow I staggered out with my heavier cases and across to the bus-stop.

'When I was four we lived here,' I thought. I was taking the same ride we took every Friday to Aunt Lyddy's with the bag of brown shrimps for tea, only now it was a smooth trolley bus instead of a rackety tram.

I got off at the post office and trotted through the back chats. I was coming home. In a way she was coming home too. Dust and bus tickets blew down the gutter. It was colder than the West Country. My arms sagged with the cases. The houses looked just the same—they still do somehow though many of the old railway cottages have been pulled down and modern rows put up with baths and fridges, they still have a strange unity. I turned into Waldron Street and put down the killer cases on the doorstep. It was going to be alright. Opposite old Lizzie's curtain twitched. I knocked the family knock.

'Go to the door, Gilly,' I heard my aunt say, 'it's her.'

Tues.

My dear Paddy,

I'm glad you received all your things quite safely and if I were you I should send your cases back the same way by rail. You could put them one inside the other and take them to the station, it would save time and a lot of bother don't you think?

I haven't been able to get your Gaberdine yet as they are not in but still expected. Dilys paid me for the petticoat I made her, at last. I wish it had jolly well come before then, we should have spent it at Solminster last week shouldn't we, but never mind we had a good day didn't we, and I thoroughly enjoyed myself.

I am enclosing a letter from Miss Tyson which came this morning. I hope you have got on alright at school. You must write and tell me all about it, I am longing to hear everything.

Arthur has been home for a few days but I shall be glad when he goes back as he is about as dumb as Billy at shopping and unless you speak to him he

217

never says a word. I have talked to him about the merchant navy but he doesn't seem to care for the idea, he says what about when you are waiting for boats in between, so I told him he could get a job during that time.

But he is pretty much the same as the rest of the Willertons, doesn't know what he does want. I'm not going to bother any further with him, he must just take his chance like the rest of them, you can't help people like that.

We went to the pictures twice last week to see Miranda *and* An Ideal Husband, *I liked the last one best. I thought the other was a bit soft. It was about a mermaid. But I remember hearing* An Ideal Husband *on the wireless, Ted would persist in saying he had seen it before, you know what he is. He still says he has, I could slosh him sometimes.*

We still have a few arguments when I get on my soapbox and then I think of you and try and hold my tongue but on the whole he has been quite passable. I miss you very much. Have you asked Aunt Lyddy about my Dalton's Weekly *to look for bungalows yet?*

I have written to Fred for Dad, I thought I had better offer. I said we should be pleased to hear from him if he could find someone to write for him.

I am trying to persuade Ted to come and see Forever Amber *tonight, but I don't know whether he will, if not I shall go with Dilys one night. I have nearly finished* Guy Mannering *and think it is very good.*

Well I think this is all for now, write again soon with lots of love from

Mum. x x x

We'd been to the pictures, all of us on Saturday afternoon and when we got back it was there on the mat inside the door, the sickly little yellow envelope. Cousin Gilly picked it up.

'It's the wrong name,' she said. 'It isn't for us. What shall we do with it?'

'Send it back,' said her father.

'I think you ought to open it,' I said. 'It might be important.'

'Perhaps we ought. I don't know what to do,' said Aunt Lyddy. Her face had gone ashy and strained. She stood there holding it by one corner. We all looked at it motionless, like a tableau I remember. 'What do you think, Gilly?'

'It ought to be opened,' she said.

'I think so too,' I insisted, my voice coming from a long way away. No one wanted it. It was an impersonal evil in our midst.

'You open it, Gilly.' Her mother passed it to her. Carefully she slit it with a knife and unfolded the square of beige paper. She let out a little cry and looked at me.

'I don't know if I ought to read it.'

'What is it?' I said. 'I want to know.'

'It says, "*Louey died this morning. Come at once. Ted.*" ' The name on the envelope was that of his first wife's relations.

28

SHE'D gone out shopping on Saturday morning. I wasn't there to push her, and she'd fallen down in the street and her blood had run out on the pavement. They'd carried her into a nearby shop but there was nothing to be done and she was dead by the time they got her to the hospital. There wasn't any pain, just her own blood choking her and I wonder what she thought, if she thought at all. It was what she'd wanted but not then, not just then and in the street, but that's how it was.

And I couldn't believe it at first; it didn't make a word of sense. I'd catch myself thinking of things to tell her, seeing things in shop windows and wanting to buy them for her. 'She'll laugh when I tell her . . .' I did everything like she'd told me, I didn't go to the funeral or anything like that—they sold her machine to pay for it and then there wasn't even a marker to show where she was.

Only she isn't there really of course. She's everywhere now, especially in these streets when December comes; under a lamp a woman's face is like hers for a moment, in profile, and then she turns. Sometimes I dream I'm back in Wortbridge and I walk into the house and there she is sitting by the fire, and she tells me it isn't true but I don't understand why I can't be with her any more. And then I wake up.

And I'm afraid too, afraid I'll forget, that's why I've tried to put it all down just as it was. But I'm not sure even now if I've got it right because there's a lot I don't remember and a lot more I don't understand. I don't know what it means, that's what I want to say. It all means something, it must do, but I don't understand it. That's partly what I'm afraid of, that I might not find out. And Aunt Lyddy can't tell me, she wouldn't even know what I was talking about.

For a long time I even thought I'd killed her because I wasn't there to look after her, to push her about on the bike, and then perhaps she felt I'd grown away from her and she wasn't needed any more, and she didn't have to go on making the effort, and I wasn't there to have a laugh and ease things along and show her it was all worth while, but then I saw people were beginning to think I was a bit touched and I thought: 'I must go on. She'd want me to go on.'

But what I really want to know is, what do I do now, what the hell do I do now? I love her but I can't go on loving her, yet what else can I do? And that's why I've put it all down too, to try and find out so I'll understand myself and know what to do. Somewhere it's there in what happened if I can only find it.

Sometimes I think everything since is a dream and that's the only truth, but when I try to tell people about it I can see in their eyes they don't believe me. But I swear it's true, every word of it; that's how it was, that's just how it was. And what the hell do I do now?

VIRAGO MODERN CLASSICS

The first Virago Modern Classic, *Frost in May* by Antonia White, was published in 1978. It launched a list dedicated to the celebration of women writers and to the rediscovery and reprinting of their works. Its aim was, and is, to demonstrate the existence of a female tradition in fiction which is both enriching and enjoyable. The Leavisite notion of the 'Great Tradition', and the narrow, academic definition of a 'classic', has meant the neglect of a large number of interesting secondary works of fiction. In calling the series 'Modern Classics' we do not necessarily mean 'great' — although this is often the case. Published with new critical and biographical introductions, books are chosen for many reasons: sometimes for their importance in literary history; sometimes because they illuminate particular aspects of womens' lives, both personal and public. They may be classics of comedy or storytelling; their interest can be historical, feminist, political or literary.

Initially the Virago Modern Classics concentrated on English novels and short stories published in the early decades of this century. As the series has grown it has broadened to include works of fiction from different centuries, different countries, cultures and literary traditions. In 1984 the Victorian Classics were launched; there are separate lists of Irish, Scottish, European, American, Australian and other English speaking countries; there are books written by Black women, by Catholic and Jewish women, and a few relevant novels by men. There is, too, a companion series of Non-Fiction Classics constituting biography, autobiography, travel, journalism, essays, poetry, letters and diaries.

By the end of 1986 over 250 titles will have been published in these two series, many of which have been suggested by our readers.